The Chocolate Money

www.**transworldbooks**.co.uk

The
Chocolate
Money

Ashley Prentice Norton

BANTAM PRESS

LONDON • TORONTO • SYDNEY • AUCKLAND • JOHANNESBURG

To my parents, Jon and Abra,
who always told me to just keep writing

TRANSWORLD PUBLISHERS
61–63 Uxbridge Road, London W5 5SA
A Random House Group Company
www.transworldbooks.co.uk

First published in Great Britain
in 2012 by Bantam Press
an imprint of Transworld Publishers

A CIP catalogue record for this book
is available from the British Library.

ISBN 9780593069981 (cased)
9780593069929 (tpb)

Addresses for Random House Group Ltd companies outside the UK
can be found at: www.randomhouse.co.uk
The Random House Group Ltd Reg. No. 954009

The Random House Group Limited supports the Forest Stewardship Council
(FSC®), the leading international forest-certification organization. Our books
carrying the FSC label are printed on FSC®-certified paper. FSC is the only
forest-certification scheme endorsed by the leading environmental organizations,
including Greenpeace. Our paper procurement policy can be found at
www.randomhouse.co.uk/environment

Typeset in Dante MT
Printed and bound in Great Britain by
Clays Ltd, Bungay, Suffolk

2 4 6 8 10 9 7 5 3 1

Part I

1

Haircut

AUGUST 1978

THE DAY I CUT my hair and *completely fuck up the Christmas Card*, I am merely bored, not *a defiant brat* like Babs tells all her friends.

It is late August. I am ten. Babs is in the kitchen talking to Andie, who comes Saturday afternoons for Bloody Marys and eggs Benedict. Babs doesn't drink alcohol. She always nurses a Baccarat champagne flute of freshly squeezed juice (grapefruit, plum, raspberry) cut with a heavy pour of Perrier. Fruit has way too many calories. I'm not even sure she likes the taste, but it looks pretty.

"So, Andie," Babs says, "we are doing the Card tomorrow. I can't decide if I should go summer or for more of a holiday feel. No matchy-matchy reindeer sweaters, of course, but maybe a tad less controversial than last year's. I know the nudity was tastefully done, but I don't want that bitch Nona Cardill writing nasty things about me in her column. That biddy probably never takes off her underwear. And all the calls from school. No sense of humor at all; no points for creativity."

All the kids in my grade at Chicago Day were really mean when our Christmas Card arrived last year. Yes, we were naked, but I was sitting on Babs's lap and covered her privates. That didn't make things any better. They said I was totally weird to have my picture taken without my clothes on. The best I could come up with was that it wasn't my idea.

"It was very avant-garde, Babs. I still have it up on my fridge," Andie says.

I think this is kind of creepy. Babs just laughs.

I'm sitting on the floor by the kitchen table, almost out of view, reading *Tiger Beat,* which has my idol Brooke Shields on the cover. Babs got me a subscription to it for my tenth birthday and it's one of the best presents she ever gave me. I watch them smoke and ash into their Villeroy & Boch plates—Babs's "weekend" china. It doesn't matter that we eat off these plates; Babs can turn anything into an ashtray. She and Andie lean into the white marble island as if they need help remaining upright. Babs wears white short-shorts and a white Playboy bunny tank top, a silver bunny head outlined on it in rhinestones.

Andie wears a brown wrap dress that is so wrinkled it looks like she dug it out from under her bed. She has Birkenstocks on her feet. When she came in, I could see the hair on her toes.

Babs is beautiful, and I wish I looked like her. She has blond hair, which she wears up in a messy French twist, and blue eyes. You might think Babs was Grace Kelly's twin if GK said words like *cock* and *pussy* and hit little kids. Babs always said she would much rather look like Brigitte Bardot, sexy, fluid, and open-ended like an unmade bed, but she doesn't have the curves to pull it off. She is very tall, five foot ten, and cut like a boy: slender hips, no butt, no boobs.

Babs's legs are right in front me, and like she says, they are so *fucking fabulous.* Her calves are shea-butter rich and smell of South African lemons, thanks to her Veritas lotion. She almost never wears pants or pantyhose. She uses their bareness to take advantage of the elements: they goose-bump in the cold, glisten in the sun, go slick in the rain. Since I am her daughter, I think she might let me touch them some time. I hope I will even grow into my own pair one day. But her body is off-limits to me. It is almost as if she were afraid my small hands would leave fingerprints and ruin them forever.

Andie isn't even remotely attractive, and this is exactly why Babs is friends with her. She has curly hair with gray in it, and big horse teeth. She always agrees with Babs, no matter what.

"That's the difference between our Card and other people's. As you know. Don't just snap something and send it to your friends. Spend some time on it. Surprise people when they open the envelope. I was thinking about a *Turning Point* theme, both of us with buns and matching leotards. But with a holiday twist. I'm afraid most people won't get it. It's just too bad we don't know Misha. Those fabulous tights."

I don't get it. Buns and leotards? Who is Misha? Since when does Babs like ballet?

"Anyone who doesn't get that movie doesn't deserve your Card, Babs."

Today, Andie is surprisingly authoritative, making up standards for Babs's friends. I think she hopes this Card will narrow the pool of people Babs likes and give Andie more of a shot. As it stands, Andie is just a daytime friend. She's never invited for dinner when other people come. But Andie thinks if she just keeps showing up, Babs will bump her up on the roster, make space for her at the table. This will never happen. Babs makes up her mind about people and doesn't allow for upgrades. Like me, Andie is taking the standby approach, but it just doesn't work. There are always better people available to take the good seats.

Babs spots me listening in on their discussion and says, "Bettina, stop hovering. Go find your own fun." Hovering is *fucking annoying,* so I stand up and leave.

Babs says things like this all the time and I am used to it. But still, I don't want to find something else to do. I'm an only child but completely lack the mythical powers of only-child imagination. Unlike Eloise, I cannot make a day out of fixing a doll's broken head or spend hours feeding raisins to a turtle.

I do have a nanny, but not the doting or fancy kind. Stacey is twenty and isn't from England, but Lyons, Wisconsin. Before coming to work for Babs, she lived in a small ranch house with her family. The average tenure of my nannies is about nine months, and Stacey has been with us for two years now. A real achievement.

Stacey's favorite parts of the job are smoking Virginia Slims menthols (Babs would never hire a nanny who didn't smoke) and speeding down Lake Shore Drive in the Pacer Babs has given her to use. She reads *Cosmo* and highlights all the passages on how to drive a man to ecstasy. She really has no interest in me.

I don't completely blame her. I am a little girl who offers no easy conversation and doesn't do tricks. I don't like stickers, don't play with Barbies, and think cartoons are stupid. What matters to me is someday being friends with Brooke Shields. Babs met her once at Studio 54 and had Brooke autograph a cocktail napkin for me. I was so happy I put it in a Dax frame along with a cut-out picture of her. This is the best thing I have.

Unlike Brooke, I am not gorgeous, or even a tiny bit pretty. I am four-three with flat brown hair that won't hold curls. Once, Babs tried to give it volume by attacking it with a curling iron, but the only thing she accomplished was burning my scalp. Babs promises that when I turn eleven, she will get me professional streaks for my birthday.

The one thing I seem to have going for me is that I'm thin, and Babs loves buying clothes for me. She spends lots of money on them: suede or leather pants she picks up in Paris, silk-screened T-shirts with Warhol prints on them, gray crinkled-silk pinafores with black velvet ballet flats. But none of this really matters. I'm a match that just won't strike.

When I leave Babs and Andie, I decide to hit the playroom in the aparthouse. Babs calls our apartment this because it's as big as a real house. Two stories, four fireplaces, six bedrooms, and eight potties. The problem is that there is really nothing I like to play with in the playroom. It's just a large space with wall-to-wall sand-colored carpeting and big toys; Babs's version of an indoor playground. There is a red wooden jungle gym with a metal slide, a sandbox filled with sand from some beach in France, and a life-size glossy black horse with a mane and tail that are made of real horsehair. Boring.

Besides the toys, there's a wooden glossy green bench that looks like it has been stolen from an actual park. The bench legitimately belongs to Babs, but it's disturbing in another way. It sports a gold plaque that says MONTGOMERY AND EUDORA BALLENTYNE. HIT THE DECK MAY 26, 1967. MAY THEY RIP.

Montgomery and Eudora Ballentyne were Babs's parents. They died in a boat accident the year before I was born. There's a glass ashtray built into an armrest of the bench. In the accident, her father was decapitated on impact. Her mother, still alive, was pulled into the motor of the boat. It was still running, and it sliced her body into bloody pieces.

Above the bench are Lucas's paintings. Lucas is Babs's first cousin. He lives in New York City, like Brooke Shields. Lucas has some kind of free pass in Babs's life. I can tell by the way Babs talks to him on the phone that she likes him in a way that has nothing to do with sex. She talks to him like she might a brother, and she once even apologized to him about something. Maybe since Lucas has the chocolate money too, he and Babs belong to the same tribe. Lucas is married to someone named Poppy and they have a son named JoJo, but I have never met any of them. Babs says Lucas hates to fly.

Lucas's paintings are abstract, mostly gray and black lines on big white boards. Even though I don't understand them, I really like them. He sends a fresh batch every two months, and Babs mails back the old ones, which he displays at a gallery and hopefully sells.

The paintings may not be that interesting to look at, but they make me feel less lonely. My family is bigger than just me and Babs. If Babs ever says she has had it with me once and for all, maybe Lucas could be my backup plan. I don't really know how I would get from Chicago to New York, but it's a start.

Babs's imagination may call the shots on the twenty-ninth floor, but I'm only an elevator ride from the real world.

Babs believes she's as accomplished as Lucas. There *are* three things she's really good at: giving parties, making scrapbooks, and, of course, doing the Card. Her scrapbooks are original in that they have almost no pictures in them. Just receipts from restaurants she has gone to and for shoes she has bought, cock-tail napkins from parties she has been to. She keeps the scrap-books in the back of her fur closet, organized by year. She has told me never to look at them; they are none of my business. But I can't help myself. I look for parts of her she does not share with me. They are the closest thing she has to a diary.

But the Card, I know all about. I look forward to it all year since it means we will spend the whole day together, posing in various outfits, trying different locations for shots. Since we have the Card tomorrow, part of me relaxes. I decide to do as I'm told and force myself to make the most of the playroom. I hang upside down on the jungle gym for five minutes, fall off the death horse twice and hurt my arm, and look at Lucas's paintings for as long as I can.

I venture into the living room. I'm not supposed to go in there by myself, but it's the best room in the aparthouse, with the most to do. It is two stories high and takes up one whole half of the aparthouse. Standing in it is like being in a Lucite box that's suspended in the sky. Instead of a solid wall, there is a huge pane of glass that goes floor to ceiling and allows for an amazing view of Lake Michigan. You can watch the cars on Lake Shore Drive go right up to North Avenue. In the summer, you can even see those women who don't have country-club memberships sitting on Oak Street Beach, slathering them- selves with cheap suntan lotion and probably reading Danielle Steel.

Babs bought the aparthouse after her parents died. Before, she lived in Grass Woods, a suburb of Chicago, on a big estate called Tea House. I'm glad Babs moved to the city and bought the aparthouse. Besides being really big, it has cool things, like the spiral staircase that winds up to her bedroom. The steps are big chunks of creamy veined marble, and the railing is a long silver tube that curves like a Krazy Straw. Straight silver bars connect the railing to the steps, and I love to stick my head through them.

I decide to risk a trip to the top of the stairs so I can saun- ter back down them just like Babs does when she makes an entrance into her parties. But my beginning is clumsy. I'm so busy looking up that I almost knock over a majolica cup filled with Babs's cigarettes and nearly step on her scrapbook scissors.

I love these scissors; the blades are long and silver like swords. The handles are gold and encrusted with diamonds, rubies, and emeralds. They are bumpy and smooth at the same time, like a seashell sticky with sand. Sometimes I put them in my mouth and suck on them. They have a metallic taste that is surprisingly sweet.

I pick them up and press them against my cheek. The longer I hold on to them, the harder it is to let them go. I spread the blades wide like legs and position them on my right cheek. They slide a little deeper into their splits, and I press them down slightly.

A piece of hair falls to my mouth and sticks to my lips. I blow it back, still holding the scissors. I pause and imagine Babs whispering in my ear, *You are such a fucking chicken.*

The words sound so real I flinch. When Babs insults me, I never answer back. I just sit there and take it, with wet eyes and trembly lips. Like someone spilled my Shirley Temple.

But since Babs is not in the room with me, I have the courage to defy her. I give a large fistful of my hair a good yank. The pain makes me feel alert. Exhilarated. I open the scissors as wide as they will go, and then bring them together with all my force. Cut. My hair is baby-fine so there is no resistance. A butcher knife slicing a birthday cake.

After about one short moment of triumph, I spiral into a complete panic. My hair's all over the blades, which are supposed to be used only to cut paper for scrapbooks. Nothing else. I bundle the amputated strands into something like a bird's nest and stuff them under the corner of the rug. This is the moment where, were I old enough, I would pause, reach for a cigarette, and have a good, deep smoke. But I am only ten, and there is no time to waste.

I wipe the scissors carefully on the hem of my dress, hold them up to the bright sunlight coming through the living room window. They look clean. I return them to the steps. I want to prove things are back to normal, so I go back to the kitchen to find Babs.

She and Andie have finished their food and are no longer talking. Andie looks nervous. She's not ready to leave and finish up her day alone. There's a lull between them, and Babs does not tolerate a lull. It's as if they are just waiting for me to walk in.

Babs looks at me and says, "What the fuck have you done to your hair?"

Babs says *fuck* all the time. It is not always a mean word, but today it is.

"Nothing," I say. I'm really surprised she can tell what I have done. I thought I had fixed the problem. But Babs can always tell everything about me.

"Bettina, lying isn't going to fly, babe." She calmly turns to the sink, runs water over her burning cigarette. Throws it in the trash.

Andie turns to me with her arms folded and acts concerned. She squints her eyes, like this development is deeply troubling to her. But thanks to me, she's suddenly in the same league as Babs. Andie would never be stupid enough to cut her own hair.

"It's not fucking *nothing*," Babs says flatly. "Your hair looks like shit. I could care less, really, but we have the Card tomorrow."

Babs is calm, and this is a really bad sign. She almost never yells when I do something wrong. The madder she gets, the more she pulls away from the situation.

Will she leave me out of the Card? This would be the worst punishment ever. Everyone knows you include your kids in your Christmas card. Unless they are dead or locked up somewhere.

Babs turns her back on me and rinses Andie's yolky plate. She normally doesn't do dishes, but it is the weekend, and there is no staff to do it for her. She hates when traces of food linger.

She starts to laugh. I know this isn't her good laugh but the laugh that means something bad is going to happen. If I try to laugh along, my voice doesn't mix with hers; it just bounces back at me. Andie acts like she is in on the joke, goes ahead and laughs too.

"Go find your fucking shoes, Bettina," Babs says.

I hear Babs on the phone when I come back.

"Geoff, we have a crisis. The kid has done a number on her hair playing home salon and we've got the Card tomorrow. There's not much to work with, but could you possibly give it your best?"

Babs flexes her toes and I hear the bones crack. She is barefoot, as usual. Her toenails are painted a tangerine orange. She always wears some cool color. She gets pedicures, manicures, and waxing twice as often as normal women. A tiny Asian girl inexplicably named Manuela comes one morning a week and uses tools that are for Babs alone.

I stand and watch as Babs waits out Geoff's half of the conversation.

"Whenever you can," Babs says. "Love you too. And you have such an incredibly perfect ass. Even better than mine."

This is Babs's way of expressing gratitude. She never says thank you.

Babs loves *fags,* as she calls them. She told me once that fags are men who have sex with other men. Each gets a turn to *put his penis in the other's ass,* was how she explained it. I had a lot of questions about how this worked. Can they get each other pregnant? And what about all the shit stuck up there? Do they have special tools to remove it beforehand? But Babs wasn't really in the mood to give more details. She just said, *Fags are the best. They actually want you to be beautiful,* and left it at that.

Babs calls Stacey on the intercom, even though her room is just off the kitchen. She drags herself into the kitchen wearing purple terry-cloth shorts and a purple T-shirt with bubble hearts. She has on her Dr. Scholl's and holds a pink can of Tab. She has brown hair that feathers off her face and huge blue eyes, like a Disney character's. Her nose is way too big though, so this ruins everything. Her last job was working at Dairy Queen.

"Yes, Mrs. Ballentyne," Stacey says, in a nice can-I-help-you voice she never uses with me.

"Stace, we have a tedious and untimely emergency."

"Really?" says Stacey, excited to be part of the drama.

"Really," Babs says flatly. She continues. "Bettina clearly cannot be trusted with a moment of unsupervised time without totally fucking up everyone's day. I know this is your day off, but you're going to have to take her to Zodiac to see if Geoff can do something about this mess."

Zodiac is on Oak Street next to the Esquire movie theater, and it takes up two floors. The outside is all glass and you can see people getting their hair cut when you walk by.

When we cross Michigan Avenue, Stacey walks very quickly and yanks my arm, like I am a dawdling toddler. Once we have made it to the sidewalk on the other side of traffic, she launches into me.

"You think your mother would have noticed my split ends," she whispers harshly in my ear.

"Do you know my last haircut cost eight dollars? And that was at Sheer Genius, where they shampoo your hair twice!"

Just before we arrive, Stacey scrunches up her hair with her fingers and pulls it down in front of her face. I know she thinks that if she makes her hair look bad enough, Geoff will insist on doing her too.

I know that our trip to Zodiac isn't going to be any fun; it's just triage at the beauty ER.

The salon has a black ceiling, black walls, and black leather chairs. The ceiling has clusters of gold stars painted on it, and low-hanging disco balls. The names of the twelve astrological signs lasso the constellations in gold script.

Geoff is busy cutting an older woman's hair and he laughs as he works. He is tall with broad shoulders and shaggy blond hair. His assistant Nikki directs us to a couch in the far corner. She tells us it will be a while.

Stacey grabs a stack of magazines and lights up a Virginia Slims menthol. I just sit there. Wait.

After two hours with no acknowledgment from Geoff, I get so bored that I finally look in the mirror to the side of the black leather couch and check out my hair. I'm surprised to see it's not such a disaster. I'm just lopsided. It's not really that ugly; it just looks kind of weird. If I wore a headband or barrette, no one would notice.

The light changes in the salon, and as we wait, I can feel the afternoon ending. Stacey's visibly upset. She pulls out two Tabs from her enormous purse and some Ballentyne chocolate: Gold Coast Chews. She rattles the box, trying to unstick the chocolate caramels from the sides, but this elicits only a few dirty looks. Even I know you don't eat candy at a hair salon. It's not a movie theater.

Stylists are packing up their stations. They put combs away and twist black cords around the necks of blow dryers; they spray their mirrors with Windex and wipe them clear of the day.

Finally, Geoff looks over at us and nods that he is ready. He checks his fingernails while I climb into the chair, like they're really interesting. Says nothing to me while I get settled. Maybe I have to start up the conversation myself? But I've never talked to a fag one-on-one. I don't know exactly what I'm supposed to say. Don't want to offend him.

He snaps a dirty cape covered with another woman's hair around my neck. He sprays my head damp with a water bottle. The shampoo woman has gone home.

"Do you have any suggestions for *my* hair?" Stacey says, moving in toward him. I had forgotten about her. She never gives up.

"Brush it," Geoff says drily.

Stacey backs off.

Geoff starts cutting or, more accurately, hacking at my head. I shut my eyes as he works. I wonder why I didn't just slice up my cheek and spare myself this nightmare.

Geoff finally stops and turns on the dryer. He does not use a brush to style my hair like he did with everyone else. He just runs the hot air over my scalp in a careless sweeping pattern like he is blowing leaves off a lawn. I open my eyes.

I try to look pleased, but this is impossible. My hair is almost all gone.

It's on the floor, mixed in with the rest of Geoff's clients' hair. Maybe if he gave me some extra time, I could sort mine out, take it home, and reattach it somehow.

Stacey looks up from the next station, where she has been busy ignoring Geoff. Straight out laughs at me. I want to throw a full can of Tab at her head.

Babs calls Geoff the minute we get home to tell him how brilliant it is. Despite the fact that the salon is now closed, he picks up. He must be waiting for her reaction.

"Very gamine," Babs says. "Jean Seberg in *A bout de souffle.* You've outdone yourself, baby."

I have no idea who Jean Seberg is, but I don't want her hair.

Babs ruffles my hair. Rubs her thumbs over my forehead as she finishes her conversation.

"Bravo, kiddo," she says when she hangs up. "The Card is

going to be spectacular. Fuck *The Turning Point*. We'll think of something else. The cut is just so damn chic!"

I want to enjoy the compliment, but part of me wonders if I have her attention only because it interests her to see me so thoroughly maimed.

2

Mack

~~~~~~~~~~~~~~~~

NOVEMBER 1979

A ND THEN COMES MACK.
    Babs has dated many men, but Mack is the first one
who lasts more than a month. I think this must be because he's
really good-looking, but Babs later explains to me what a *fucking genius* he is in bed.

I meet him at the very beginning of their affair. One night,
Babs goes out to some charity ball. It's for a cause she has no
interest in: endangered animals or homeless people or something else that won't result in a building being named after
you no matter how much money you give. But she goes anyway, partly for the goody bags. *Love a good freebie,* she always
says. When she goes to parties like these, she never takes a
date—she *likes to keep her options open.*

I am up in my room reading one of the Little House on the
Prairie books. It's a bit childish for me, but I love the way the
whole family gets along. They live in a small cabin and buy
almost everything they need at one store. I start to think maybe

the problem between Babs and me is the aparthouse and that she almost never takes me with her when she goes shopping. Around eleven P.M., I hear the elevator. I wasn't expecting Babs back so early. Usually when she goes to a party, she hits the discos afterward.

I decide to go down and see her. I love it when Babs is dressed up. She's so glamorous I can't believe she is my mother. I was eating dinner when she left, and I missed my chance to say goodbye. As I walk down the stairs, I hear two people talking: Babs and some man. Their voices are sliding into each other's, overlapping but not breaking into the other's.

"A tour . . . ?" says Babs.

"Yes [laugh]," says the man.

"I'm not being a good hostess. I'll get you a scotch . . ."

". . . If I want it. No, thanks . . ."

". . . That's not what you came here for . . ."

"And?"

"And?"

They both laugh.

"Will you be spending the night, O hapless one? Rehash?"

"Yes, missed the train to Grass Woods."

"Penalty for that. Where's wifey? Are you being naughty?"

"She took the car, early. Headache."

"Pity."

"Maybe not . . ."

Laugh.

Laugh.

Silence.

When I finally get to the bottom of the staircase, Babs and the man she was talking to are kissing. He has his arms on her back and is running his fingers up and down, even grabbing her tush. His hands make a shushing noise as they travel over the fabric. Babs is wearing a floor-length blue sequined dress.

I know it is Bill Blass because she once took me through her closet and taught me how to recognize all the designers. This man's a few inches taller than Babs and is wearing a tuxedo. When they break away, in the few seconds before anyone says anything, I see the gold studs holding his shirt closed and know his tux is not a rental.

"Bettina, darling," Babs says with enthusiasm, "I want you to meet a friend of mine."

There's no awkwardness in her voice about what I have just seen. Babs never gets embarrassed. She's probably happy I watched her kissing such a good-looking man.

"This is Mr. Morse," Babs says. I approach him to shake his hand.

"Come on, Babby, enough with charm school. It's Mack," he says.

This makes me happy because when grownups tell you to call them by their first names, it feels like they are including you in stuff. Not that he would let me watch him kiss Babs on purpose, but maybe I will get to hang around when they have a nightcap.

"Nice to meet you, Mack," I say, glad to put my hand into his warm palm.

"Mack" feels smooth coming out of my mouth, but then I look at Babs and it dries up, withers. She has not signed off on this transaction.

"Manners, Mack. Manners. She's eleven, not forty."

I'm not sure if I'm supposed to redo our introduction. But Mack is unfazed. He ignores Babs and winks at me.

"My son, Hailer, is eleven too. Great age."

I don't see what's so great about it, but I'm stunned by how easy it is for him to forge ahead without Babs's approval. No other grownup I have ever met would talk to me if it meant making Babs mad.

I nod my head. Want to see how far he will go.

"I have known your mother since before we were eleven. We went to Grass Woods Academy together. And my wife, Mags, and I bought the house your mother grew up in. You should come see it sometime."

This whole conversation is getting weird. How can he make out with Babs and then talk about his wife? Maybe it has something to do with his looks. Even though Mack is a grownup, I am still in awe of how handsome he is. Eyes the color of the psychedelic blue popsicles you eat only in the summer, and tousled blondish-brown hair. He is about six-two, but his tallness is not intimidating like Babs's is. It inspires salutation. If I threw my arms around his neck, I'm sure he wouldn't push me away. He has probably had a whole lifetime of Getting Away with Things.

But I'm still surprised he would attempt this defiant behavior with Babs. Especially since he says he has known her so long. I look over at her. She has lit a cigarette and is ashing on the floor. Staring at him, deciding what to do next. She grabs his arm, pulls him to her, and kisses him on the back of the neck.

"Mack, let the kid go to bed. I know you want that scotch."

He turns toward her and laughs.

"At your beck and call, madam . . ." He smiles at me and follows her into the living room. I watch as they leave.

Late, late that night, Babs comes into my room. When she wakes me, I think it is to brag about Mack and what a good time they had. Instead she says, "Bullet point: When you try and flirt with one of my beaux, you don't look precocious, just stupid. Mack's a gentleman so he will put up with your bullshit. But hands off. Just so you don't make an ass of yourself. Got it?"

I start to explain, then leave it at a nod. She is already half-way out the door.

In theory, I'm supposed to make Babs more attractive, not less so. She has a home life and no ticking bio clock. She had her tubes tied right after she gave birth to me. Her doctor challenged her on this before delivery. Said he felt uncomfortable performing this radical procedure on such a young woman. But the chocolate money won out. Babs donated a million dollars to completely redo the maternity ward, and now her womb is permanently closed for business.

In late November, Babs and Mack have a fight. When I awake the morning after, I know immediately that something bad has happened. The mood of the aparthouse has shifted. The air has that closed-off, heavy feeling. I search my brain for things I might have said. Any small messes I might have made. This is ultimately a futile activity. If Babs wants to be mad at me, she can always make up a reason.

At dinner that night, she tells me what happened. It has nothing to do with me. Thank God.

"Bettina," Babs says, "etiquette lesson. Mack is hopeless when it comes to gifts. Last night, I am on my hands and knees, waiting for Mack to come from behind and fuck me in the ass. He reaches for some K-Y from his briefcase. If he wants a smooth ride, he has to buy the gel himself. I don't do supplies. When he is digging around for the K-Y, I see a box wrapped in glossy white paper with a little card stuck on it. First mistake. Never attach cards to big-deal gifts. I see the lavender bow and know he actually went to Guillard. Guillard! Predictable. Fucking crap. I know he is making an effort, so I decide to give him some credit. I say, 'Someone has been shopping.'"

I have no idea what K-Y is, but I am certain by the way she keeps repeating *Fucking Guillard!*, fast and loud, that things did not go as she planned. The gift's not for her.

"Mack says, 'Yes, Mags's birthday is coming up.'

"Thank God, I think. Really. No opening the stupid box and faking all of those thank-yous. Time to get back to what we were doing. But talking about the gift kills his erection. I decide to give him a breather and say, 'I don't give a fuck who it's for. I just want to know what it is.'

"He says, 'Tahitian pearl necklace.' But I know he doesn't have the dough to get anything good. Something that will piss other women off when Mags wears it. I bet the whole damn thing will fit in her fist. This is getting boring so I snap my fingers and say, 'Enough!'

"He gets back on the bed. I decide to roll over and wrap my legs around his neck and squeeze tightly. He rubs the jelly on his dick and I glide it into my vagina. My ass is no longer available. Let him try that at home."

The next day, Babs goes out and buys herself a pearl necklace with diamonds. She shows it to me the minute she gets back. The pearls are huge, like bits of gray hail, and the diamonds are like bright rays of a silver sun that would slice your neck if you put them on too quickly.

She lets me hold the necklace and tells me conspiratorially, "Now, these pearls are what you are supposed to get. A man should stick with a floral arrangement if they're out of his league."

The day after that, I go down for breakfast. Lily, our cook, is there, making me cinnamon oatmeal. Lily is my favorite person in the whole world. I love her even more than Brooke Shields. She is black, grew up in Tennessee, and always calls me "sugar." Her hair is dark and streaked with gray. She's heavy and her face isn't pretty, but if I could choose another mother, Lily would be it. Lily's worked for our family since Babs was eighteen. She's the only person who isn't afraid of Babs. Lily has Jesus.

I sit down at the empty table. Stacey's allowed to sleep in since I can get myself dressed and ride the bus to school. Lily walks over to me and says, "Your mother is going to be gone for a few days. She went on a trip with Miss Tally to Paris."

Tally has replaced Andie in the friend department. Thank goodness for this. Tally is pretty decent to me. She also has a daughter, Frances. We're the same age, and she's nice too.

Their trip is a surprise to me. Usually Babs talks about her trips way in advance, shows me maps and the restaurants in the Michelin guide she has circled. She told me once that she's going to take me with her to London. On the Concorde. She hasn't told me when, but I'm still pretty excited about it.

"When is she coming back, Lily?" I ask.

"Probably Friday or Saturday," she answers as she clears my plate. This is special treatment; Babs always makes me do my own dishes. When she goes on a trip, it is a minivacation for me. Lily and I play kings' corners and read Ann Landers in the paper. Stacey is also pretty nice to me. She lets me make ashtrays for her out of sparkles, glue, and old Mountain Dew cans. We even watch TV together.

No matter how much fun I have, I still miss Babs. Eagerly wait for her to come back.

Lily comes into my room that night to tuck me in. As soon as she leaves, I sneak into Babs's bedroom. I love to touch her things. Pretend I'm her.

Babs is in her peach period. Her room is completely ripe with it. Peach doesn't make sense as a Babs color. It is too muted. Evokes the offensive notion of fruit. But peach is more sophisticated than orange. It costs more money, and most women don't think of it when they decorate.

Babs's bedspread is silk. My fingers glide quickly when I trace patterns into it, usually my name. Her pillows and sheets are from Léron. A single set costs as much as a wedding dress. The linens all have beautiful designs: flora and fauna, ribbons with *Babs* sewn across them. Delilah, our maid, changes and irons them twice a week, but they still smell like Babs. I lie down on her bed and fall asleep almost instantly.

Someone wakes me up later that night. Before I can even orient myself, I am afraid. Instinct.

But this time, it isn't Babs. It's Mack. He rubs my head softly. Waits patiently for me to emerge from my sleep. Completely unlike Babs, who always rips me from my dreams whenever she comes to my room for late-night chats. Mack. My first time ever alone with him.

He comes to the aparthouse so often that the doormen just let him up. Without buzzing. I'm surprised I sleep through his arrival. Usually, I know immediately when he comes to see Babs. He focuses her energy. Directs it away from me and pulls it all into himself. Mack nights are the only ones when I'm able to fully relax. As long as Mack's at the aparthouse, rolling about in her bed, Babs will not seek me out.

My eyes open, blink slowly. Mack touches me gingerly on the shoulder. I sit up. The room is dim, but not completely black. The light from the hallway spills in over the bed, breaking the dark into shapes. Mack leans into me and our noses are so close they almost touch. His breath hits my face. My eyes smart. He must have been out drinking.

Mack's wearing a khaki trench coat. Carrying a briefcase. Blue suit, white dress shirt. His clothes look crisp and pressed despite the hour. Maybe this is a trick only people with money can do. Mack comes from the "old" kind. Anonymous. Unlike Babs's, it has no title. Just old, as if it is sitting in an attic somewhere. Dusty but viable.

I look up at him. He's more handsome than anyone in the movies. He runs his hand through his hair, messing it up a bit. A tic Babs finds annoying. *If he needs to occupy his hands, why not take up smoking, for fuck's sake?* I like to watch him do it. It's as if he knows he's better-looking that anyone has a right to be and is trying to handicap himself. Allow others a shot at the game.

"Baby, where is Babs?" Mack begins.

I already know his voice intimately. I hear him ask Babs to make him drinks, hear the strained chords he sings when he and Babs sleep together. The fact that when he talks to me he now calls her "Babs" and not "your mother" like he did when we first met makes me sad. Now even he knows that Babs is always and only Babs. She never alters herself, even for me. Also, I don't care much for the nickname "baby." Coming from him, it is not intimate. Just a lazy word he throws in when he talks to girls he doesn't owe anything to.

"She hasn't returned my calls the past couple of days," he continues. "I was worried."

I want to tell him that Babs isn't someone you worry about. Instead I say, "She's not here." I'm afraid if I give him too much information up front, he will leave.

"Where is she?" Mack asks.

"She's mad at you," I say, hoping this will buy me some more time.

"Why?"

"The other night. When you brought the present."

"I don't get it."

The necklace episode has gone over his head, but I still have his attention.

"How do you know?" he asks.

I roll off the bed, get Babs's pearls from her vanity. Bring them to him.

Babs left them behind when she went to Paris. I found the necklace coiled in the top drawer of her vanity, tossed among her eyelash curlers and lipsticks, like a forgotten string of Mardi Gras beads. I have visited it twice since she left. I want to try it on, but I'm afraid I might break the clasp. I touch the pearls carefully. They are smooth and cold, like frozen grapes.

I'm not that surprised to find them there. Babs will probably never even wear them. Whatever satisfaction they gave her died the moment the salesclerk returned her credit card and went to help the next customer. In Babs's mind, pearls are not sexy. No matter how pumped up hers are, they do not have the power to cut like other gems. After all, they are round. Too female. Too passive. Vulnerable to perfume, scratches, chlorine. Babs thinks pearls are stupid.

"See?"

Mack sits down and takes the necklace in his hands, holds it by one end to assess the weight. As if it were an animal she has killed.

"This is some necklace. Why do you think she's mad if she went out and got this for herself? I'd say she must've been having a pretty good day."

I want to change the subject, but what else would interest him? If I were old enough, I might lean in for a kiss. But he is only sitting with me because he wants to understand Babs.

Mack is so busy trying to figure out why Babs has gone and left an eleven-year-old girl in her place that he does nothing to break the silence either. He touches his watch. It has a round face, black Roman numerals, and a black croc strap. There is a groove cut into it, slicing the band where Mack fastens it.

Finally something to talk about.

"Can I see your watch?"

He takes it off and hands it to me. I put it on. It is heavy and big on my wrist and twists around like a bracelet. I feel nicely weighted down wearing Mack's watch and want more than anything hold on to it forever. But somehow I know he will never leave the aparthouse without it.

I take the watch off, flip it over. There is an inscription on the back: *April 11, 1966. MHM & MTM.*

"I got this as a gift," Mack says, seeing me mull over the words.

"For your birthday?" I ask, knowing that Mack's birthday is in August. The day after Babs's.

"When I got married."

"From your mom?" I pretend to be eleven now, even though I really am.

"From my wife." He almost winces when he says this.

For just a tiny moment, I think he might actually take his shoes off. Lie down on the bed and go to sleep with me. Let me hold his hand. Maybe he will even hold my hand back. His chest is so broad, his pressed white-collared shirt so fresh, I just know it smells like fall. I want to bury my head in it and nod off, if only for an hour.

But he stands up. Buttons his coat and picks up his briefcase. Bends down and kisses the top of my head.

"Good night, babe. If Babs calls, tell her I miss her."

I whisper, "Good night, Mack," and he walks out the door.

After he leaves, I find a quarter on the bed. The coin is shiny, like it was just minted. It isn't the watch, but it's something. Mack hasn't given it to me, but I haven't stolen it. It's an exchange born of the moment.

I have that quarter for almost six months before I lose it.

3

The Daddies' Breakfast

DECEMBER 1979

Every year at the beginning of December, the sixth grade at Chicago Day hosts the Daddies' Breakfast. The fathers are invited to come to the cafeteria before school starts and feast on pancakes, waffles, bacon, and cinnamon rolls. Students decorate the dining hall with red and green paper neckties, hand-drawn portraits of their dads. The day we're supposed to begin working on these, I wonder how I'm going to get out of it.

My homeroom teacher, Wendolyn Henderson, goes around the room handing out white doilies for the daddy heads to go on. She gives me one, not knowing what my deal is. All the other girls and boys around me pick up markers, start working. Wendolyn comes back my way.

"Bettina, you better get going," she says to me. Authoritative.

Where am I supposed to go? I want to say. Instead, I reply, "I'm sorry, but I can't."

"What do you mean?" she asks. "It doesn't matter if your family has an unconventional situation."

"Huh?" I say, then realize she probably thinks my parents are divorced. I decide to just smack her with the true situation.

"I don't have a dad."

Wendolyn is now frustrated because she believes I'm holding out on her.

"Is he dead?" she asks without emotion. Just trying to get the facts.

"I'm not sure," I say truthfully. Wendolyn looks down at me, annoyed. She thinks I'm just looking for attention. Have roped her into a game of twenty questions.

"Are you adopted?" she ventures.

"No," I reply.

"Well, then you must have a dad," Wendolyn says, as if this is the only solution.

"I do, I guess," I admit, "but I don't know who he is. My mother has never told me anything about him."

School is the only place where I refer to Babs as "my mother." My calling her Babs would not go over well with Wendolyn. Like my dad situation.

"Hmm," Wendolyn says, still not quite believing what I have told her. But she has twenty other kids to manage and can't waste any more time on me. She takes a moment and then comes up with a solution I can tell she is proud of.

"You can always invite your mother," she says.

I don't want to tell her that Babs doesn't get up before noon. Certainly not for breakfast in a school cafeteria. I pretend inviting Babs is a good idea. I pick up my marker and get to work on my invite.

Wendolyn returns to check on me. She sees my picture of Babs and nods her head in approval. Babs would laugh in my face if I brought this home. When Wendolyn isn't looking, I crumple it up and throw it away.

· · ·

School over, I arrive home and find Babs in the living room, smoking her Duchess Golden Lights. Doing nothing else. This is enough of an activity.

I am loath to interrupt her. I hang back, let her continue.

When Babs smokes, it is a gorgeous gesture. Babs is not athletic, but the way she handles a cigarette reminds me of the way players at Wimbledon work their racquets. Every June, she and I sit inside and watch it on TV.

When Björn Borg stretches up to meet the ball on a serve, he throws his whole weight behind it, hits the sweet spot, and sends it across the net to the precise patch of grass where he wants it to go. When Babs picks up a cigarette, she doesn't hunch into herself as if it were a private activity. She opens up every inch of her body to the action, and anyone watching can experience it with her. She takes the cigarette between her lips, draws a long inhale, and sucks the smoke deep, deep into her lungs. There is a flinch of pleasure when the nicotine hits her bloodstream, but she is always in complete control when she exhales. Steady. Unrushed. Even. When she blows out the sweet mix of smoke and air she has alchemized inside her, it is completely intoxicating.

I approach. She sees me and says, "Bettina! School?" Cheery voice. An invite to talk to her. I revel in it and join her on the couch.

Maybe Wendolyn Henderson's dumbfounded reaction to my dad situation will make Babs laugh. Babs hates Wendolyn. Says she is a simpleton who cannot possibly comprehend our universe. Wendolyn is also fat. Two strikes against her.

"We had to make invitations to the Daddies' Breakfast, and Miss Henderson doesn't believe I don't have a dad."

"Wendolyn's complete lack of imagination aside, of course you have a dad, Bettina. You just don't know who he is."

"Why won't you tell me? Please." I risk asking, even though

I have gotten nowhere with this subject in the past. Today I can't help it. Seeing all my classmates make invites really got to me.

"I can't, Bettina. We promised we would keep it a secret."

This is more information than I have ever gotten from her. He knows I exist. I wonder if he's a dad of someone at Chicago Day and doesn't want to risk his marriage.

"But I won't tell anyone. I promise. I just want to know," I say.

"I told you. It is one of those things that is just none of your business."

If it's anyone's business, it is surely mine. I feel tears coming. I am one sentence from knowing, but Babs will not budge. And I can't think of anything that will force her to. I really do want to have a dad with me for the breakfast.

Babs sees that I am upset and inexplicably does not mock me for this. She takes my hand and we walk upstairs to her room.

"This should make you feel better," she says.

She reaches into a drawer in her room and pulls out what looks like a silver coin. She hands it to me.

"Your father gave this to me. You can have it."

It's a medal; on the face is a relief of two griffins ringed by Latin words. The back reads *Latin Composition I, 1958*. It is heavy in my hand, and I trace my fingers over the griffins.

I don't dare ask any questions, afraid that Babs will think better of this gift and snatch it back. Instead she says, "He won the Latin prize when he was a senior in high school."

This coin is potent currency for me. It's the first thing I've ever had that belonged to my father and perhaps a clue to finding him later. At eleven, I don't yet have the resources to go looking. Maybe that's why Babs gave it to me.

I say, "Thank you," as if this coin is enough. As if it could come to the Daddies' Breakfast with me and count as a person.

If Babs were another type of mother, at this point we would hug. But I know her limits. However, maybe I can ask for just one more thing.

"Babs, will *you* come to the breakfast?"

"You know I don't do breakfast, Bettina." Her tone is now cross, verging on offended.

I really don't want to be alone at the breakfast. I come up with an outlandish idea, but it just might work.

"Can I ask Mack?"

"What?" she says, as if I have asked to eat her cigarettes.

"Mack, you know . . ."

"I fucking know who Mack is. Of course you can't ask him. Mack has his own stupid kid to deal with, and this is not *Fantasy Island*. He is *not* your dad, and the sooner you forget this crap, the happier you will be."

"I wouldn't tell anyone he was my dad. Just a friend of the family." I can't get this scenario out of my head.

"Bettina, Mack is not a family friend. He's not even my *friend*. We are fucking. That's all. Even we don't do breakfast. And he barely knows who you are. *Point finale.*"

I don't tell Babs about our night together. As much as I want the actual Mack to come, it's more about having a grownup with me. I will look like a complete loser if I show up alone.

As if she can read my thoughts, Babs says, "The parents at Chicago Day don't matter. They're a middle-class clusterfuck. You could just go by yourself. But you aren't gutsy enough."

She's right about that.

Then Babs offers up a solution. It's depressing, at best, but it will save me from total humiliation.

"Why don't you ask Stacey? I fucking pay her way above her skill set, and while you're at school, she does nothing but watch soaps and practice smoking in front of the mirror."

As much as I really don't like Stacey, she's better than noth-ing. But she'll be hard to explain to Wendolyn. Almost none of my classmates have nannies. A few have them, but only because both parents work, and even then they are called babysitters. Not permanent; just filling in until Mommy and Daddy get home. And in any case, the father would still make time to come to the breakfast. Even if it meant missing a cou-ple of meetings. Bringing Stacey is like showing up with the doorman.

But of course I take Stacey to the breakfast. She seems thrilled to get out of the aparthouse and fill in for Babs. She trades her tight jeans and Dr. Scholl's for an old red silk dress, a hand-me-down from Babs. I am almost touched that Stacey thinks to dress up.

The cafeteria smells sweetly of syrup and sugar. The sev-enth-graders serve us as we go through the buffet. Despite my worries, the students are so excited to be with their fathers they hardly notice I have brought my twenty-one-year-old nanny. And unlike the mothers at Chicago Day, the dads will not tuck this fact into their brains somewhere, eager to gossip it about later. No, the daddies are thinking about their children, then getting back to work. But Wendolyn notices, and this time she seems to actually feel sorry for me.

4

Sex at Our House

T HAT WINTER, BABS SLEEPS with Mack all the time. He's over at the aparthouse constantly. It is late at night when he comes, and early in the morning when he leaves. I'm supposed to be sleeping, but on Mack nights, I sit by the door of my bedroom. Listen.

They no longer confine themselves to her bedroom. Just start on the back stairs. Sisal with the steepest incline. As Babs and Mack crawl up them to her bedroom, I can hear Mack's steady humming and Babs's puncturing expletives: *Jesus! Fuck! Finger my cunt!* When Babs's door clicks shut, I take their place on the staircase. Mack usually leaves a shirt behind. Babs tells me later she likes to suck on his nipples.

I run my hands over the shirt's cuffs and finger the buttons one by one. Sometimes I give them tiny kisses, being careful not to get spit on the edges and leave marks where there should not be.

Mack's shirts smell so good. Nothing overwhelming and obvious, like Babs's perfume. Just clean and woodsy like moss.

I know I don't smell like anything yet. I'm always tempted to take off my nightgown and wrap my naked body in the shirt. I just want to feel like some part of this man sleeping with my mother belongs to me.

But I never dare. If Babs ever caught me touching Mack's stuff, she would just laugh and say, *Oh, dear,* in a pseudo-pitying way. As if she had caught me trying to eat the oranges off the chinoiserie wallpaper in the powder room.

After dinner, once Lily has cleared our plates and Stacey has gone to her room, Babs tells me almost everything they do on those nights.

"Bettina," she says, "what is going on between me and Mack is very educational. You need specifics, not that bland shit they'll teach you at school."

I really don't want to know all the details, but Babs launches right into them anyway.

"When the time comes for you to have sex, I don't want you sitting on your hands, fucking baffled. Oral sex, very important. First, the name. When a man sucks on your clitoris, you should call it *admiring the centerfold.* Much, much better than *eating you out* or *going down on you. Giving a blowjob* is also stupid. Refer to putting a dick in your mouth as *raising the mast.* Or something like that. Blowing has nothing to do with it."

I wonder if I'm supposed to be taking notes.

She continues. "Remember that every man's different. You can't just get lazy and have a pat formula. Mack, for instance. He likes to be licked rather than sucked. Except at the very end, when he is close to coming. Then he wants his penis to be worked over like a pacifier."

She reaches for a cigarette. I don't like the idea of Mack's penis in Babs's mouth. I worry someday she'll get mad and bite it off.

"You must pick a man who knows how to properly admire

your centerfold. This is the easiest way for a woman to come. But a man who has even the slightest skill in this area is rarer than you think.

"Mack, thank God, knows exactly where the centerfold is and isn't intimidated when he gets there. A lot of men make a quick pit stop at the centerfold because they think they have to but clearly would rather be elsewhere. Sucking on your breasts or grabbing your ass. Never waste time on a man who is afraid to put his mouth between your legs and fucking Wimbledon it like a true pro. Point, set, match. Mack admires my centerfold until I've had two or three orgasms. No self-respecting woman should settle for less. That's just laziness on someone's part."

Another night, Babs continues with more of her sex life. Tells me they often leave the aparthouse and go to Hopse-quesca, Mack's country club in Grass Woods.

"We have the place to ourselves," Babs explains.

"Mack parks his golf cart in the woods by the sand trap on the eighth hole. I wear tennis outfits. My legs look fabulous, and Mack can quickly flip up the skirt. He just wears his boring preppy uniform. Khaki pants, needlepoint belt. A button-down shirt. Penny loafers. No socks.

"Then there are the damn pennies," she continues, "those 1909-S VDB wheat-backs. His grandfather gave them to him on his fourteenth birthday. Before he left for Cardiss. He's worn them in every pair of loafers since. Sentimentality in shoes. Stupid."

I don't like to hear any criticism of Mack. Especially about something so trivial as his shoes.

In the end, I don't mind knowing what goes on at Hopsequesca. When you are eleven and your mother tells you things, you think these are things you should know.

But already at my age, sex doesn't shock me. I've read Babs's copy of *The Joy of Sex* cover to cover with all of those gross drawings of naked adults. Underarm and pubic hair every-where. I'm also not one of those dumb kids who think grown-ups are hurting each other when they moan or who get scared when they hear them yell out as they come. In fact, I know all about orgasms. I masturbate every night in the bathtub before bed. It makes it easier for me to get to sleep.

Babs, for all her power, has yet to catch me at it, this thing I call *chasing the smash*. It's not that she would disapprove; rather the opposite. She would think it was a much better afterschool activity than ballet or tap dancing. But I don't want to tell her about it. It's a secret I keep with myself.

My technique is, as far as I know, specific to me. I lie flat on my back in the bathtub with the tap running and let the water hit the small, hairless mound between my legs.

I know from my reading that my vagina is tucked inside my body and that the spot the water is hitting when I tilt my hips upward is my clitoris. But in the tub I use my own vocabulary, make my own rules. I just think of the whole area the water touches when I masturbate as my me.

The my-me bedtime ritual feels so, so good. A steady pres-sure of warm water starts with a small tingle, which grows and grows like a balloon until there is an enormous pop. But the pop has no punctuation. It just flows from my me up between my hips, like an enormous spill of water.

At the moment of a smash, I press my hands against the sides of the tub as hard as I can. Steady myself to keep the enormous throbbing from propelling me out of the tub. A child gone overboard. I also brace myself to keep my me there for as long as possible, to see how much intensity I can with-stand before pulling away. I learn that there's no limit to the amount of smashes you can have. My record is four.

If I have enough smashes, I fall asleep easily, without the intrusion of dreams. Without smashing, I usually nightmare.

In such dreams, I'm usually naked, hunched on the floor in the middle of a crowded black-tie-one-on (what Babs calls formal parties). I'm wearing some of Babs's drop-dead jewelry, perhaps her pissed-off-at-Mack South Sea pearls. The pearls are always twisted tightly, in a chokehold around my neck. Then I realize I'm about to be trampled by the heavy dress shoes and pointed high-heeled stilettos the grownups wear. They don't mean to hurt me; I just happen to be in the way. They walk on my body while I suffocate. I always feel vulnerable and half-me the days after these dreams. I need to smash, smash myself extra hard and good to make this horrible dream go away.

I am absolutely sure, however, that the idea of *chasing the smash* did not originate with me. I have the strong impression that when Babs was pregnant with me, she didn't have sex, just masturbated. Since Babs and I were one body (or as close to it as two bodies can ever be, one body not merely penetrating but actually *floating inside* another), I was rocked to sleep by her smash. Now I do it alone. A kind of gentle womb-breaking, my own invented version of birth.

When all the water has drained, I pull myself over the side of the tub and rest on the bathmat on all fours. I'm usually too far gone to walk. I wait a little to dry so I don't make a puddle and slip on the marble floor. Then I crawl to my bedroom, my bony knees relaxing when I make it there.

My bedroom has white wall-to-wall that approximates bunny fur: soft and vulnerable, like the down of a newborn's head. My bed is a queen-size canopy, but it is about as far as you can get from the pretty-pink-princess version all girls my age are supposed to want. It has a hard green wrought-iron lattice with angry leaves sprouting from the posts. They twist themselves into threatening vines. The top of this mean bed is covered with white mosquito netting. In an animated version of my life, where I talked to mice or had singing dwarf friends,

Babs might be a fairy godmother who sewed this net to protect me from hostile creatures. The sad thing is, as it stands, the netting is just a creative touch she can show off to friends.

When we are eating dinner, Lily always sneaks up and prepares my room. Stacey can't be bothered. Lily turns down my bed. Leaves a fresh Lanz nightgown folded on the pillow. Babs forbids me to wear underwear to sleep. She thinks every vagina needs to air out after being cooped up all day.

Lily always leaves a Splush on top of my pillow. A Splush is a pebble-size bit of dark chocolate wrapped in purple tinfoil with a gold *B* stamped on it. It is my absolute all-time favorite Ballentyne product. It is one of the poshest chocolates in the whole line. A bag of them costs twelve dollars.

Despite the renowned ecstasy of this top-shelf chocolate, it's not something I'm supposed to indulge in. Ever. Babs doesn't let me eat chocolate or any sweets, no matter what. She refuses to have a fat daughter, and I don't dare do anything to risk such a fate.

I always carefully unwrap the Splush Lily has left for me, but I never put it in my mouth. Just smell it. I don't want to disappoint Lily, so I leave the tiny bits of purple-tinfoil wrapping on my bedside table so she can see it in the morning. As for the chocolate itself, I wrench open my window and hurl it outside into the night.

I sometimes wonder what becomes of all of these discarded Splushes. Do they hit the people walking below on Walton Street on their way to Water Tower Place for a movie or dinner? If someone gets hit, does he think a bird has pooped on him or maybe that he has been assaulted by an angry pellet of air? But really, I couldn't care less about the subsequent trajectory of the chocolate. I am smashed and Splush-less. I've earned another night's sleep in my own bed.

5

Thrash

JANUARY 1980

I HAVE SWIMMING PRACTICE AFTER school. Leaves me physically spent. My body and hair are stripped of dirt by the chlorine, and I decide not to take a bath and smash. Read a book instead. *Madame Bovary*. In English. It's a hard book, but I am picking away at it the best I can. I do know some French, but not enough to read *MB* in the original.

I have spent every June, July, and part of August since I was five in Cap d'Antibes living with Cécile, a cousin of Babs. *I need the summers off,* Babs says. It is the best present Babs has ever given me. I'm adding French to my skill set and can use it throughout my life. Even though Babs goes to France pretty often, she makes no effort to learn the language. The way she talks resists translation.

Cécile is from Babs's mother's side of the family. Like Babs's mother, Eudy, Cécile is a great beauty, but she is middle class, which Babs considers the same as being poor. Poor might be interesting, but it is not fun.

I'm still reading when Babs comes to my room for a chat.

Mack must have taken the night off. She saunters over to my bed, wearing only her bra and underwear. Carries a goblet of Perrier with a lime in one hand and a fistful of Duchess Golden Lights in the other. I take it Babs has a long conversation in mind. She would never pace her smoking to match the length of our exchange should it get interesting. She has a stack of mags tucked under her left arm, and she spreads them out on the end of my bed. *Vogue. W. Harper's Bazaar.* She sits down next to me.

"I've been thinking. We haven't been putting enough effort into your shoes. People always notice what you have on your feet. This might be the key to your popularity at school."

I doubt it, but when Babs proposes a project, I always count myself in.

She continues. "I thought you and I could go through these, find ones that are downright fabulous. You and I can hit Saks or even I. Magnin tomorrow and buy them. This is worth missing school for. Finding your size shouldn't be a problem. There are many women who have the bad taste to be short and have small feet. I've already marked a few pages I like."

I pick up the *Vogue,* ignoring the models' tiny bodies and concentrating on their feet. I flip through the pages and see green suede boots, red satin high heels, black lizard flats. Even if I don't really like any of them and can't imagine wearing them to Chicago Day, I'm still excited. Babs shops without a budget, and we could spend all day together amassing things. Babs is deep into *W,* circling her favorites.

I move my book away from where we are sitting. Try to hide it from Babs. She hates when she catches me reading. Says I'm showing off. Not working hard enough to make friends. I don't even mark my place. I would trade Emma's adventures for shoes with Babs any day. Unfortunately, *Bovary* slides off my bed into the space next to the wall where I've stashed a ginger ale. I hear the can thunk against the wall as it tips over. The sticky pop must now be pooling on the expensive bunny-fur carpet.

Babs has ears like a deer. She hears the can spill too. She crawls forward on my bed. Reaches down and pulls the can up slowly, as if she were fishing garbage from a dirty lake. She examines it for a moment, then hurls it at the wall.

I watch the can fly across the room. It leaves a stain on the silver-lamé wallpaper. More damage than I have done to the bunny-fur rug.

"What the fuck, Bettina. You know you are not supposed to have drinks or food in your room."

She lights up a cigarette, rips the *Vogue* from my hands. Waits for a response.

I think if I handle this right, we can get back to the shoes. Surely more fun for both of us. Rarely, but sometimes, I can sway Babs by using the right tone.

I say, "I'm sorry, Babs. I just thought I'd be really careful, and there wouldn't be a problem."

No such luck. She is still staring at me with dull, flat eyes. I have ruined the shoe project. All for a ginger ale.

"The ginger ale is for Lily. Do you know how many calories are in a single fucking can? Not to mention the fact that you tried to sneak it. I fucking hate sneaks. I wonder what else you have hidden in here."

I try to reach out and touch her wrist. Keep her from leaving the bed. Useless. The ship has sailed. I just have to hope that daybreak will come as fast as possible and provide a benevolent shore. Babs loves to stay up all night working on various projects, but she always calls it quits before Lily wakes me for breakfast. Her idea of being a civilized person.

"Take off your nightgown, Bettina, so I can see you have nothing hidden in there."

I do as I'm told. Am now naked on my bed. This might be enough punishment to inflict for most people. Not Babs.

She stands up, walks over to the armoire where I keep my clothes. It has a *The Lion, the Witch, and the Wardrobe* feel. Big enough for me to hide inside. Sometimes I do. Not tonight. There will be no hiding tonight.

She opens the door and pulls at the top drawer. She grabs fistfuls of my socks and brings them over to the bed. Begins unballing them. She carefully reaches her hand inside each one where my feet normally go, checks that there is nothing tucked in there.

"I know how sneaks work, Bettina. They pick the places where most people would not think to look."

I begin to wonder if I have indeed stashed something important in my socks. But no. The only thing I truly value, my autographed napkin from Brooke taped to her picture and framed, is on my desk. Not hidden but in clear view. Maybe this will add points to my honesty column. Maybe Babs will see it and be less mad after all.

But she is just getting started. After the socks, she goes through my underwear. It is all the same, white cotton bikini briefs. No Disney princesses, Pooh Bears, or Tinker Bells for me. She takes each one out and stretches the elastic and then smells the place where my crotch would be.

I'm still not old enough to have anything but immaculate underwear, even before it is washed. I always wipe carefully whenever I go to the bathroom. Am not yet burdened by all the messy emissions of a menstrual cycle.

Babs is so thin that she almost never juices or has a monthly period. She eats so little that she rarely has a bowel movement, and when she does, she takes long showers and scrubs her anal region clean of any traces of excrement. The only thing that taxes her panties is use. When the elastics start to give, Babs cuts up her underwear with a pair of kitchen scissors and buries them in the trash.

She does this to stop the *freaks out there who want to whack off with the lingerie of chocolate-heiress pussy.* Once, I dug a strip of her panty fabric out of the garbage. I made it into an anklet and wore it in the tub while I chased the smash. I was so worried she would find out that I threw it away two days later. I guess I am a sneak and a liar after all. Babs does have to be on her guard, protect herself from me.

I watch as she moves on to the pockets of my pants. It's strangely comforting to see her take such an interest in my things. In me.

By three A.M., everything I own is in a huge heap in the middle of the floor. Babs seems happy with her work. Another opportunity to use her parenting skills to turn me into a decent human being.

She's finished. Maybe we can get back to the mags. Wrong. She still has one thing left to do.

Babs walks over to my desk. Picks up the picture of Brooke. "How stupid of me," she says. "I almost overlooked Brookie."

Babs undoes the frame. My picture of Brooke and the autographed cocktail napkin go tumbling to the ground.

I try to think of something I can offer her in place of Brooke. But I'm naked. Have nothing. And Babs does not give options.

Don't, Babs, don't, Babs. Please don't.

Babs throws my treasures on the bed by my feet.

"So, babe. An eye for an eye, I think."

She turns back to my desk and picks up a pencil. I wish she would take the pencil to me. Poke me in the cheek with it, maybe. Write some obscenity on my forehead. But no. She goes right for the picture of Brooke and scribbles all over her face.

Babs gains momentum. Presses harder. Makes deep grooves in the picture. She keeps going until Brooke's whole face is covered with marks. Brooke looks like she has really bad acne. *I can always get another picture,* I think. *This isn't so bad.*

But Babs isn't done. She picks up the cocktail napkin. Brooke has actually touched this. It's irreplaceable. It's the very best thing I have. She reaches down to the side of the bed where the ginger ale spilled. Pats the wet spot with the napkin. She holds it up. I can see that Brooke's signature has run to the point of being illegible. I can live with this, I think. Brooke still took pen to this small napkin. It's still worth something. But there are to be no consolation prizes tonight. Babs holds the napkin to my face. She rips it up until it is just white strips. Just like her old underwear.

"See! This is what it feels like to have someone fuck up your things. But now you can take inventory. Keep the things you want and throw the rest away. I will bring up a garbage can from the kitchen. When you are done, your closet will be neat as a pin, and getting dressed will be like shopping at Saks! Everything will be in its place with only the things you like to choose from."

She leaves to get the garbage can. I'm not sure if I'm allowed to put my nightgown back on or if I'm supposed to tackle this project naked. I give myself a minute to consider this. I look at the magazines, which are still sitting on the end of my bed. I wonder if we'll ever get back to the shoe project. Probably not. But I was so close.

Later that night, as I sift through the huge mound of my things, throwing most of them away because I am too tired to put them back, I discover that Babs has left behind one important thing. Her cigarettes.

I take one of them in my left hand, put it to my mouth. Light it. The inhale is disgusting. The nicotine hits my bloodstream so fast my head reels and I clutch the post of my bed. I take it from my mouth. Come up with another idea. I can't help but be angry at myself for having caused the whole room-thrash.

I stretch my right leg out. Bend over and look for a good spot. My wrist is off-limits. Babs has given me too many how-tos on death to do otherwise. *If you are going to slice your wrists, make sure you know what you are doing. There is nothing more pathetic than ending up in the hospital because you didn't do your homework.*

Babs is pro-suicide. Has no patience for depressed people. *If you can't get out of bed, just bag it altogether.* No patience for the very old either. Too many of them linger. Pooping in diapers, sporting ugly bruises and nasty brown spots on their papery skin.

If she sees a burn mark on my wrist, she will think it is a childish attempt to off myself. So I push the lit cigarette into the flesh just above my right anklebone. No blood. Just a round, red tattoo. Babs will never be able to strip me of this.

It hurts, but not really.

6

The Hangover-Brunch Cruise Party

APRIL OF THAT YEAR, the affair is still going on, but there's something different about it. Mack comes to the aparthouse less often. Babs is alternately restless and bored. When she's had enough, she decides to throw a party.

Babs's parties are a big deal. Everyone wants to get invited. There's always a theme and you have to dress accordingly. The key is getting all the details right. Even more important than who you invite.

Babs calls this one the Hangover-Brunch Cruise Party. Since Babs doesn't drink, she's never hung over. But she isn't against other people drinking. She says most people she knows are completely boring unless they drink. Sober, they are too worried about what other people think. Are not *fearless*, like she is. I'm not fearless either. Babs is excited for the day I start drinking for real. The way Babs thinks about drinking is kind of hard to explain, but I get it. Babs has rules for herself, and rules for everyone else.

Babs would never be caught dead taking a cruise. They are middle-class tacky. Brunch is a whole other level of disgusting. Breakfast and lunch *at the same time.* Going back as often as you want for more, wielding tongs at those steaming serve-yourself stations. Waiting for a "chef" wearing a paper hat and rubber gloves to hack off slices of ham from a communal slab. The whole thing is on par with rats feeding in the dumpster at the IHOP.

But all this is fodder for a *damn good time.* Hangovers before a party, a cruise without a boat, brunch before bed. An alternative universe where Babs is in charge.

Babs is always in charge of my universe, of course, but in the months that lead up to the party, things are much easier for me. I get to help Babs get ready for the party. School is just something I do between our work.

Each invitation to the Hangover-Brunch Cruise Party is an intricate package. Babs and I assemble all three hundred of them ourselves.

Most nights we are up past two. I don't mind missing out on sleep. I'm good at gluing and organizing. Can keep going while Babs takes smoke breaks.

The first component is the actual invitation, which Babs has printed up on round cardboard coasters. The coasters are ringed with sketches of orange lifesavers that say *SS Babs.* The details of the event are printed inside the ring of the lifesavers:

Go Overboard with Me
At a Hangover-Brunch Cruise
100 East Lake Shore Drive
7:00 P.M.
Saturday, May 17
Dress: Naughty Nautical

The second item we include is a clear Lucite cube filled with a viscous blue liquid. It transforms into crashing waves if you shake it. We glue to the top of each cube a little plastic cruise ship and tiny plastic people lying facedown, as if they have fallen into the sea. Then we add to the package a shot glass for each invitee, with DRINK UP, THROW UP, SHOW UP printed on it in the same font as the invite. Finally, minibottles of rum, scotch, and vodka. A pouch of Hawaiian Punch mix and one of Tang as mixers. Drinks of choice for tacky people?

The RSVP cards are touristy it's-better-in-the-Bahamas-type postcards, stamped and addressed to Babs. There are three reply options:

    __ Will rally
    __ Still passed out, have to pass
    __ Party pooper

I'm not sure who's going to check the party-pooper one. But Babs sends some invites to people she knows won't get the joke, won't come. She wants them to admit that they can't handle parties like hers. I look at the guest list and see that *Mr. and Mrs. McCormack H. Morse III* is on there. I wonder which box Mack and Mags will check.

We put all the items that make up the invitations in mini– leather suitcases. Babs writes each invitee's name and address on a small rectangular piece of heavy cream stock. Babs has beautiful handwriting.

I get to slide the pieces of paper into orange leather luggage tags from Hermès, each of which has *SS BABS* printed on it. Babs always gives a practical souvenir of her parties, something people can actually use after the party's over. I like to think that years from now, if anything happens to Babs and I want to track down people who knew her and might remember me, I can just go to airport baggage carousels and look for these tags.

When we are done, Babs's chauffeur, Franklin, and I spend several days driving around Chicago and the suburbs hand-delivering them. Each morning, Babs charts the route we are to go by placing numbered stickers on a street map and corresponding stickers on the cases. This is way more important than school. Babs doesn't even bother sending Wendolyn a note to explain where I am.

Babs says Franklin and I have to drop the invitations off because the post office would crush them, but I know it's more than that. Babs bought herself a new car for Christmas. For it to be admired properly, everyone has to see it. It is a toffee-colored stretch limo. Full bar, TV, and lights that run down each side of the interior of the car, like a landing strip. You can dim them or put them on full strength, depending on your mood. There is a phone with buttons that light up when you dial. Babs cranks Lionel Richie or Kool and the Gang when she rides around in the *stretcher,* as she calls it. Sometimes she doesn't even go anywhere in particular, just cruises. I have seen cars like this only on TV. It makes me feel like Babs is a movie star.

The license plate on the stretcher just says BABS. Riding in it makes me feel like I'm part of Babs in a way that nothing else does. It has her smell: the sweet toasted mixture of Duchess Golden Lights and Georgette Klinger perfume. When the car is idling, I feel like it is Babs breathing.

When Franklin and I get to a stop, I run around back, find the case, and give it to the doorman. If we are in the suburbs, I take it to the front door of the house. Then it's usually a housekeeper who comes to the door, but sometimes there's a mom in a sweaty tennis outfit or scruffy gardening clogs. She'll generally say, "Thank you, Bettina," which surprises me, since I don't know any of them. Then I realize the woman must recognize me from our Christmas Card.

If Babs's parties were run-of-the-mill, if people just got invited over for food and drinks in normal clothes, these women might consider inviting Babs and me to their houses for dinner. Let me play with their kids. As it stands, they treat Babs's parties like going to the circus. You take in the show, enjoy yourself. Don't wonder what happens to the monkey in the stupid outfit once you leave.

Babs does invite a few out-of-towners. She wraps their cases in layers of orange-and-white-striped tissue. Places each in a large cardboard box. We get those RSVPs back, and most say yes. Even her cousin Lucas from New York is coming, with his wife, Poppy. They are going to take the train here and then leave the next day, since Lucas has a gallery opening to go to. Cécile and her husband, Luc, say no. Babs says it's because they can't pay for the plane ticket from France. Typical.

The night of the Hangover-Brunch Cruise Party, the apart-house doesn't look like a place people live in. Babs is always big on decorations, but for this party, she makes structural changes. The huge pane of glass is removed from the living room, leaving just a slim balcony and air where the window used to be. Lake Shore Drive is blocked off, and helicopters with huge hooks carry the glass panes down to the beach. They are then wrapped up and lifted to some warehouse. It takes two days and the kids are all talking about it at school.

When I am older, I tell stories about this party, and people never believe this part.

"But you lived there," they say.

"It wasn't permanent," I reply.

"What if it had rained?" they wonder.

"I don't know. It didn't," I answer. They still can't get over it. Sounds crazy, not fun.

An hour before the guests arrive, everything is perfect. The aparthouse looks just like a cruise ship. All the furniture's gone from the first floor, replaced with boat-y, cruise-y things. There are rows of deck chairs with orange-and-white-striped towels folded on them. Their canvas backs billow with the breeze blowing off the lake. There is large aboveground pool filled with aqua-blue water, with two ladders to get in.

Babs is disappointed with the pool. She says it looks more Wisconsin-backyard than *Love Boat,* but I'm still impressed. I climb up one of the ladders. Three female mannequins float facedown in the water, wearing only bras and underwear. The kind women wear in *Playboy.* See-through in the back; silk bows or intricate lace in the front. Babs doesn't wear things like this. Says men who get off on this kind of lingerie have to work to maintain erections or tend to prematurely ejaculate. I wonder if she bought them herself or sent Stacey to Victoria's Secret.

The mannequins' synthetic hair and plastic limbs give them away. They aren't real people. But the effect is still creepy. I get off the ladder. That night, I hear some people saying the pool is just in bad taste. Especially since Babs's parents drowned. I feel embarrassed for Babs. But why did they come? Why not just check the Pooper option on the invitation? Stay home. Everyone knows Babs always does things like this.

Waiters and waitresses dressed up like the crew of a cruise ship are already hard at work. They walk around with brown plastic trays and order pads. Getting the mood right before anyone arrives. They balance piña coladas and daiquiris, concoctions with fruit and straws in them.

Babs absolutely hates straws. They are for lazy people who

can't be bothered to lift glasses to their lips. For fat people who need to get in as many calories as fast as possible. Perfect for the party. But whenever we go to a restaurant, Babs makes me take the straw out of my glass. Put it off to the side. I feel bad because the discarded straw always leaves a wet spot on the tablecloth that seems sloppier and more offensive than the straw itself. Reminds me of the wet stick oozing from a deflated condom I once found out on the back terrace of the aparthouse after a party.

I do it anyway. Babs says you can always tell how a person has been raised by what he or she does with a straw.

I appreciate what the waiters are doing. I am in what Babs refers to as my actress period. I make up elaborate routines to the albums of Broadway shows Babs has seen in New York City. She gave me a pink boom box for Christmas. One of the best gifts ever. I spend hours in my room, practicing. Babs likes the music I choose. Songs with swearwords in them. Ballads sung by men about love affairs gone wrong.

A week before the Hangover-Brunch Cruise Party, Babs rewards my efforts.

"Bettina," she says, "why don't you do one of your little numbers at the party for my friends? You work so hard on them. I just know they must be amusing."

"I would love to, Babs." Trying to sound professional, not excited.

My current repertoire is from *A Chorus Line.* I especially like a song I call "Tits and Ass." It's about a woman with a body that no one likes. She can't get famous until she buys new parts for it. I've memorized all of the words. When I lip-synch, it really looks like me singing.

When I practice, I think about Mack watching me. Imagine that he will clap louder than anyone else. Get me a drink of water when I'm done. Let me sit on his lap while Babs talks to her other guests. I'll impress him in a way I failed to when we were together on Babs's bed.

The night of the party, Babs and I get ready with Tally and her daughter, Frances. Tally's real name is Natalie. She started calling herself Tally after the divorce, thinking people would take her for a different person. She and Babs go on fun outings together. Take exotic trips. Their favorite thing to do is a game called speed shopping. They agree on an amount of money—say, ten thousand dollars—and go to stores like Gucci. See who can spend it faster. The only rules are that you cannot use a personal shopper and have to buy things that you will use. No returns allowed.

Tally has another vocation apart from these activities, which is a first for a Babs friend. Tally writes the Diary of an Heiress series: a Rolodex heiress who travels the world, works low-paying jobs just for fun, and sleeps with men she meets along the way. Tally's written five of them so far. They piss Babs off. She claims Tally has no talent and does nothing but poach Babs's experiences. But more than a small part of her likes to see herself in print, so she lets it go.

Babs's bathroom is as much a room as her bedroom or the kitchen. It has plush peach wall-to-wall. A peach marble bathtub. Matching pedestal sink. There's also a brown suede sofa covered with peach-tasseled silk pillows. You can't sit on it when you're wet, but it looks cool.

Tally is sitting on the sofa, smoking. She wears a white silk robe trimmed with fur. Matching mules. Babs is stationed at her vanity getting hair and makeup done by *the boys,* Geoff and Jasper. Her robe is not belted. We all have a good view of her sheer skin-colored lingerie. It does nothing to hide her nipples and pubic hair. She always gets ready like this, so it's not shocking. Babs has no private parts.

Frances and I are sitting Indian-style at our mothers' feet. I love Frances. I don't have to explain Babs to her. She doesn't talk a lot and is always willing to try out my ideas.

Geoff has pulled Babs's blond hair up in a messy twist. Strands are falling about her face. Bobby pins are jabbed in at odd angles. Now, she is moving on to makeup. Babs has her eyes closed, her face open to Jasper.

"Jas," she says, "the idea is to make me look hung over but still up for a good fuck. Disheveled, but not dirty. Think about last night's makeup, a short press in the pillows, and a gooey app of gloss as touchup. Also, we are on a cruise, so turn up the tacky."

Jasper laughs and applies foundation. He picks up some rouge from Babs's second drawer and smears it across one cheek like a gash.

Frances and I are also wearing robes. But they are part of our costumes, ordered especially for the party. Blue and white stripes, and short, falling just over our fannies. On the back, they say ss BABS, CREW. Underneath, we wear white bikinis that have blue sequin Bs on the triangles where boobs are supposed to go. We get to wear blue high heels, and we have jobs to do.

Frances's pocket is stuffed with Alka-Seltzer and aspirin packets. She's supposed to give them out as people arrive. I have two Rx pads with the names of drinks on them, ones that Babs has invented: hula happiness; decadence on deck. I'm supposed to hand one to anyone who looks sober or not completely into it.

We also get to have our makeup done, but only after Tally and Babs are finished.

Just then Lily comes in carrying a silver tray. I can always tell when she's coming. Her pantyhose rub together at her thighs when she walks and make a swishing sound.

"Here you are, Miss Tabitha," Lily says.

On the tray is a large crystal pitcher of ice water. The ice is not in cubes, like regular ice, but in disks that have arched holes, like sand dollars. The water can pass right through them. Sliver-thin rounds of oranges, limes, and lemons float on top. A delicate wineglass flanks the pitcher. The glass is wide and deep like a pregnant tulip might be, frosted with cold. A bunch of frozen purple grapes huddle in a silver bread basket, and a pair of silver scissors is tucked inside to cut them off their stems. Three squares of dark chocolate the size of butter pats sit smack in the middle of a Bernardaud dinner plate. Babs's pre-party dinner. Always the same.

"Thank you, Lily," Babs says, her eyes still closed.

"Lily," Tally says, eyeing the tray, "I would love a glass of white wine, please. Two ice cubes. Some potato chips. With Dijon mustard and a side of cayenne pepper. And a Mint Milano cookie."

Tally's just making this order up as she goes along. Wants to look like she's as specific about food as Babs is. But even I know you don't put ice cubes in wine.

Lily takes her seriously and says in a respectful voice, "Yes, Mrs. O'Mara."

She looks at me and Frances sitting on the floor. I see her wondering about our shoes. I don't feel as excited anymore. When Lily looks worried, I start to get worried too. It's as if she can see something coming that I can't.

"Miss Tabitha," she says, "should I get the girls something to eat?"

"In the kitchen, Lily," Babs says. "I will send them down when they are finished. Just make sure they don't get in the way of the caterers."

"Yes, ma'am."

"Where is Stacey?"

"I believe she is getting ready."

"Ready? For what?"

"For the party. She told me she would be just a minute."

"Tell her to get her ass up here. I need her to rub the girls down with coconut oil. She is probably going at it with her home waxing kit again. She seems to think that we're really going on a cruise and that she'll be sitting by the pool tanning her armpits. I'm all for authenticity, but not on my dime.

"And I really don't give a fuck what her bikini line looks like. Plus, the last time she took off almost half of an eyebrow, and I can't have people working for me looking like that."

"Yes, Miss Tabitha." Lily looks down at me again. I know she loves me no matter what, but I'm afraid one day she'll go and find people to work for who don't use swearwords.

Lily picks up the pitcher and fills Babs's glass. No matter how many times I have seen Lily do this, I'm still in awe of how precise it is. How beautiful.

I decide that I'll concoct a special drink just for Frances and me. It'll have a lot of alcohol. We don't want to look sober or detached. At least I don't. I'm not entirely sure about Frances. She still orders chocolate milk when we go out to eat with our mothers. When it arrives, Babs always looks at me. Does an eye roll that says *Can you believe we are with these stupid fucking people?*

Jasper finishes Babs's cheeks and reaches into his makeup case for a pot of blue eye shadow. The blue is the color of cotton candy, gaudy but sweet and edible. Not a Babs color at all. Looks like something Stacey would wear.

Jasper smudges a heavy layer of the Stacey blue on Babs's eyelids and then dusts each one with silver sparkles. When he's done, Babs looks like she has been iced with cupcake frosting. I wonder if, later on in the evening, Mack will suck on these delicious-looking eyelids until his lips and teeth turn blue.

I want to casually ask Babs if Mack is coming to the party; she hasn't mentioned him once and I am worried this means something. But I don't dare. Babs knows I am rarely if ever casual about anything. She has emphatically told me that I'm to have nothing to do with him. If she senses I'm too interested in him, she might take away my dance number. Send me to my room so I will miss the whole party.

Babs opens her eyes. Leans into the mirror and checks out Jasper's work.

"Jesus Christ, Jasper! You nailed it. If I weren't the fucking hostess of this itty-bitty boat bash, I might just head over to Randy's and see if they would hire me for the twelve-to-eight shift.

"Think of the possibilities. I could pour coffee and take down orders on those little pads. Who eats in the middle of the night anyway? I just adore those gold-tin ashtrays they have. I've always wondered if they throw them away or wash them for reuse."

Randy's is the all-night diner on North Avenue, right across the street from Chicago Day. A lot of moms have breakfast there after dropping their kids off. I'm not quite sure how Babs knows so much about it.

Tally laughs.

"It would be *so* interesting, Babsy. I know a lot of hookers go there after work."

Tally calls Babs Babsy because she thinks it is a good nickname. But Babs isn't the kind of person you make up names for.

"Hookers are not interesting, Tally. Drag queens, yes. That's art. Hookers are just women who fuck men for cash. Where's the story in that?"

Diminished, Tally pinches the neck of her cigarette with her thumb and forefinger, lifts it up to her mouth. She can't even get smoking right.

"Well, Babsy," Tally begins tentatively, trying to regain her footing. Babs would probably be more inclined to take Tally seriously if Tally leaned forward and kicked the back of Frances's neck.

"I wasn't necessarily thinking about what they *did,* but they would surely be interesting people to *talk* to."

Babs just says,

"*You* go to Randy's dressed like a hooker and see what happens."

Forty-five minutes later, Frances and I are as heavily made up as the grownups. Sparkly eyes and gooey lips. Just off-kilter. Just like Babs. Our hair is teased high on top of our heads, and Babs has Jasper smudge gray eye shadow under our eyes so we look tired.

Stacey finally arrives with two bottles of Coppertone and rubs the lotion into Frances's and my skin. She gets all the spots. On the soles of our feet and between our fingers. As if we are really just children going to the beach.

Frances and I are in the kitchen, surrounded by the catering crew. We each have a plate of brunch cruise food: pineapple, watermelon, strawberries, and mango. Slices of bacon. We eat carefully so we do not smear our lipstick. When we are through, I'm going to get our party drinks made. It is almost seven o'clock. People will be arriving soon.

I go to the living room. Frances follows closely behind. In addition to the waiters, there are now several photographers wearing Polaroid cameras and leis with real hibiscus around their necks. There are tan women wearing grass skirts and bikini tops. Undulating their hips. Peter Duchin plays "Escape (the Piña Colada Song)," with the din of ukuleles in the background. There are at least six ukulele players wandering through the aparthouse strumming "Tiny Bubbles." I wonder where Babs found all these people.

I walk over to a young male waiter. Hawaiian shirt, khaki shorts, and flip-flops. I know he won't question whatever I order. At his age he has no paternal instincts. Does not know that twelve-year-olds are not supposed to drink booze. I take a few moments to come up with something unique. I remember that Mack always drinks scotch. A good place to start.

"Excuse me," I say. "I would like two scotches, no ice, with a splash of lime juice and ringed with sugar."

Frances isn't expecting this. For once, she challenges me.

"Bettina, that is disgusting. I'm not going to drink that."

"Just wait. You'll see."

"Coming right up, pretty lady," the waiter says, totally in character. "Enjoying the cruise?"

I follow him to the bar. It's right next to the railing of our "ship." I feel the breeze coming off the lake. It's a good feeling, like we are moving, going somewhere. I just know Mack is going to show up. Even Mags wouldn't miss this. The thing about Babs's parties is that you don't have to like her to enjoy them.

The waiter puts the drinks in large tumblers, stirs them slightly. Hands them to us. Then he slaps me on the fanny. Disturbing. I don't want anyone grabbing me. Unless it's Mack.

Frances is unable to drink more than a few sips.

"Bettina," she says in a stupid whiny voice, "this is gross. I want some pineapple juice."

"Just drink it," I say impatiently. "It will make you feel good."

"No," Frances says insistently.

"Okay, then I will just drink yours." Now I wonder what the whole point of Frances is. She's a party pooper all the way.

I line the cups up on a side table. We sit in adjacent deck chairs. I sip my drink slowly. I have Frances's there should I need it.

The guests start to arrive. The mood shifts. The staff's no longer practicing. They're in full swing. People splash their hands in the swimming pool. Accept leis from the cruise director, a skinny woman in a blue linen dress who greets them in the aparthouse foyer.

More and more people board the SS *Babs*. All the guests look like they're really into it. The costumes are excellent: floor-length muumuus, cheap swimsuits, fanny packs and new white sneakers.

My scotch and lime juice doesn't taste as bad as it might have. I finish half a cup. My brain is now gently loosened in my head. It seems to just be floating there, untethered from anxiety and fear. I want to shout, *Babs! I get it! I am not a stupid drunk like most people!*

Babs is in the middle of the crowd. She's wearing a white bathing suit with a plunging neckline and a captain's hat. Navy blue fishnets and matching stilettos. She's smiling, talks to everyone. Welcomes them onboard.

I leave Frances and her pineapple juice. Get up to do the task Babs has given me. After being fondled by the waiter, I'm afraid to start with a man. I approach an unattractive woman who is dressed in a floor-length muumuu, not quite long enough to hide her open-toe sandals. The polish on her toes is chipped. How can anyone go to a party and not properly groom her feet? This evening is not a come-as-you-are, wasn't a surprise. She had plenty of time to book a pedicure.

She clutches a white vinyl purse that is way too big for evening. Is the purse part of her costume? It looks like something you could buy at Woolworth's. Or does she use it in real life? Given the toe situation, I doubt she has gone all-out and bought a new purse for the party. She definitely needs a few stiff ones.

I reach in the pocket of my robe. Rip the top page off my Rx pad. "Shoot yourself up with sunrise surprise." Seems pretty funny to me.

I hand it to her and she reaches into her white purse for glasses. The look on her face tells me immediately that she's of the camp bothered by the mannequins floating in the pool. She holds the paper between her fingers like it is a used piece of toilet paper. She can't bring herself to hand it back to me. She's looking for a place to throw it away.

I want to ask for it back, since I think it's a good one, but I don't. I start to walk away but she grabs me by the shoulder.

"Your mother should be ashamed of herself. You shouldn't be here giving out things like, like this." She holds the paper up to my face. As if I've not read it, do not understand what it means.

"Babs has crossed a line. Yes, she has . . ." The woman shakes her head. Walks away from me. Women like this really make me mad. As outraged as she claims to be, she won't confront Babs. She won't call the next day to follow up. She will go through the buffet line. Grab some cinnamon buns, scrambled eggs with melted American cheese. Maybe even dance a few rounds. She might complain about it to her husband in the car, then leave it at that. She'll still show up at the next party. Well, aloha to her.

I try not to let her get to me, but unlike Babs, I don't like pissing people off. I continue to circulate through the crowd but don't hand out anything else.

The scotch starts to hit me a bit harder. The guests begin to blur together. Only one couple stands out. He wears a faded T-shirt that says FIJI, broken-in blue jeans, and white Converse sneakers splattered with paint; she has on a blue wrap dress with white anchors on it and blue pumps with short heels. She has opted for nautical, he for Caribbean cool. They skipped the naughty part of the dress code. Who are these people?

They walk over to me. The man is tall but bends over carefully and takes me gently by the shoulders. Nothing threatening. There is something familiar about him, but I can't figure out what.

"Bettina," the man says. It's a statement, not a question. His pretty partner (wife?) smiles kindly. I don't know what to say. They're in no rush to join the party with the other adults. They want conversation. With me. I wait.

"You are beautiful, like your mother."

I want to say, *I'm not. We look nothing alike.* But I like the comparison too much. The compliment.

He takes in my costume. Continues. "You're a sport to go along with all this." As if I had a choice. Are these new friends of Babs I don't know about?

The man is handsome, but not at all like Mack. He has blond curly hair that is on the long side. His eyes are also different. They are not blue but brown, like mine. His energy is charged but diffuse. Enough of him to go around. The woman with him is more contained. She'll make careful choices about whom she talks to, won't use swearwords. Not sanctimonious, just ladylike.

"Thanks," I say.

"I'm impressed you can walk in those shoes," the woman says. "I am always terrified of falling over." More than fear keeps her from these cheap high heels. She's just being polite.

"I practiced a lot before tonight." I don't want her to think I normally wear shoes like this. Part of me, however, knows that they are not paying attention to me because of my face or costume. They are intrigued, curious. What is it?

He removes his hands from my shoulders. Takes a pack of cigarettes from his pocket. He is still staring at me. This is beginning to get awkward.

He senses my discomfort.

"I'm sorry, Bettina. I've heard so much about you I forgot to introduce myself. I'm your cousin Lucas. And this is my wife, Poppy."

I knew they were coming, but I was so busy thinking about Mack I forgot. What has Babs told him about me? It could be anything. Since Lucas isn't on Babs's men-to-fuck list, there's no risk of scaring him away. She can tell him everything about life in the aparthouse. Kid included.

I want to ask them what they know, but the party is too loud. This would be a sit-down-on-the-couch conversation. I'm tempted to at least show them my room. Tell Lucas how much I love his paintings.

"Where's Babs? We've been upstairs to change but haven't officially checked in," Lucas says affably.

So Lucas is more like Mack than I thought. A few kind words and he's ready to move on. I'm just an interesting pause before they lose themselves in the party. No matter what I say or look like, Babs is always the one they want. I point vaguely to the middle of the crowd.

Ten o'clock. It's dark outside, but the aparthouse is lit up by tiki lamps. Mack still hasn't come. If you didn't know Babs, you would think she didn't care. But I watch her from my deck chair where I've retreated to drink more scotch. Can tell by the slight tremor of her right hand when she smokes that she's furious. I sit by myself and just watch. Frances has gone to Stacey's room to watch TV.

I want to go to Babs. Tell her what a great party this is. She catches me looking at her and strides across the room to me.

"Bettina," she says, "you're on. I know how much work you've put into your routine. It'll be a huge smash. You're my daughter, after all. Great pins, especially in those heels."

I sit up. My dance number! Mack isn't there, but at last I can do something to make Babs feel better. Except the scotch I've been nursing suddenly turns on me. When I stand up, my head spins. I have the urge to throw up. But I can handle it. I go up to my room to get the *Chorus Line* cassette. Stop at the bathroom for a tinkle, hoping to flush some of the scotch out of me. I want to douse my face in cold water but can't risk smearing my makeup. I just look in the mirror and think, *I can do this. I have practiced so much.*

I take my place at the top of the spiral staircase. The same one where I cut off part of my hair. But this is a do-over. It will have a happy ending.

"Ladies and gentlemen," Babs says, "as captain of this cruise ship, I have the privilege of presenting you with some entertainment from one of our crew members. My daughter, Bettina."

Everyone stops talking. They all clap distractedly until they see me at the top of the stairs. Then their energy collects and hits me full force. I'm no longer on the fringe of the evening, a mere party helper, but inside the party itself.

"Hit it, Bettina!" Babs shouts, smiling up at me and punching her right hand in the air.

I clutch the railing. The queasy feeling hasn't passed. I wait a beat, as Babs has taught me to do, before cueing the music to begin. Then I lift my head, look out at the audience. The music starts. I'm off.

> *Dance: ten; looks: three.*
> *And I'm still on unemployment . . .*

I shimmy my hips and take off my robe. Show off my bikini. The matching high heels.

> *Dancing for my own enjoyment.*
> *That ain't it, kid! That ain't it, kid!*

I point my fingers in the air. Try to hit every beat as I lip-synch. Still feeling unsteady. People are laughing. I worry they think I'm a bad dancer. I continue anyway.

Dance: ten, looks: three,
Is like to die!
Left the theater and
Called the doctor
For my appointment to buy . . .

I am moving much more slowly now. I stop worrying about the dancing part. I just have to get to the bottom of the stairs. Babs hates quitters. The guests are all still laughing.

Tits and ass.
Bought myself a fancy pair.
Tightened up the derrière.
Did the nose with it.
All that goes with it . . .

I have five more steps to go. Five more steps. I look at my feet instead of the people. I can't really hear the music any-more. It's just a large ball of sound rolling around in the air. I wish I had a slugger's bat to hit it away from me. I'm almost at the bottom. Have almost finished. But I don't make it. Instead, I trip and fall. Not just a little fall either. My head hits the edge of the bottom stair and my legs go flying over it. I feel a giant thud, then something breaking open. A wetness.

The music keeps going but I just lie there on the marble floor. White bikini and blue high heels askew. I'm spread out every which way, as if I've hit a rock while skiing. There's a searing pain in my head that's so bad I almost can't feel it. My cheeks burn. I know everyone's still standing there, watching

me. I can't let them see me cry. I want to lie there until everyone goes home. They can step on me. I don't care. Then I will
sneak back up to my room. Avoid Babs. Replay the nightmare
and wonder how I could've come up with such an idiotic plan.
If I'd just followed Frances's lead, I wouldn't be in this mess.
She is probably still watching TV in Stacey's room, drinking
her pineapple juice. Eating green Jell-O with orange Life Sav-
ers floating inside it.

I feel a hand on my back; it strokes me gently, then takes my
right arm to pull me up. I can't see anything at first because my
face is covered in blood. It pours out of my forehead and blurs
my vision. *Babs,* I say to myself. For once, she feels bad for me.
Is going to tell me it's not a big deal, not a fiasco after all. I did
my best.

I'm looking at the floor and see her blue stilettos next to
mine. Then something weird happens. I see the hands touching me, holding me up, and realize they're not hers. I look up
and I see him. Mack.

He grips my arm with a gentle pressure. Makes sure I don't
slip in the blood and fall again. He pushes my hair off my
face. I can't really see him clearly, but I take in that he has not
bothered to dress up, is wearing one of his plain white button-
downs. It smells like all his other ones and makes me cry. I
lean into him. Put my face above where his heart is, sobbing.
If Mack had come earlier, Babs probably would've forgotten all
about my dance number. None of this would have happened.
But he's here now. Has finally come to my rescue.

I feel another hand on my arm. It yanks me away from Mack
and toward the kitchen. Babs. She must be mad because Mack
got to me first. Wants to claim her rights as a mother. Comfort
me. Mack follows us through the swinging door. We're still
walking when Lucas and Poppy run in behind us.

Three other grownups are in the kitchen, but in this

moment, it is just us: Babs and me. There is a pause. And then. And then. Babs draws her right hand back, swings it forward, and smacks me, hard. Across the face. I almost fall again, but she holds me upright with her left arm. Smacks me again. This stings but is more alive and precise than the sloppy blood pouring from my forehead. If the smacking didn't hurt, it would feel good. Each one contains more force than Babs has ever directed at my body. Both times her hand hits my cheek, the contact makes us one person. I can feel her energy and her hatred. Her effort also feels like love.

Babs lets go of me. "Bad move, babe. You fuck up and fall. You bleed all over Mack's shirt. You blew it."

She's right. I have nothing to say.

Lucas steps in. "Jesus Christ, Babs. She's only a kid. What's the matter with you?"

"She's *my* fucking kid, Lucas. I can do what I want."

"No, you can't."

"Fine," Babs says, looking at Poppy. "Take her with you to New York, *cuz*. I don't really care. See for yourself how much fun a twelve-year-old girl can be."

Mack is still standing there, in on it. Unlike Lucas, he says nothing, and I can feel him pulling away. Probably thinks this has turned into a family argument. Doesn't want to intrude.

"Babs, quit with the drama. No one is going anywhere. Just watch it," Lucas says.

"*Drama? Watch it?* I'll show you drama."

Is Babs going to smack Lucas? Throw something at him? Whatever she has in mind, Lucas backs off. He takes Poppy's hand.

"Look, it's over. No one fell off the ship. Let's go dance to the Duch and pour pink champagne over people."

Babs pauses. Then says, "Sounds fab." Babs has Mack and

Lucas. A swinging party and a hot outfit. Not worth wasting time on me. She moves on.

"Bettina, go find Lily and have her clean you up. Put some regular clothes on. Party over." She walks to the living room. Lucas and Poppy follow behind her. Case closed. Lucas is Babs's cousin. A Ballentyne, after all.

Mack hangs back.

My blood is all over the front of his shirt. My red handprints smear his pants. Traces of it on his wrists. There must even be spots on his watch. I have his attention; I've made an impression. He is completely disheveled and looks spent from all the excitement.

Mack comes closer to me. Leans in and kisses my forehead. He gets some of my blood on his lips and wipes it away with his hand. It just keeps coming.

"Feel better, Bettina," he says. I think he might take my hand and walk me up to my bathroom. But no. He is still just there for the party.

Lily puts me in the bath, holds a washcloth to my head to stop the bleeding. Wipes my face clear of all traces of makeup. She dresses me in jeans and a T-shirt. Suitable attire for a kid to wear to the hospital to get stitches.

When we leave, it is close to eleven. The party has slowed down a bit. No longer frenzied, but mellow. Babs and Mack are talking intensely in the corner. Leaning into each other. If people were not there, Mack would be at the point of kissing her. Or maybe not. Maybe it is the other kind of talking. Supremely private but signals that things have come to an end. I don't know.

Lily and I spend almost all night in the ER. I get fifteen stitches in my head. The nurse gives me a small pink stuffed elephant with a red bow. An odd receipt.

When we get home, it is almost four in the morning. The party's over. Cleaned up except for the missing windowpane. But not everyone's gone. By the front door, two white canvas high-tops. Lucas's. He and Poppy must be asleep in the guest room. I kick the shoes and they fly in opposite directions, no longer a pair.

Next to them, Mack's penny loafers, with the S VDB pennies, and his blue blazer. I walk over to Mack's pile of things and stick the pink stuffed elephant in his pocket. I mean to say *Thank you* and *Don't forget me*. Wonder what he'll do with it when he gets home.

The next night, Babs takes me out to dinner. No Stacey. Just the two of us. She orders me the shrimp cocktail and filet mignon. We barely talk. Babs says nothing about my stitches. She eats her entire salade niçoise and even one bread roll. Lets me get the bananas Fougères for dessert. No mention of my getting fat. Not one word.

7

Breakup

Two weeks go by after the party and no Mack. I still don't know what they were talking about when I left to get my stitches but decide it couldn't have gone well, even if he spent the night. Babs told me once that just because someone wants to fuck you, it doesn't mean he wants to be in a relationship with you, or even that he likes you. *You shouldn't read too much into these things.* So I'm not sure Babs really misses him or is that surprised. But people can't just leave Babs whenever they want. Only she gets to decide when they go away.

One night before dinner, Babs and I are in the kitchen pulling out her parents' pale blue linen placemats. Babs claims there's so much good stuff and Lily doesn't rotate enough. We hear the elevator. Babs just keeps on stacking cloths for the table.

Then we hear him.

"Babs?" he says, footsteps coming our way. "Are you here?" Mack.

Babs is wearing an aqua-green silk robe. Her hair is wet and she has no makeup on. At first she says nothing, waits for him to come in. Then:

"Yes. Jesus, Mack, if I knew you were coming, I would've put a face on. It's been kind of a clean-out day around here." She leans in to kiss him but he turns his head so her mouth lands on his cheek.

"What the fuck, Mack? Why such a goddamn prude? We've kissed in front of the kid before, remember?"

He looks at me, his smile more like a wince. "Hey, Bettina," he says, only now registering that I'm there, looking on.

"So where the fuck have you been? Are you here for dinner?"

"Let's take this into the living room."

"Oh, there is a *this*. No. *This* can stay right in the kitchen. I want Bettina to see how a man acts after he gets the lights fucked out of him and then decides he's going to take a breather."

"You know I don't want just a breather. We did this already. It's over."

"So why the fuck are you here?"

"I came to get my cuff links. I wore them here about a month ago, and I can't find them at Tea House anywhere. I must have left them."

Babs starts to laugh. "You're telling me you're doing a drive-by for your cuff links? Bullshit. I would have sent them, you know. But they're not here, babe. Delilah would have found them when she cleaned my room."

"Babs, Mags gave them to me for our anniversary. Maybe I could have a look? Under the bed, perhaps?"

"Go fuck yourself."

He reaches for her hand but she snatches it away. Then she actually puts her arm around my shoulder and gives it a squeeze.

"Bettina and I are very busy. If I find them, I'll call."

Mack starts to say something, but stops himself. He does not have the vocabulary for this kind of situation. He leaves the aparthouse empty-handed. Babs doesn't give out goody bags.

We are seated for dinner, food served. Babs goes back to Mack's visit.

"He says it's *over.* I don't do *over. Enough,* maybe, but *over* makes it sound like a bad movie. I just know he got an ultimatum from Magsy and was afraid that if things didn't cool down between us, she would kick him out of Tea House. This is just bullshit. She would never dirty her hands with a divorce, and she knows Mack will pull this shit again. Three minutes of missionary just isn't going to do it for him."

"So," I say, "you think he will come back?"

"I'm sure of it." She reaches into the pocket of her bathrobe and pulls out three gold nuggets in the shape of knots. Dumps them in her ashtray. Keeps smoking.

I want to stick my hand in there, grab them. But I just watch as she covers them with ash.

"The question is, will I take him back? I'm not big on playing the do-over card."

I want to stick up for him, tell Babs Mack is worth waiting for, but I keep my mouth shut. I might make her mad if she thinks I'm not completely on her side. I just stare at those gold knots and wonder if I can rescue them when we are finished with dinner.

"On one hand, it would be stupid to deprive my centerfold of his talents, but on the other, I can't have him thinking I'm that easy." She takes another drag of her Duchess Golden Light, then grinds it into one of the cuff links.

"I give it two weeks before he comes back. Plenty of time to figure out what to do."

"Sounds good, Babs," I say. As soon as she stands up, I will collect those cuff links, sleep with them under my pillow, like a prayer. She lights another cigarette.

I start to feel desperate, wanting dinner to end. She said he'll be back at the aparthouse in two weeks and I just know she will take him back. No need to discuss other possibilities. But the cuff links. It is painful to watch them sitting there, buried underneath a heap of butts. As if she has been searing Mack's wrists.

Finally, she pushes her chair back. I start to relax but then see that she's taking the ashtray with her. I get up and follow her toward the powder room. She turns and sees me.

"Normally, my girl, I like to potty alone, but you are onto something. This is different." She takes my hand, balances the ashtray in the other hand. We go inside.

"Mack fucked up. Sure, he will come back, but in the meantime, I'm not a safe-deposit box. But big picture: If a man ever takes a hiatus on you, never give all his toys back. Don't get sentimental and stash them somewhere. Throw them away. He will know. Not the specifics maybe, but he will be able to tell. That in the end, you have won."

The last word is barely out of her mouth when she dumps the contents of the ashtray into the toilet. The cuff links sink and I hear them hit the porcelain like tiny pebbles. The cigarettes float on top, like fallen leaves on a lake. Babs grabs the silver handle and flushes.

I wonder if she's right. It seems to me that you should save sacrificial gestures like this for when things are really over.

Three weeks later, Babs finds me in the playroom. Says, "Field trip. I want to show you where I grew up, Bettina."

Babs and I settle ourselves into her red convertible Jag. Set off with a picnic basket packed by Lily the night before. She tells me we are going to stop by Tea House, then go to the

Grass Woods cemetery and have a picnic on Eudy and Mont's graves. I don't think this through. Forget that Mags and Mack live at Tea House and probably don't want a Babs drive-by. And normal people don't have a picnic in a cemetery. But I'm so happy to spend the day with Babs, I just go with it.

I am wearing a pretty if slightly babyish sundress that Babs bought me the day before. Pink and white checks. Brand-new white sandals. Babs has on white shorts, a Lilly Pulitzer print top, and a pair of lime-green Jack Rogers. Her legs are tan and toned. You can see a line in her outer thigh as she works the gears. Her toes are painted a whisper pink. Matches her shirt. Her blond hair is down and pushed off her face with enormous Jackie O. sunglasses. The whole effect is completely Grass Woods. As if the town is a club with a strict dress code. It's unlike Babs to dress to please people. She must have a plan.

She plays the latest Stevie Wonder and balances a cigarette deftly between her lips. We go up Lake Shore Drive to Sheridan Road. I watch the progression of houses. Small, modest. Then they begin to swell. The lawns get bigger and bigger the farther we are from the city. Like they finally have room to stretch out and breathe.

Babs has put a six-pack of ginger ale on the floor by my feet. She tells me I can drink as much as I want. I haven't had lunch yet and am hungry rather than thirsty, but I drink at least three cans. I keep looking at Babs to see if this is some kind of trick, but she does not flinch when I crack one open. She even smiles.

We pass Evanston, Kenilworth, Lake Forest. Finally, we arrive at Grass Woods. No cars in the parking lot of the train station. None of the men are going anywhere. All of them at home where they're supposed to be.

Babs follows a few long winding roads. Stops at a house with an enormous gate. It is open and Babs pulls in, crunching the driveway as we go. It is a magnificent house. Salmon-colored with black shutters. The house is big and solid. Looks like it could stand up to her. Babs would not be able to remove the windows, turn it into a cruise ship, dance about it in a white bathing suit. Tea House is on steady ground, immutable.

Babs parks the Jag right inside the gate. Gets out and drops her cigarette onto the gravel driveway, still burning. A calling card. I'm fairly certain Mags does not smoke.

Babs puts her hands on her hips and leans against the car, confident and still, like she is in some kind of ad. She lights another cigarette and takes in her surroundings. Beside us is a sort of guardhouse. There is one car nearby. A brown station wagon. Babs told me once that Mack drives a green Austin Mini. He must not be home. Thank God.

She runs her hand over the hood of the station wagon, says, "I bet she picks him up and drops him off at the station in this ratty old thing." She laughs with a snort.

I don't need to ask who she is talking about. Babs is single-minded in her interest in people. For now, *he* always refers to Mack and *she* to Mags. I have never met Mags. But something tells me I am about to.

I have to go to the bathroom. I've been so busy taking it all in that it comes on me in a giant rush.

"Babs," I say, "I need to pee."

One problem that will solve another: we'll have to leave Tea House to find some restaurant where I can go potty, which means we can avoid Mags altogether. Babs just stands there, nods.

"Just go up to the front door and knock," she says. "I happen to know there are plenty of bathrooms. After all, I grew up here. There's a powder room in the front hall."

"I don't know the people who live here," I say, even though of course I do.

"Don't be such a fucking chicken. If you have to go, go!"

"Will you come with me?" I ask, knowing what the answer will be. On second thought, having Babs as escort might not be such a good idea.

"Nope. This is your deal, babe," she says, like I have brought this on myself. Which I guess I have.

I try not to panic. I consider my options. I can pee right where we are standing. No. I can approach the house more closely and pee somewhere on the lawn; no one will see, then I can get back in the car and we can drive away.

Babs waits.

I begin my walk toward the house. My stomach lurches as I go. I know Babs is watching me, the way you're supposed to with young children. Then she's gone. I see her get in the car, back out on the crunchy gravel, drive away. I now have two problems. But I have to go so bad I am afraid I will wet myself if I don't get to the house soon. I start to run.

All of a sudden I see her. Mack's wife, Mags. She emerges from a side door of Tea House. She is wearing khaki pants, a pink-and-blue Liberty print shirt, and gardening clogs. She is so beautiful and looks so nice, I want to cry. Like the affair is my fault. Her dark hair is pulled up in a loose chignon, and her eyes are a clear blue. Like a lake that has no swimmers. She has a visor on, and her face is unmarred by the sun, but her arms are tan. She holds her hand up to break the sun's glare.

"Can I help you?" I know Mags sees me for what I'm not. A run-of-the-mill twelve-year-old girl in a pink-and-white sundress. A friend of her son, Hailer, perhaps.

"Um, I just need to go to the bathroom really badly." I forget to say *please*. That's how bad I need to go.

How did you get here? I know she wants to ask but doesn't. She's a good mother. Can see how bad I need to get to the toilet.

She takes me inside the house. There is a powder room just off the front hall, as Babs said there would be. The toilet is a rose pink. I sit down. Make myself comfortable. Release my breath as a strong steady stream of pee hits the bowl. I finish. Wipe myself, pull up my underwear, and go to wash my hands. There are monogrammed linen hand towels carefully folded on the sink. *MMM*. Margaux and McCormack Morse. Problem. I do not want to mess them up, but don't want to look like I didn't wash my hands.

I run water from the tap. Pick up a bar of rose glycerin soap from a white porcelain dish on the sink and scrub my hands with it. When I am finished, I dig my index finger into the soap and drag it across. It leaves a long scratch. Mags will be able to tell I have used it. I have manners. I am conscientious about hygiene. I wipe my hands on my dress, leaving wet streaks.

The front hall of Tea House is messy with shoes and coats in a way that the aparthouse never is. I spot a blue sweater. Cotton roll-neck, about my size. It's folded carefully on a frayed antique bench. Directly underneath there is a pair of children's Topsiders. A red, blue, and yellow plaid cap. Hailer's? I want to pick up the cap, take it with me back to the aparthouse. Maybe go to sleep wearing it.

Mags is standing outside the front door. I try to be as nice as possible. Hope to get out of there without causing any problems.

"Thank you for letting me use the bathroom. I really appreciate it."

"Feel better?" Mags asks. I want to say *Not really*, but I don't. I won't get a tour of Tea House after all. I have a use-the-bathroom-only ticket.

She takes a step in my direction.

"I'm sorry, but I just don't understand how you got here." The tree in the front garden blocks my view, but I can feel that

Babs has come back. I don't know what her next move is. I just focus on Mags. Want to say something that will make sense, to come up with a story that will satisfy her.

"I was driving around with my mother and I had to go to the bathroom and she pulled into the driveway of what looked like a nice house. She saw the car out front and knew someone would be home." Even though Babs often calls me a liar, everything that I have said so far is true.

"Why didn't your mother drive you to the door?" Mags asks.

"Um"—I think quickly—"she had an errand to run." Not true.

"Oh, that's silly," Mags says. "I'm sorry you had to walk."

"No, it's okay. Thank you," I say. "I should get back to the car." I know Babs is waiting for me. Getting impatient.

I turn to walk away, but Mags grabs my arm.

"Wait; why do you look familiar? Maybe I know your parents?"

"I don't think so," I say. Really not true.

"What's your name?"

"Bettina." Wrong. I should've made something up, kept working in the lie column. Mags releases my arm as if I have burned her. Probably wishes she had told me to drink the toilet water rather than pee in it.

"Bettina?" she asks, just to make sure.

"Bettina," I repeat.

Mags's eyes are no longer friendly or maternal.

"Bettina," she says. "You should not go to strangers' houses. Even when you need to use the powder room. That's not how we do things in Grass Woods." She is holding a trowel firmly in her other hand, digging her fingers into the handle. *Throw it at me,* I want to say. I have no good answers.

She turns her back on me and walks toward the side entrance of the house.

"Have a nice day," she says flatly, kicking the dirt off her gardening clogs as she goes inside.

"Thank you, Mags," I say, trying to tuck an *I'm sorry* into this goodbye.

She snaps around and looks right at me. Had she been another type of woman, this is the moment when she would have yelled.

Instead, she just says, "It's Mrs. Morse. You need to go now. Goodbye, Bettina."

I watch her disappear into Tea House. I go back down the driveway to find Babs.

She's leaning over, picking some dandelions from the lawn. She really does look like she belongs here.

She looks at me. I have my pensive face on. Thinking about Hailer. Where is he? A tennis clinic at Hopsequesca? Sleep-away camp? I finally met Mags, but now I realize the one I really wanted to meet was him.

Babs slides into the car. I do the same. She lights up a ciga-rette and pauses before starting the car.

"So," she says, "how was it?"

"Um, fine." I'm not sure what to say.

"Did you see her?"

"Yes."

"What did you think?"

"She was pretty." Since Babs is beautiful, I don't think she will mind my assessment.

"Pretty shitty. Everyone in this village looks the same. And they all share the same brain. They aren't smart like you. They flip through coffee-table books and believe they are actually reading. Go to the ballet or opera once a year and think they are cultured. There's got to be more going on than pretty. Did she talk to you?"

"Yes. She was mad that I was there."

"I thought as much. These women are vicious. Now you know why Mack comes to the aparthouse. You were brave to go in there. But Tea House is beside the point. I wanted you to see firsthand how limited these women are. Never, ever live in the burbs. All the fucking tennis and golf. Gardening and driving their nasty kids everywhere. The only time they orgasm is when they have star fruit at Oscar's Market. Thank God I got out."

Everything she has described to me doesn't sound that bad, but there is nothing for me to say. We leave Grass Woods once and for all.

Back at the aparthouse, I know Babs is waiting for an angry response from Mack. Anything to bring him back, even if it's using me to mess with his wife.

I imagine the rebuttal she has planned:

My mother installed that goddamn toilet. What's more innocent than a child asking to use the bathroom?

But there is to be no confrontation. Weeks and weeks go by. Mack still does not come.

8

Funeral

TWO MONTHS AFTER WE visit Tea House, Mack dies in
a car accident. He slams into a tree on his way home from
Aces, a Grass Woods bar. The hood crumples, and his face
smashes into the steering wheel. Too much scotch.

I think of the velocity. Mack moving, then Mack not. All of
that energy absorbed in that tree. Speeding in his Austin Mini,
no seat belt. Completely reckless. Completely Mack.

Babs gets the news from Tally. Babs doesn't cry. At least not
in front of me. She tells me death happens. There's no need to
get all *fucking dramatic* about it. There will be a funeral. Plans
to be made, outfits to be purchased. Babs sees the service as a
kind of party. All those people gathered together and dressed
up to say goodbye to one of their own.

The service will be held in Grass Woods four days after the
crash. There'll be a casket. Closed, since Mack was so badly
mangled, but his body will be there nonetheless. Like some
kind of rotting, putrid guest.

Babs never even considers that it might not be appropriate for her to attend the funeral. She dons a black linen shift, a color she hates because so many women favor it. Wears her big black sunglasses and carries a pack of tissues in a black clutch. The pearl necklace she bought to get back at Mack is around her neck. Maybe she's sentimental after all.

She insists on bringing me, though from what I gather, most people don't take kids to funerals unless they are related to the deceased. She dresses me in a pale pink linen dress with pink petals sewn around the neck, like I'm some kind of accessory, a bow perhaps, for her flaxen hair.

I don't want to go. After our trip to Tea House, Mags knows who I am. If I show up at the church, it will upset her. Part of me also believes Mack's death is my fault. If I hadn't fallen at the Hangover-Brunch Cruise Party and bled all over his clothes, he might have come back to the aparthouse. He would have been having sex with Babs in her bed that night, not drinking at a bar and then driving. I'm sure the whole smacking episode did the relationship in. More than he could handle. The bloody shirt too hard to explain to Mags.

Franklin drives us up to Grass Woods in the stretcher. When we get to the church, Holy Trinity, we are late. There's no one outside, and the big white doors are shut. Babs thrusts a bouquet of white roses into my hands.

"Bettina, these are for Mack. I hate those stupid arrangements propped up on plastic legs. Makes the casket look like it's in the winner's circle at the Kentucky Derby. I want you to put this on the coffin. Understated, but tasteful."

Horrifying. I don't see how I'll be able to get them up there without everyone, especially Mags, looking at me.

My hair's pulled back in a bun. I look like I am going to a ballet recital, not a funeral. Babs holds my hand as she calmly walks up the steps, as if we really are here just to pay our respects.

We walk in. They are in the middle of "O God, Our Help in Ages Past." Babs gives me a shove to continue forward into the church and now I'm on my own. She stands resolutely in the back.

I walk up the aisle. People stop singing. Stare at me. I focus on the casket. Worry about my bouquet. There is nothing else on top of the coffin. It's just shiny and black like a piano. I'm almost there when a hand grips my wrist. Prevents me from walking farther. It belongs to a handsome preppy man who looks like Mack. But most of the men in the church do.

He pulls me away. I see Mags standing in the front pew. Her arm is draped around a boy about my age in a blue blazer. Hailer. His hair is dark like hers. His head is down; he looks at the floor. He's quite thin, like Mags. I see his shoes. Penny loafers. Holds a golf ball in his hand. Probably one Mack played a course or two with. Mags turns her head to look at me, but I don't dare meet her eyes. I pray she sees this for what it is: me sent on another mission by my mother.

The man—Mack's brother? cousin?—gently leads me off to the side of the front pew. As if he means to redirect me, not scold me. For a second, I think he's going to escort me to a seat. Help me get settled. Instead, we keep going to the back of the church. I still have the bouquet. The stems of the roses are wrapped in pink ribbon over the green tape. Its thorns neutered in a silk cast. These are the same type of roses I saw in Mags's garden on my visit to Tea House. Looks as if I've stolen them.

We make it outside the church. I think of Hailer sitting inside. He's possibly the only one in the church who did not look up to see me. I remember the plaid hat I saw in the front hall at Tea House. Is it still sitting there? Or do you have to get all new clothes when your father dies?

I walk by myself to the stretcher. Babs is sitting inside. She probably went back to it the minute I began my walk down the aisle. She'd made her point. No need for another scene.

The engine idles and she's sitting in the back, smoking leisurely. She studies the program for the service as if it were a *Playbill*. Fingers the stock.

"Cream is iffy," she tells me. "It says 'wedding.' I would have gone with stark white. Also less feminine. And the font—a tad too informal. What the hell was she thinking?"

She holds it up to the light and inadvertently ashes on her black dress. She brushes herself clean with the program in her hand.

We're not moving. Franklin knows better than to drive without instructions. Babs could easily say *O'Hare* or *Newport*. She finally looks up at me. Sees the bouquet. Not pleased. At all.

"Bettina," she says, "you were supposed to put the damn thing on the casket. Even handing it to Mags would have been a nice touch. Mack actually liked you, you know. This was your chance to say thank you. I am going to have a lot of men in my life. Not many of them are going to give a shit that I happen to have a kid."

She looks out the window. Is she going to make me go back inside, try again? The only thing I know for sure is that my bouquet of roses won't be coming home with us.

"Maybe I could just leave them on the steps?" I offer.

"No," Babs replies. "Someone would trip over them and fucking sue me."

I study the hearse parked just in front of us. Maybe I can give the flowers to the driver and he can put them on the coffin. At present, he has nothing else to do.

"Bettina, he's not a fucking florist," Babs says. Reading my thoughts, as usual.

I would eat the roses if I could. I know plan B isn't going to be any better than the first.

It is a bright day with hard shadows. I think of how many fractured nights of sleep Mack had before this eternal rest. Sex, showers, leaving the aparthouse at three, four A.M. Two women. Two beds in one night. Exhausting.

Babs says, "Oak Lawn," and we're off to the cemetery. Franklin knows exactly where it is. He drove Babs there when Mont and Eudy died. Two caskets, two hearses.

We pull into Oak Lawn. Inch down a long driveway. Babs signals to Franklin to stop and we get out to walk. Babs is wearing her *ladylike heels,* and they dig into the ground like golf tees. She pulls a heel out of the wet grass with each step. It rained the night before, and the outdoors seems to stick to us. My pink ballet flats are now a smudgy brown. They look like Babs bought them at a thrift store.

Maybe we are going to visit Eudy and Mont. Leave the flowers on their graves. But when we had our picnic on their plot after our Tea House visit, Babs didn't bring a bouquet. She thinks leaving flowers for the deceased is dumb. Dead people can't enjoy them, and the flowers just wilt and die. So why am I carrying roses for Mack? No clue. We're walking in the opposite direction of where my grandparents are buried. I can't see precisely where we are going yet, but I just know.

Here we are. There is a white tarp surrounded by freshly dug ground. There's a man standing over it, walking around the perimeter. As if it's a swimming pool and he doesn't want anyone to fall in. He's wearing a short-sleeved checkered shirt, khaki pants. Has short gray hair, thinning a bit. Babs walks right up to him, puts her hand on his shoulder.

"Hello, Carl," she says.

"Tabitha! Well, hello," he says, glad to see her. His eyes get all soft and there's a tenderness in his tone that surprises me. But there's no way Babs has slept with him. He is way too old and not good-looking enough.

"How are you?" He reaches out with one hand, soft and wrinkly with age, and touches her. I have never seen someone so comfortable in her presence. He must remember when her parents died.

"They don't often go two together," he says to me, softly but kindly. I now realize he sees Babs as no one else does. Abandoned and lonely. An orphan. She holds Carl's elbow and dabs a tissue at her eyes. But there are no tears.

"Mack and I were close. Especially after the sale of the house." She says this like a normal person would, even, but tinged with sadness. "He was good to Bettina. I didn't want to take her to the funeral—that would be too much—but I thought we could come and say goodbye before everyone else gets here, after the service. You know our parents were such good friends. He was the brother I never had."

Carl nods. Like this is really true. He seems to be the only person in Grass Woods not to know that Babs and Mack had an affair. Or maybe he just has things in perspective. Knows how everything turns out in the end. He strokes her hand.

"Of course, Tabitha. Take your time. I'll leave the two of you alone. I need to get a drink of water myself. I'll be back in a bit. The rest shouldn't be along for another half an hour or so."

Carl gently pats my cheek and walks away. I'm still holding the bouquet. Am not clear where all this is going. Is Babs going to make some kind of weepy speech? Seems unlikely. Mack's gone. *Time to fucking move on.* She looks at me.

"Put the flowers in the grave. This is much, much better."

This seems easy enough. I bend down. Set the bouquet

carefully on the white tarp that shields the hole, the six-feet-under. But the flowers look haphazard sitting there, like someone tripped and dropped them. Not at all deliberate.

Babs says, "No, not there. *In,* not *on* the grave."

When I look up, she stands so tall, despite her sinking heels. For a moment, I am actually afraid she will push me in. That I will be stuck and Mack's coffin will be lowered on top of me. I might scream, but no one will care enough to pull me out.

But Babs doesn't touch me, just says impatiently, "Bettina, goddamn it, put the flowers in."

I can tell Babs wants to be done with it and get the heck out of here. I slide back the tarp and drop the flowers in. I can't see them land. Don't even hear a thud.

Babs bends over me, hurls something in. Looks like a fistful of marbles, all attached. I look up and see that her neck is bare. The pearls. The flowers will rot, but the pearls will always be there. They will lie under Mack's casket like tiny rocks. Irritate him forever.

We see Carl slowly walking back, shading the sun with his eyes. Babs strides to him. Grabs his hands.

"Thank you," she says quietly, as if we had really just been standing there saying a prayer. Thinking sad thoughts.

"You're welcome, Tabitha," Carl says evenly. He looks at me a little too intently. Maybe he saw what we did. He gives us a little wave goodbye. Resumes his post by Mack's grave. Babs turns and begins the walk to the stretcher. I follow. Then look back. Carl is still watching. Maybe he's wondering which one of us is going to die next.

Part II

9

Cardiss

SEPTEMBER 9, 1983, IS a bright, crisp day in Cardiss, New Hampshire. The leaves are green and sharp. The trees robust, sturdy, and tall. The sky has none of the dampness or gray tones one might expect to find across the pond in an English boarding school. I am fifteen when I arrive as a sophomore, or a Lower, in Cardiss-speak.

Cardiss presents the same front to everyone who arrives there. It is beautiful in this way. It looks like a college, only smaller. The buildings are red brick with white marble steps. There are Latin sayings over most of the doorways. Lawns sprawl for the mere experience of sitting on them. Attractive boys and girls lounge, books and binders open, as if they were sunning themselves on an academic beach.

I don't go back to Chicago before starting Cardiss. Babs says, *It's your deal, babe, you are too old for me to unpack your clothes, help you with your bed.* She has no interest in watery coffee and meeting all of the chipper parents who want to make small talk. But she does buy me a silver-and-gold pen from Tiffany.

Has it engraved with my initials. I plan to save it for exams. She also hands me a large check for tuition and airfare, and a wad of traveler's checks to cover expenses for the whole year. It makes me feel independent. And sad.

After three months in France with Cécile, I fly directly from Paris to Boston. I take a cab to campus, about forty-five minutes away. Most new students arrive with their parents. I worry people will feel sorry for me, coming alone; will wonder about the cab. But the driver takes me right to the front gates of campus and pulls away before anyone can notice.

I have one small bag. A Louis Vuitton duffel I bought on rue Georges V. Babs hates LV. Thinks it's tacky to have logos stamped everywhere. Makes you look like you're trying too hard to prove you can afford something expensive. But I like the bag. It's completely incongruous with the things the other kids bring. Trunks filled with new sheets, down comforters, flannel PJs, stereos. My duffel, I hope, makes me look cool. Like I have purposely opted out of such teenage clutter. Chose to bring a few pants and tops from agnès b. and Petit Bateau because that's what I like. But the truth is that I don't have a clue what you're supposed to wear at boarding school. I don't know anything about the bluchers, rag socks, flannel pajamas that the others have. I didn't have the catalogs to order them from. I do bring the silver medallion of my father's that Babs gave me. I have yet to try to find him, but maybe I will now that I am at Cardiss. Who knows. It will change things between me and Babs and I'm not sure I am ready for that.

I check out the map of campus that's just past the front gate. According to my acceptance packet, I'm not assigned to a dorm but instead to a house called Bright. The idea is appealing: a small cluster of girls living in a real house with one female faculty member, generally a younger woman without a spouse or kids. Just starting her tenure at the school. The problem with the houses is that, unlike the dorms, they have a small number of students living in them, between four and six per house. Less margin for social errors.

Bright House is a two-minute walk from the front gate. I find it easily. It is white, two-storied, with black shutters. The front door is propped open. Just a screen door divides the inside from the outside. I walk into a living room that looks like it belongs in a tired B & B: dilapidated couches, worn shag carpeting, and a TV. There is a woman standing in the middle of the room tapping a clipboard with a pen and, as I soon find out, waiting for me.

Miss McSoren, whose power over me is also explained in my acceptance packet, scribbles something on the paper attached to her clipboard. She looks about twenty-seven and has short brown hair. I know instantly (the rigid way she holds the clipboard?) that she will never have any children. She sports a khaki skirt, open-back clogs, and a pink-striped oxford shirt that has been ironed. She wears small crescent-shaped earrings. No makeup.

I expect her to smile but she approaches me briskly and sticks out her hand. Firm, businesslike.

"Bettina, you're the last to arrive."

It's just after three. I thought we had all day to get there.

"Sorry," I mumble.

"I'm Miss McSoren. Head of Bright House. I also teach French and coach field hockey."

I want to like her, but I don't. I know Miss McSoren has probably learned French at some all-women's college and spent her junior year abroad in some provincial town like Rennes. I bet she can expertly navigate all of Molière and Camus but has never bothered with *Paris Match,* my favorite mag. I know Babs would laugh at her, and this makes me want to too.

One of my French teachers at Chicago Day, Madame Coutu,

wore blouses so sheer we could see her nipples, the skin of her back. Our fifth-grade class was shocked and embarrassed. Babs was thrilled. Now that I am older, I can see what Babs was getting at. Can you really be a good French teacher if you have *zip sex appeal?*

"So, you're from Chicago," she says.

I've been too busy with my critical assessment to offer up any pleasantries. I smile, but again, I'm disappointed. I never know what people expect me to say to that. I don't really consider myself *from* anywhere, at least nowhere anyone else lives. Babs is the country I come from. That's the only way to explain it. I gather up my hair, which is now far past my shoulders, and tie it on top of my head in a knot. I nod and say, "Yes. And you?"

"Bangor," she answers, but it's clear from the clipped reply that I'm not supposed to be asking her personal questions. She gestures for me to follow her up the stairs.

"Your roommate, Holly, is already here. Dinner's at six and we'll be having a house meeting afterward, at eight. You still have some time to unpack."

Holly, I know, is Holly Combs from Iowa City. There was a tiny index card in my packet with this scant information about the girl I will be sharing a room with for the next nine months.

Miss McSoren talks over her shoulder as she climbs the stairs. Her bare legs are perfectly smooth and have the sheen of carefully applied lotion. I bet she shaves them on a schedule. Never nicks herself with the razor. Never has to scramble for toilet paper or Band-Aids to stop the bleeding. I have been using the same disposable razor for about six months and it never gets all the hairy patches. I just can't keep up with my body.

We reach the landing. The door to bedroom number one is open. There's a man in there, wearing khaki pants and a blue golf shirt. Must be Holly's dad. He's tightening the screws on the legs of her desk chair. He is large and mostly bald, working up a good sweat. A woman has her back to the door and is arranging things in a closet. Must be Holly's mom. She hangs dresses with dresses, skirts with skirts, so that Holly can find things easily when she gets ready each day. She arranges clear stacking boxes that hold coiled belts, socks, tights, and hair accessories. I have never seen a couple working together on behalf of their child. Holly's mom is about the same width as Holly's dad. She has shoulder-length brown hair kinked from a perm. She turns when I reach the bed that is to be mine. She has already finished making up Holly's. There's a large blue dolphin on the comforter, and sheets with waves on them. (I later find out that Holly was a star on her swim team back home.) In the middle of her pillow there is a ratty teddy bear wearing a T-shirt that says GO HAWKEYES!

Holly's mom wears a pink pantsuit and white Keds. Opaque pink lipstick that makes her look like she has been eating Cray-Pas.

"Bettina!" she says with such friendliness that I am completely bewildered. She pulls me to her, and her body is big and soft, like a sofa. She is not shy about smothering me with it. Holds the back of my head and presses me even closer to her. I'm sure I will leave an imprint once she releases me.

"We have been waiting for you! What a wonderful time you girls will have!"

I look for Holly, who is nowhere to be seen. Holly's mom looks around me as well. I, too, am missing a person.

"Where are your folks?" She says this in such a way that it's obvious she has no doubt they will be along shortly. I just need to place them somewhere on Cardiss's campus, attending to something else.

"I came by myself," I say. Leave her to make up a reason why my parents aren't there.

Holly's mom eyes my solitary duffel. Sees the standard-issue sheets folded on my bed, grayish white with PROPERTY OF CARDISS stamped on them. There are two maroon blankets next to the sheets that seem to promise all the comfort of burlap sacks. The LV bag does not register. For all she knows, I bought it at Kmart. Given these facts, Holly's mom makes a quick calculation. It is the wrong one, but generous all the same.

"Oh, lots of students come by themselves. Airfare can be expensive, as is renting a car. We drove our own. I'm so relieved that we all have the same *values*. Holly didn't know what kind of roommate she would get. There are so many students here that come from important families, and Holly was worried she wouldn't fit in. I said that everyone was just here to get an education, that having money or not doesn't matter in the end. That there is just too much work for people to care about things like that. But I must say, I am more than a little relieved that you are from the Midwest too."

It's funny the way she says it. Like the Midwest is a small town where no one has any real money and everyone gets along. I nod in reply, though it is completely untrue. But I am certainly not going to bring up the chocolate money. Only Babs can be a *fucking chocolate heiress* with impunity. It would be social suicide for me to bring it up.

Holly's dad stands up from his crouch by the chair. He strides over, pumps my hand.

"Tell her, Donna."

"What?"

"What Holly thought about Bettina."

"Oh, no, Dennis, it's stupid."

"No, it's really funny if you think about it."

I look at both of them: open faces, shining. Wait.

"When we got the card with your name on it, Holly thought

you were related to Ballentyne chocolate. That you must have pots of money and live in a fancy apartment." Donna starts to laugh.

Her presumption pisses me off. It's true, of course, but it is my secret to tell. It's not a *really funny* one, no matter how you think about it.

"I told Holly she would be lucky because your family would probably send you big care packages of chocolate. Chocolate is Holly's favorite food. I make brownies every Sunday night, and by Tuesday morning, they're always all gone."

"Not true!" I turn to see Holly standing in a peach robe, her long brown hair dripping wet. She wears teal flip-flops and carries a metal bucket that holds all her bathroom amenities. She's beautiful. I can't believe she left her parents unattended. Trusted them to be alone with her things. Make first impressions on the people who will make or break her Cardiss experience.

"My favorite food is ice cream, *then* chocolate!" She laughs. I see that her wet hair is making small puddles on our wooden floor. She is shorter than I am, probably five-four to my five-seven, but she looks more developed. She has boobs and hips, while I do not. I've gotten my period, but I have still not achieved a woman's body. My fat has not distributed itself into come-hither sexy parts. It's as if my hormones have gone on strike.

Holly's eyes are brown, like her hair. There is a lightness and sweetness in them that makes them pretty. She looks wholesome, pastoral. Like a character in a Hardy novel but no one I have ever seen in real life. She's near enough that I can smell her shampoo. It has a fruitiness to it. Probably some variation of Herbal Essence that comes in a pink or green bottle with complementing conditioner. In France, you buy shampoo at the pharmacy. It's so expensive you are only supposed to use it once or twice a week. I hardly even bother to do that. Instead, I wear a heavy mist of Coco perfume, but with my smoking, I never manage to smell clean the way Holly does, standing there with her parents.

"As for the brownies, Jenny helps." Holly puts the bucket with her bathroom things on top of her dresser. Begins toweling off her hair. Her towel is white with pink trim, and I can tell by the crisp white color and the way the threads are not matted together that it is new. Bought especially for her Cardiss room. A reminder from her parents that she hasn't been permanently exiled from her home in Iowa City. When she comes home, all of her old things, towels and sheets included, will be waiting for her.

I look at Holly and try to initiate a casual conversation even though we have not yet been introduced. I'm still pretty dismal when it comes to making friends with girls my own age.

"Is Jenny your sister?"

"Best friend," Holly and her mom say in unison, then laugh at their synchronicity.

"Jenny and Holly have been best friends since kindergarten," Donna continues. "I'm really surprised she didn't sneak into the car with us. Holly has already written her twice since we left."

I picture big bubbly writing and envelopes with stickers. Purple ink.

"Holly is going to bankrupt us with all that postage."

"Mommy, stop! You keep blabbing on about me like I am not here."

Mommy? Is she fucking kidding? I have taken to swearing, speaking Babs's language. At my age, it is not clumsy, awkwardly precocious. Instead, it gives me an edge.

But I can't be completely cynical about Holly's Mommy. I

still don't even get to say Mom when referring to mine. Suddenly I feel like I have been cruelly tricked. I thought the whole point of boarding school was that there were no parents.

Holly walks over. Gives me a hug. I'm somewhat stunned but hug her back. Her robe is damp, but her body is still warm from the shower. I want to put my head on her shoulder and just let it stay there. I am so tired. But I pull myself away. Sit down on my bed. I want, *need,* a cigarette but know Holly and her mommy will be horrified if I light up in the dorm room. This is probably one of the best thing about Babs. If she were there, I would go right ahead. She would join me and later we would laugh at this earnest family from Iowa.

Holly doesn't seem to notice my change in mood. She confidently walks over and grabs my hand.

"Bettina, I'm so excited we are going to room together! It's going to be the best!"

I add exclamation points and double underlines to my growing list of her epistolary faux pas with Jenny.

"Mom, let's give her the present!" Holly points to her closet.

Holly's mom winks and digs in the back of Holly's clothes. Hands me a fat cardboard tube with a red bow. I go from being disdainful to completely ashamed. It never even occurred to me to bring something for Holly. *That's my girl, self-absorbed as usual.* But it's not like we're at a birthday party. It's the first day of school. Not standard practice, as far as I know, to bring a gift. Still, I could've easily bought something, anything, from the duty-free at Charles de Gaulle. A mini Eiffel Tower? A pack of cards? But these people don't even know I spend my summers in France. Have the chocolate money to travel outside Illinois. Didn't come by Greyhound to Boston but flew internationally and then took an eighty-dollar cab ride to get to school. But Jenny would have brought a gift, I know.

I undo the package. It is a three-by-five-foot hook rug in Cardiss colors, a big gray *B* for Bettina, I presume, rising from a background of maroon threads.

"Thank you," I say with as much enthusiasm as I can muster. I'm not exactly sure what the fuck it is or what I am supposed to do with it.

Holly whips one out from another tube. It has a gray *H* on it.

"Aren't they great? My mom made them herself." She puts hers down on the floor beside her bed. "So our feet won't get cold in the morning."

I kneel and follow her lead.

"See, it's just like being in a hotel!" she adds.

More like a Barbie House, if Barbie lived in a ranch and made her own curtains, I think. But really, I'm touched.

"They are great," I say slowly. "Thank you," I add again, inanely. "I'm sorry, I didn't . . ."

Holly's mom grabs my shoulder. "Don't you worry, my dear. We had fun doing it! Two are just as easy to make as one. What's important is that you girls stick together. It's going to be a lot of work this year, and I know there will be some richies who won't be nice like you are. You're going to need each other."

Holly's dad comes over to us and takes out his wallet. He pulls out two ten-dollar bills. Gives one to Holly and one to me.

I am mortified. Try not to take it. Shake my head and wave it away.

"Now, Bettina, this is nothing," he says. "Just a little money so you can get a poster for the wall by your desk, and maybe some snacks at the Cardiss Grill." He takes my hand and puts the money into it. No way I can give it back.

I have a thousand dollars in AmEx traveler's checks stuck in the *Marie Claire* in my duffel. I know Holly will find out about the chocolate money eventually, and then she and her parents will hate me for taking their money. But I can't think of a way to explain this to them. Say no. I decide to just take the ten dollars and give it back at a later point. Maybe when her parents leave, I'll just tell Holly I can't accept it. It's way too much. Or I could use it to buy her something, the present I didn't think to arrive with.

I set the money down on the empty wooden desk that is to be mine and say, "Thank you very much." They all look at me strangely, and I realize I've made another faux pas. I'm supposed to put it in my pocket or safely tuck it in a wallet. Normal people don't leave money lying around.

I pick up the ten quickly and stuff it in my duffel. I will not unpack the things I've brought until Holly's parents have left. *Bonjour tristesse,* an ashtray in the shape of Sacré-Coeur, a carton of Marlboro Reds. The green bomber jacket I bought myself from a shop near the Sorbonne, the kind all the French students wear. I'm sure the strange foreign things I've brought will make them want to take back the hooked rug.

An hour later, when Mr. and Mrs. Combs are ready to leave, Holly and I walk down with them to their car. The green Jeep Cherokee has some dents in it. There are crumbs on the floor mats. In the back seat, there's the September issue of *Glamour* that Holly must have read during the long car trip. Holly's dad gives her a big hug and goes to work unlocking the door. Holly's mom fishes in her bag, rooting through keys, breath mints, loose change, and lipstick to pull out a small pack of Kleenex. She puts her hand on the back of Holly's neck and pulls her close. They touch foreheads. An alternative form of kissing, I suppose, a mark of togetherness. Holly's part of her mom. First a tender plan, then a girl birthed and cared for.

Holly starts laughing and crying. She grabs her mom around the waist and puts her face on her shoulder. Holly's mom's chin quivers and she dabs at her eyes with a small piece of folded Kleenex. At first I feel the tiniest bit of contempt. I've never cried when saying goodbye to Babs. Not even when I was five and went to France for the summer for the first time. I thought I was just brave, more mature than other kids. Now I know it was because there was nobody to cry back.

I'd wanted to avoid this scene. Stay in the house and smoke a cigarette, but Holly's parents insisted I come. They want a picture of the two of us in front of Bright House. Roomies on our first day of Cardiss. They will develop the film when they get home and put the picture on their fridge. Or Holly's mom might even have it printed on a mug and take it to work with her, to whatever stupid job she spends her day doing. Holly and her mom break their embrace, both still crying and laughing. Holly grabs my hand, and we strike a pose against the door of Bright House.

Holly is wearing jeans and a maroon Cardiss sweatshirt with a hood. Her feet are still bare. It is almost five, but the sky is still light as day. I have yet to shower after my flight. Am still wearing the gray agnès b. T-shirt and black linen pants with black Converse low-tops that I pulled on over twenty-four hours ago. As Holly's mom works to focus the camera, I realize I do want to be in this picture after all. I have never kept a friend for more than a year, but this beginning suddenly seems promising. Perhaps because it's stripped of Babs, I have just a little bit of faith in it.

Holly puts her arm around my shoulder. Her parents seem a bit too friendly, but I remind myself that the Combses would've acted this way with whoever turned out to be Holly's roommate. They're just trying to provide Holly with some sort of insurance that her year will go well. Again, I feel very, very tired. I didn't sleep on the flight. Have now been awake for what seems like two days. I smile for the picture, but it is all I can do to return their hugs goodbye. Some small part of me wishes that if I went back up to my room I'd find Babs there, making up my bed with sheets she bought from Marshall Field's. Adorning my desk with a real leather blotter and pencil cup. Babs loves an opportunity to shop, and I can't believe that she has passed this one up.

10

Meredith

Holly and I go back up to our room and see that the door next to ours is open. We walk over to investigate, hover in the doorway. Two girls sit on the floor in the middle of the room, talking.

"I think I should just break up with him. It's the beginning of the year and better to act before all the top guys get taken."

"But he *is* a top guy. And you've only been dating five months. Plus it would piss off your parents."

"I don't care. I'm not going to date someone just because I've known him forever. That would be, like, pathetic. And I don't do charity cases."

"Cape is hardly a charity case. He's one of the best-looking guys at school and he really likes you."

They notice us, halt their conversation.

"Come in!" one of the girls says. We do, and I'm not sure whether we should sit or stand. Sitting seems to indicate an intimacy Holly and I don't yet share with these girls, and standing just seems awkward, like we are at a cocktail party and have not been offered drinks. Better to err on the side of a flyby than to act like we know them, like we really belong. We stand.

The girl who invited us in has long blond hair, which is wet. She wears a white terry-cloth robe with the initials KIM monogrammed in light peach. She is very tan, a tan that suggests not lying in the sand but letting the sun chase you because you have lots of great things to do. Waterskiing. Sailing. Whacking a tennis ball with a taut racquet.

She has a pedicure. Not the do-it-yourself kind either. Her toes are immaculately painted a baby blue, the color of hydrangeas. The skin around her heels is smooth. She's slathering her legs with a white cream. Her application is so generous that I can smell it where I am standing. Honey? Lavender? Unlike Holly, she isn't just getting cleaned up for dinner. She is Getting Ready. I'm not sure what motivates her. A standard she generally maintains? The male population of Cardiss?

I wonder if there are many girls like her at Cardiss. If so, I don't have a chance. I thought we were supposed to focus on getting good grades, not on winning a campus beauty pageant. I might be fluent in French and I can read a three-hundred-page book in a day, but I don't own a blow dryer and my makeup is old and caked in my cosmetics bag.

The other girl in the room seems more like an accessory to KIM than a person in her own right. She is whittled down to bones, sharp and angular, just like the models in *Vogue*. In this New Hampshire setting, however, she doesn't look fashionable. She looks ill.

Their room is decorated in such a way that it seems they've lived there for years. I wonder how they have achieved this on the first day. There's a Persian rug and upscale magazines strewn about the floor: *Vogue, W, Vanity Fair, Tatler.* A huge advert for Pommery champagne takes up half the wall over one of the beds, and there are books stacked in rattan baskets that are placed around the room. You could just reach in and pull one out if you were in the mood for a good read. I spot *Middlemarch, Madame Bovary* (in English, I note), *Lolita,* and *Great Expectations.*

Their beds have beautiful comforters. KIM has a snowy-white down duvet and white scalloped pillows. There are also baby pillows with her monogram in peach. On her wooden bedside table (it looks like an antique and must have been sent from home), she has silver frames with pictures of people I take to be her parents and friends from home. There's also a silver julep cup that holds a dozen black felt-tip pens.

The skinny girl's bed is covered with a maroon paisley bedspread and has green pillows. I recognize these as Ralph Lauren. The lack of frills indicate they were designed for a boy, but they look intense and cool to me.

Holly is weirdly quiet. I am not sure if she is suddenly missing her parents or—seeing this room—reconsidering the foot warmers her mom made. I see her pull at her sweatshirt and tug it down toward her waist. It has a fabric panel to put your hands in, and a hood. It seems it's no longer as comfortable.

KIM breaks the silence. "You must be Holly," she says, looking at her. "And you Bettina."

"How did you know?" Holly says.

"No offense, but Iowa City looks different from Chicago."

I want to say *How?*, fishing for the compliment, but I don't want her to insult Holly.

Holly, however, is eager to play this game, to show that she is just as able to pick up things about people without being told.

"And you're Kim?"

"Kim?"

"It's on your robe."

I wince for Holly.

KIM laughs. "No. Kim? Can you imagine? I'm Kingsley Meredith Ivory. But I go by Meredith."

"Oh," says Holly, both sorry she guessed wrong and confused about why.

"I'm Jess," the other girl says, sparing Holly any further embarrassment. "Join us; sit."

I like her. She's doing her best to make us feel comfortable despite Meredith. Holly and I sit. The four of us now form a circle on the floor. Part of me wishes we could avoid any further conversation and just play duck, duck, goose.

Meredith says, "You'll see that Bright is much better than a dorm. We don't have to wait for the shower, there are no dud girls, and Deeds pretty much stays out of our hair."

"Deeds?" I ask, not sure if she is a student or a teacher.

"Deirdre McSoren. Our resident dyke, dorm head, whatever. Don't walk around in any state of undress. I caught her checking out my tits once. Totally freaked me out. But you will see for yourself at our dorm meeting tonight."

Jess laughs. She wraps her hands around the front of her chest, as if to protect herself. Her boobs are even smaller than mine. Her laugh is more like a cough. There's no levity in it; just hard air pushed out. She's eating baby carrots from a ziplock bag. Seems to take no pleasure from them, as if they were medicine instead of food.

Meredith turns to Holly. "So, Iowa, we were just discussing boyfriends. Do you have one?" Meredith is just like Babs. Boys are really the only thing that counts as interesting.

"No."

"Why not?"

"Well, I went to junior prom with Stan, but it was more of a friend thing."

Meredith gets excited about this. I can see why. Proms represent so much optimism. All those corsages and puffy dresses. No exposure of legs or cleavage, just miles of satin hanging down the girls' bodies, like curtains hanging to the floor. Makes me want to vomit. I know Meredith has never been to one.

"Stop right there. Prom? I must know all." She looks at Jess and they both smile as if this is the funniest thing they have heard in years. I take the fact that they start on Holly as kind of a compliment, as if Meredith divines I am going to be a harder case. I am and am not. I want Meredith to like me, but I will put up a bit of a fight. Fuck with her superiority just a little bit.

"Well, seniors get to have theirs at the Hilton, but the rest of us just have it at the school gym."

"Do the seniors get the marquee outside by the highway? Does it say 'Congratulations, Graduates!'?"

"Yes!" Holly says.

"I've always wanted that for my wedding," Meredith says, as if letting Holly in on a big secret. I want to both smack Meredith and laugh at the joke.

"My aunt Deb and uncle Ray had that. I don't think it's that big of a deal. I mean, I think it comes with the package when you rent the venue." Holly sounds as if she is really trying to pass on information to Meredith. Reassure her.

"Venue! Did you hear that! Iowa's quite a little hotelier. I'm impressed. So, back to Stanley." Meredith is now really into the game. "Did you fool around in the back of the car?"

Meredith's question elicits the intended response from Holly. She is completely shocked.

"Of course not," says Holly quietly.

"No?" Meredith continues. "Why not? Not the right *venue?*"

"No, I just don't . . ." Holly looks to me. I don't come to her rescue. Am I just as mean as Meredith, or am I worse because I don't really care? The fact is I probably have less experience with boys than Holly has. Babs taught me what to do with a boy, but not how to attract one.

"Oh, dear." Meredith is determined to keep this drama going. "Don't worry, you will have plenty of opportunities at Cardiss." Suddenly, she turns to me. "Shut the door."

I get up to do so. Think about walking out of the room before Meredith torpedoes me. But I find Meredith strangely comforting and decide to stay.

Meredith grabs a beach towel, blue with white stripes, from underneath her bed and throws it at me. This towel also has her monogram on it.

"Put this under the door frame, will you? Deeds has gone out for her daily run and I need a smoke. Open the window while you're at it."

Meredith reaches under her bed again and pulls out a plastic Hello Kitty box that contains a pack of Marlboro Lights, a pink Bic lighter, and a glass ashtray. At least I'll finally get to smoke. I am almost dizzy from lack of it. Meredith's ashtray is the size of a coaster. It's heavy like a paperweight, and it has two orange interlocking Ds. I recognize it immediately. Babs has the same one. It's from Doubles, a private club in the basement of the Sherry-Netherland. A smoking kit, I think to myself. How cute.

Meredith tips the pack to Jess, who takes one. Then holds it in the direction of Holly, who waves it away. Meredith gestures to me, but I shake my head and reach down the front of my shirt. Pull out a leather pouch that I wear around my neck in lieu of a purse. It holds my Marb Reds and a gold Cartier lighter that Babs gave me for my thirteenth birthday. The lighter was expensive. You could buy a whole season of clothes for what it cost. Like most things Babs buys for me, this purchase was directed at pissing people off. She knew the other mothers at Chicago Day were horrified that I smoked, and this was her way of saying she didn't give a fuck. I know Holly does not recognize that it's Cartier and probably thinks the gold is fake. Hasn't figured out yet that I am not on scholarship after all. Meredith does recognize it though, and I can tell she is impressed.

I turn the box of cigarettes upside down and begin slapping it on the palm of my hand, packing the tobacco. Meredith stares at me for a good three seconds and then says, "Nice, Bettina. I didn't expect a Chicago girl to smoke." Like the Combses, she thinks all midwesterners are nice and follow the rules. At least the big ones.

"I picked it up in France," I risk. This isn't the story I signed off on with Holly.

"Did you go to Paris on a trip with your school?"

"No. I have family there."

Meredith puts her cigarette in her mouth. I can tell she smokes for effect, not for the nicotine itself. She is overly dramatic when she lights up. Doesn't seem to pull hard enough to fill her lungs. But the gesture works on Holly, who seems a bit let down that I smoke too.

Meredith seems intrigued by my answer.

"Do you speak French?" Jess asks.

"Yes. Fluently."

"Perfect," says Meredith. "I got a C in French last year. Spoiled my average. Deeds doesn't give any points for being in her house. You can help me."

"Sure," I say. Who knew my smoking and French would actually get me places?

"Okay," says Meredith, "I want to get back to what we were talking about before you came in. I have a big decision to make, and want to see what you think.

"Last spring, I started dating this boy, Cape. It was supposed to be a test drive, but he thought we were buckling in for the long haul. He's from New York, like me, and I've known him forever. He's hot, but major needy."

"Cape?" Holly asks. "As in Cod?"

Poor girl. She still gets it all wrong. Doesn't understand how esoteric preppy nicknames are. I know about them from books and always wished I had one. Maybe Meredith will give me one someday.

"No," Meredith says, trying hard not to laugh. "When he was little, he wore his Batman cape all the time, even to bed, and his mother nicknamed him Captain Cape. It became just Cape and all his friends have called him that ever since.

"Anyway, after dating all spring at Cardiss, we both spent the summer in East Hampton. One night, I decided to take it further, and it was just a disaster."

Holly looks up at her, considering. She has never met this kind of girl before. One who has a summer house and can discard boys on a whim. Didn't even knew they existed. But she knows this is her chance to join in, redeem herself for being from Iowa City. She is, after all, a good listener.

"So what happened?" she asks.

Pleased by the suspense she has created, Meredith takes a deep drag from her cigarette, attempts to inhale the smoke from her mouth in through her nostrils. Meredith has probably practiced this many times in front of a mirror at home. The effect's not lost on Holly. She will probably try a cigarette by end of term.

"Well, Holly, I'm not sure." Holly looks so happy that Meredith has finally called her by name, she almost claps. "But I'll tell you. See what you think.

"It is the last week of summer break. I'm at Pruett's house, drinking B and Ds. It's past midnight when Cape comes in and asks me if I want to go for a walk on the beach. He never drinks, which is kind of boring, but whatever."

"B and Ds?" Holly asks, determined to master this new language.

"Bacardi and Diet Cokes. Anyway, Cape and I drive to Maidstone to take our walk. I have a pretty good buzz and am thinking about maybe going for a swim in the ocean. I start to take my top off, and then I trip. But because it's Cape, I don't feel embarrassed at all. He takes my elbow, and once he's sure I'm steady, he leans into me and says, 'Meredith, I think I love you.' He then reaches over and starts petting my hair like I'm some kind of cat. I think this is just too funny and start to laugh. But because I know that is just too mean, I put my hands up to my face and make it sound like I'm crying."

"Crying?" Holly says. I know that Holly, like me, has yet to elicit such a declaration of love from a boy, and we are both eager to hear the rest of the story.

"Then Cape puts his arm around me and starts kissing my ear. I can't stand ear kissing. All that spit and heavy breathing. It's like porno for dogs. I just want him off me, so I push him back into the sand, unbuckle his belt, and give him the best blowjob he has ever had. I'm really good at blowjobs. They are like my specialty."

I'm really good at blowjobs. They are like my specialty? Jess has a neutral expression—I know she has heard this story before—but Holly's face is all pinched together, as if she is trying to figure out just how many blowjobs Meredith has had to give to make them her "specialty."

I can tell Meredith likes our interruptions; they add to the suspense.

"I'm good because I don't get distracted; I'm totally single-minded about the whole thing. Sometimes guys try and touch my tits when I blow them, thinking they're giving me something for my effort. Like it is some kind of pay-as-you-go, but I'm just like, No, don't mess up my rhythm. So of course, with

Cape, the harder I suck him, the more sentimental he gets, calling me Mere with these little *oh!*s and whimpers in there.

"I think this is a major victory for me, because if you saw him, you would think he was cool and could keep his shit together during a blowjob. But when he comes, he keeps gulping air and making these little noises. I swallow, of course. That's one of the things that make me so good. It's really almost the same as warm salt water, but thicker, like salad dressing. Then I put everything back in his boxers where it belongs and zip up his khaki shorts. Cape pulls me up next to him and kisses the top of my head, my cheeks. I think he's going to cry for real, which is just not my thing. After about five minutes, he seems composed and ready to make another speech. I can't deal and tell him I really need to get home."

I start to feel sorry for this boy she has made cry on the sand, even though I have never met him.

I say: "I know what you mean. It's so lame when guys don't know you're supposed to take turns. You go down on him; he goes down on you."

Meredith looks slightly off balance, as if I'm Cape reaching for her breasts while she's trying to tell her story.

"Exactly, Bettina," she concedes in a flat voice before proceeding. "Anyway, the next day, there's a poem from him in my mailbox. A poem! Written in pencil. I hate poetry, even pencils, so I don't even read it. He calls that night, and I let Mums take the call. I just don't want him to embarrass himself any more. I mean, he is really good at soccer and will be captain of the lacrosse team next year, I'm sure of it. But for fuck's sake, have some dignity, dude. He sent another Poem by Cape to our apartment in NYC but I didn't call him. Instead, I brought it to show Jess. It's a classic."

Meredith gets up and walks over to her desk. She opens the top drawer, pulls out an air-mail envelope, and tosses it to me.

Unlike Meredith, I like poetry. Would love for a boy to send me a poem that he wrote especially for me, even if I had to give him a blowjob first.

There's an onionskin piece of paper tucked inside the envelope. The writing is in dark black pencil, but the letters are cramped together, as if they had not been given the chance to stand and stretch.

> *I think most about your ankles,*
> *The way the bones kiss when you stand.*
> *Or perhaps the backs of your knees:*
> *They are so lovely and vulnerable,*
> *As if they await a press of my thumbs,*
> *To make you fall to me.*
> *Or maybe your beautiful hair—*
> *You are so generous with it,*
> *Leave strands of it on my sweaters*
> *When once it filled my hands.*
> *I save every trace of you as if it were a relic*
> *For you are my goddess.*

Meredith watches intently as I read it. She is like a cat after all, leaving a fresh kill on the doorstep. Despite what she says, I know she thinks the poem is good, or good enough to impress other girls. Otherwise she would have tossed it. But I pretend to agree with opinion.

"You are totally right. Poetry is stupid. It's for people who are too lazy to write good prose. And who wants to be told her hair sheds? I mean, the guy does seem weirdly hostile and angry. I would stay away from him."

Meredith practically snatches the paper from me and hands it to Holly, who reads it and puts her hand over her heart.

"Oh, Meredith. I think it's sweet. What are you going to

do?" Holly asks, enraptured by the game, even though I know the blowjob story threw her for a loop, forced her to reconsider her past and possible missed opportunities.

I'm now the crazy woman in the park. The one who spits and curses even when you give her change.

"Are you going to see him again?" Holly asks.

"Of course," Meredith says as she stubs out her half-smoked cigarette.

"He goes here. Lives in Wentington, the dorm next to ours," Jess says, showing Holly and me that she has the inside scoop. Or maybe part of her job description is to keep the conversation going when Meredith is busy attending to other things, like putting her smoking paraphernalia back in her Hello Kitty box.

"Goes to Cardiss?" Holly asks. Even though Jess has already said this.

"You got it!" Meredith replies, taking over.

"Cape?" Holly asks, making sure she understands.

"Yes. You just can't let him know I showed you his poetry. He would be horrified."

Meredith and Jess laugh.

"Have you seen him yet?" Holly has grabbed hold of this drama like it is the rope of a ski tow pulling her into Meredith's inner circle.

"Nope," says Meredith. She takes the envelope from me and Cape's note from Holly and puts them back in her desk's top drawer. "I mean, really, these poems can't go on, it's too embarrassing. But maybe I can fuck him in the shower."

"In the shower?" Holly says, bewildered. Even though Meredith is comfortable using the word *fuck,* I am fairly certain she's still a virgin. Something about the way her robe is so tightly belted and the perfection of her white bed.

"I've never had shower sex," Meredith continues. "It just

seems like something cool to do. I mean, one of the best things about living in this house is that our bathroom door actually locks. I know it would totally freak Cape out, but he would go for it. I also have a sweet tan."

I am half tempted to tell Meredith that sex in the shower is better in theory than in reality. Babs explained to me that given the space, the only position that really works is for the woman to bend over and take it from behind. You end up staring at the soap and conditioner. It's next to impossible to smash, and soon you just want to get the thrusting over with, it is so uncomfortable.

Instead I say, "It's really hard to get a condom on once you are in there. Make sure Cape puts it on beforehand. Also, you might want to give him a blowjob first so he doesn't come too quickly."

Meredith looks at me, stunned by my tips. Then she pats my knee, almost grateful for the information.

"Thank you, Bettina. I'll give you all a full report."

Holly's now both awed and unsure. Can she be friends with Meredith and me, people who have apparently actually touched a penis? I'm pretty sure she thought we would be talking about classes. Or maybe other girls on campus.

Meredith dismisses us, as if she's a therapist and our time is up.

"I have to get dressed for dinner. You two probably have some unpacking to do."

She swoops the blue-and-white towel up from the floor and throws it onto her bed. As we leave, I notice a field hockey stick leaning against wall near the door. I know Meredith probably runs her tan legs off wielding the stick to bring Cardiss to victory, but it still has the menacing air of a weapon.

It is now almost six, time for dinner.

When we get back to our room, Holly takes off her Cardiss sweatshirt and puts it neatly back into her closet. She pulls out a white shirt that has a tiny pink flower stitched over the left breast, probably from the Gap but more feminine than the sweatshirt. She is now Trying.

"Holly, that shirt is really pretty," I say.

She smooths it down, since it is wrinkled from the trip.

"Thanks, Bettina," she says. "You can borrow it sometime."

Then she continues. "Bettina, do you think most girls here are like Meredith? I mean, she's so rich and has done so much, and I've only kissed one boy."

"What makes you think she's so rich?" I ask, wondering what Holly has picked up on. I can tell Meredith's family has some money, but nothing compared to what Babs has.

"Her robe, for starters."

"You have a robe, Holly."

"But hers has her initials on it."

"Holly, a robe is just a towel with a belt around it. You could get yours monogrammed too if you really wanted."

"But I don't even have a middle name. And Meredith has one name for dressing up and one for every day."

"Would you really want to be called Kingsley?"

"Well, no." We both laugh.

"Bettina?"

"Yes?"

"Why do you smoke?"

Because it is the only thing I have in common with my mother and it makes me feel less alone. But I opt for the next true answer.

"Because I've never been good at sports and it keeps me from gaining weight. My mother hates fat people."

I suddenly remember that Holly's mother's heavy and wish I hadn't said this. But she doesn't seem to notice.

"Do you miss her? And your dad? I think you were brave to come alone."

Of course I miss Babs, but that has nothing to do with homemade brownies and cozy hugs. I just say what Holly wants to hear.

"Yes. But my dad doesn't live with us."

"Do you see him often?"

"Never." Of course I mean *I've never seen him in my life,* but Holly does not need to know that.

The look on Holly's face is of both pity and shock. In addition to believing in my imaginary Greyhound ride from Chicago to Cardiss, she now has the idea that Babs is a hard-working single mom scraping to make ends meet. How could there be any other explanation? Holly seems stumped as to how she can make me feel better about my hard-knock life. She picks up her brush and decides to change the subject.

"You must have gotten a good package. And that's a big deal."

"Package?" I'm lost. We haven't been at Cardiss long enough to get mail.

"It's okay if you don't want to tell me about it. I've just heard it's harder to get in if you need one."

I still have no idea what she is talking about. I decide to pretend I do and just deflect the subject back to her.

"Did you get a big one?"

"Yes. My mom told me not to mention it because it would seem like bragging, but I got tuition and board. My parents just have to pay for books and other supplies."

Fuck. I should have told the Combses the truth. Holly and I can never be good friends now. Part of me will always be lying to her.

Meredith pokes her head in. She is wearing a long Laura Ashley skirt that goes to her ankles, sweetly feminine with white and blue flowers. A navy blue short-sleeved Izod and navy blue flip-flops that match her shirt perfectly and show off her hydrangea-blue toenails. It's normal to want to be as beautiful as Meredith is, but I am also strangely jealous of those toes. Does Cape notice how perfect they are? I decide she must have an entire wardrobe of polishes: light pink to match Mumsy's peonies, solid white to match the color of their house in East Hampton. I think about water beading on them during her shower sex. If she actually does it, that will probably be the best part of the whole thing—her glossy toes repelling the water, retaining their unchipped shine. But who will maintain them in this boondocks New Hampshire town? Maybe Jess is good at application.

Her blond hair is pulled up in a ponytail, and she has on a smear of pink gloss. The kind that is extra-gooey and comes in a tube with a wand. Jess follows closely behind. She's wearing a black linen skirt that hits her ankles. She has on a long-sleeved green T-shirt. Bluchers on her sockless feet.

"Hey, guys, want to come to dinner?" Meredith asks.

Holly puts her brush down, says, "Yes." Without the exclamation point. She's a quick study.

I feel the fatigue come back from earlier. I just can't make myself go.

"I am going to stay and finish my bed. I'll meet you there."

The three of them look at me strangely. You never turn down an opportunity to be included. Even if you have just met these people and you've been friendless for the past two years and it hasn't killed you, you still rally when they ask you to come to the dining hall. But I need a break. Just can't.

"Okay," Meredith says, "knock yourself out." She leaves, and the other two follow her.

I finish my bed. Start on my duffel. All of my clothes fit in two drawers of my dresser. I have gotten into the French habit of wearing the same outfit three days in a row. Seems much easier.

I strip naked, grab one of the white Cardiss-issued towels, and head for the shower. I don't have a bucket like Holly's, so I cradle my toiletries awkwardly in my arms. The towel barely fits around my waist and I have no robe. But I'm used to being topless. At Cap d'Antibes, nobody under thirty wears a bathing-suit top on the beach.

The bathroom in Bright looks like one any American house would have. Unlike in France, the toilet is next to the bathtub, so you are forced to both shit and clean yourself in the same space. The bathtub has a white canvas shower curtain, like the sail of a ship, and it's stamped PROPERTY OF CARDISS on the corner. There's a heavy white scale by the door with big pink flowers stuck on it. I'm pretty sure that this belongs to Meredith. Jess probably has one stuffed in her closet somewhere that is perfectly calibrated. For her use only.

There's a medicine cabinet above the sink with nothing in it. This depresses me. I'm not looking for pills to steal or even dental floss, but this emptiness seems to prove that even though Bright looks like an authentic middle-class American house where a real family with four daughters might live, it's still just a facsimile. I turn on the shower, and as I wait for the water to get scalding hot, like I like it, I get the cigarette and lighter I have tucked away where my towel hits my left hip.

There is no bathmat. I sit on the cold tile floor. Ash into the toilet. I always smoke in the bathroom, before and after showering. It's really my favorite place to do it. The whole ritual is the closest thing I have to meditating. It almost makes me feel safe.

After about a minute, there's a knock on the door.

"Bettina?"

I feel the floor around me, worried that water has splashed out of the tub and might be leaking. That I'm making a mess.

But the floor in the Bright House bathroom is dry. Relieved,

I stand up and open the door. Completely forgetting that I am still half naked and holding a cigarette in my left hand.

It's Miss McSoren. She's wearing running clothes, and her short hair is damp with sweat. She wears the more feminine running socks, the kind that do not cover your ankles, with a Nike swoosh on them. I hate socks like this.

She stares at me for a second and then tries to stand up even straighter to assert some kind of authority. Even though her posture is perfect, we're exactly the same height. I remember what Meredith says about her sexuality and try to cover myself up. My cigarette crosses right in front of her face and I almost burn her cheek.

"Bettina," she says, stepping back from me. "It is dinnertime. You should be at the dining hall."

"I'm sorry," I say, "I was just so tired from the flight and didn't have a chance to get clean. I was talking with Meredith and Jess and . . ." I notice Miss McSoren's cheeks and nose are dusted with freckles. She looks much younger than I originally thought. She stares at the cigarette. Having almost seared her face, I'm now getting smoke in her eyes, hair. It's seeping into her pores that are open from her recent run. I doubt smoking makes her feel protected and peaceful. I don't know if I should turn my back on her and toss the cigarette into the toilet, or just hold it down by my side until she leaves. She didn't expect to find this. Didn't think she would have to face a disciplinary situation on the first day of school, or maybe ever. I think her strategy was to be severe and distant up front so as to discourage any defiant behavior down the road. I say, "I'm sorry." Start to cry. I am almost naked, barely covered by a towel, holding a cigarette. I've been at Cardiss only three hours and already everything has gone wrong. "I'm allowed to smoke at home," I manage to get out.

Miss McSoren takes the cigarette. Enters the bathroom,

turns on the faucet, and runs it under the water. She rolls the now soggy butt in some toilet paper and tucks it in the pocket of her running shorts. Reaches over and turns off the shower.

"Pull your towel up," she says. Doesn't mention the cigarette or the crying. "As I said, you're not to be in the house during mealtimes. Take your shower, but then get dressed immediately and go to the dining room."

Strangely, I feel a bit let down that Miss McSoren doesn't punish me. She would've punished Meredith, who would have complained about it but bragged too. Meredith is too much a part of Cardiss, and not punishing her would undermine the whole structure. But me, I have just washed up here and inevitably will wash back out. My studentness somehow counts less than others'.

But I haven't been at Cardiss long enough to understand the magnanimity of Miss McSoren's gift. Only later will I find out that smoking in a house is a pretty serious offense. It's a huge fire hazard, and the school could lose its insurance. Anyone caught doing it is put on probation. Just a tiny step below being kicked out.

But now, I pretend to be grateful and say, "Thank you, Miss McSoren."

She flashes me the hint of an angry look. She doesn't want to be thanked. That would imply that I owe her something, and she does not want the responsibility.

11

Meeting

SEPTEMBER 1983

I MEET UP WITH THE Bright girls at Oakley, the dining hall on our side of campus. It's mostly empty by now. Meredith and Jess linger over coffee in Styrofoam cups while Holly looks on. I wonder if they're waiting for me or just engrossed in conversation.

The dining hall is divided into two identical halves. I later find out that you always sit on the same side of the dining hall. Seats are not assigned but taken out of habit. Each half contains a hot-food line and its own salad bar. There are floor-to-ceiling windows and you can see students walking on the path outside. There are wooden circular tables as well as long rectangular ones.

I'm not really hungry, so I make myself two pieces of toast with butter and grab a cup of coffee. It looks so weak, you would probably have to drink seven or so cups of it to achieve the buzz of one espresso. I walk over to Meredith, Holly, and Jess and take the empty seat at their table. Meredith says:

"Bettina, you just missed Cape!"

"He's really cute," Holly adds.

"Don't worry, he'll be at breakfast," Jess says.

As if I came to the dining hall not to eat but to examine Meredith's beau. I'm curious, of course, but not obsessing over it. Babs would say, *Moving on—next?*, as she always does when she's bored with a conversation. I hope one day soon the Bright girls and I can play boy-spotting with a guy I like, who whimpers over blowjobs and writes poetry. *Sure, that will happen* hits me inside my head, right behind my eyes. *Fuck off, Babs,* I want to say, but part of me believes this.

Later that night, we gather in the living room for our house meeting with Deeds. On a side table, there is a bizarre assortment of snacks: Three bananas. A handful of baby carrots. A white paper plate with five chocolate chip cookies. Root beer. Even though we're not inclined to eat the cookies, it seems strange that there's not a whole batch. Did Miss McSoren bake only five? Or did she get them from a nearby dorm that had oodles of them? One more indication that she has no maternal instincts.

Deeds stands in front of us, wearing the same outfit I first saw her in and once more holding a clipboard. Is she going to take attendance even though there are only four of us in the house?

Meredith and Jess once again sit on the floor, and Holly and I are cross-legged on the sofa. We don't yet know that we will spend almost no time in this room. It is only for receiving visitors and the occasional phone call. No one at Cardiss watches TV. There is just too much work.

Deeds begins.

"First of all, I want to welcome Holly and Bettina to Bright. You can come to me with any questions, or just ask Meredith or Jessica. Since we are such a small house, we don't have proctors. You have to see me each night to check in, and check-in is at eight.

"I want you each to read the C-book, but I will go over the big rules. No smoking or drinking on campus. No boys in your room unless it's during visitation. Then you have to have lights on, door open, and three feet on the floor."

I wonder about this. What does *three feet on the floor* mean? Where does the fourth foot go? Will Deeds walk by and check that we are complying with this? If we aren't, what will the punishment be? It doesn't really matter because I know nothing can be worse than a Babs deluxe room thrash. Do you have to leave if your roommate has a visitor? Where do you go? The living room? What would Deeds do if she caught Meredith fucking Cape in the shower? Would that be worse than my cigarette?

She continues. "You can study at the library until ten if you get permission beforehand."

Will she check the library? She seems thorough enough to do so, although I bet she wants to be on deck at the dorm.

"Any questions?"

Holly raises her hand.

"Are we allowed to take baths?"

I don't understand why anyone would want to. Does she think this is a hotel?

"Yes, of course, but not in the morning when everyone showers."

I want to look like I am participating. Redeem myself for the smoking incident.

"Do we have to go to bed at a certain hour?"

Jess and Meredith giggle.

Meredith says, "You wish. Sometimes you'll have so much homework, you'll stay up all night."

Miss McSoren doesn't expect feedback from us. "No. If you are old enough to be away from home, you can regulate your own sleeping habits." At least Deeds won't be waking me up in the middle of the night. I sense from her rigidity that she gets her eight hours.

She waits for more questions, but we have none.

"That's it," she says. "I'll leave you to get to know one another." Holly takes a cookie, gets crumbs on her T-shirt. I want one too, but Miss McSoren's offerings are too pathetic. Meredith declines. Seems to be watching me.

12

Boys in Blazers

SEPTEMBER 1983

I WAKE UP EARLY THE next morning, around six, due to the jet lag. The starchy sheets and itchy blanket make me wonder at first if I am in some kind of hospital. Then I look over at the bed next to me and see Holly sleeping soundly. I badly need a cigarette. Smoking is now like breathing to me. It steadies me, helps me clear my head and get my balance. After my run-in with Miss McSoren, I don't dare risk doing it in the bathroom. I decide instead to take a walk. Yesterday evening, I read in the C-book that students are allowed outside after five A.M., so I figure I'll find a nice bench somewhere on campus and have a cigarette. I slip on my pleated skirt and a yellow button-down and go outside.

The New Hampshire morning air is crisp but not quite cold, like a lake in summer. No one else is up that I can see. I walk for a bit, not really knowing where I am going, since I missed the campus tour the first day. I see identical red-brick dorms and concrete paths cutting through the grass. The library is in the center, a huge red building with round windows. One of the things that drew me to Cardiss, besides the fact that Mack and my grandfather went here, was this library. It's bigger than any other prep school's; has the most books. Behind the dorm farthest from Bright is an expanse of playing fields. These seem too open to risk a smoke on, and it would be almost sacrilegious to put out a butt on the grass. I keep walking until I get to a river lined with green benches. Just like a regular park.

I find a suitable bench. Take a seat and light up. I feel lonely sitting on this bench. It reminds me of the one in the apart-house. But I am no longer a ten-year-old, bored in the play-room. New problems. I inhale sharply, think about Meredith and her stupid relationship with Cape. Even Holly has a better chance with someone like him than I do, even if she's from Iowa. I am not sweet, or even hard in the right way. I'm cynical, but not dark, funny. I'm there on the bench for about an hour before I head to breakfast. I scan the dining room and spot Meredith, Jess, and Holly sitting at a different table from the night before, a long one filled with other students. I help myself to coffee and Raisin Bran with skim milk and join them.

"Hey, Bettina! Where were you?" Holly asks.

"I couldn't sleep and took a walk," I say, not wanting her to know I was suffering from jet lag.

"I can barely get out of bed at seven," Meredith says. "You're an inspiration."

"Hardly," I say, looking around at the others at the table, wanting to ask, *Who are these people?* There must be about fifteen students sitting there, boys and girls. I have never eaten breakfast with boys. Almost all of the students have wet hair. The boys wear blazers and ties, the girls skirts and slim-fitting T-shirts or oxfords. They are the best-looking bunch of teenagers I have ever seen. They seem to have some kind of hall pass from acne, and their bodies don't pull at their clothes. There are too many of them to make introductions, so I just sit there.

No one seems too interested in my arrival. I wonder if Cape is among them. Judging from the way that Meredith calmly spreads cream cheese on her bagel, I think not. How could you not perk up if a boy you gave a blowjob to was eating at the same table, even if you claimed to be on the verge of breaking up with him?

But I'm wrong. Another boy arrives at the table and says, "Hey, Cape! Summer?"

"Good; you?" He's just three seats down the table from me. Has brown hair that falls in his eyes, which are an intense blue. White oxford with a navy tie that has lobsters on it. Thin wrists and long fingers. Totally put together, except his fingernails. The nails, and the skin around them, are savagely bitten. I realize that while you can be fluid during the summer, admit attraction and even love, at Cardiss, you hold such things in check. You have to live with these people, after all, and you have to tuck the vulnerable parts of yourself away. All the drama is secondhand, recounted and then rehashed during intense conversations in the dorms. I wonder what Cape's thinking. Does he try to make eye contact with Meredith, or is even that small gesture too much of a risk? I turn and begin asking Holly what classes she will be taking, not wanting anyone to think I'm checking out Cape.

When the bell rings, we exit the dining hall and walk quickly to class. I haven't had time to buy my books, so I just carry an empty straw bag that I picked up at the stalls in Paris. I worry Holly will think I can't afford them and try to lend me money. I have a little schedule of all my classes that reads like some kind of treasure map. First is English 212 with Mr. Donaldson, room 42, Fielding Hall. I hope he's more inspiring than Miss McSoren.

The classrooms at Cardiss are all alike, except for the science ones. Each contains a large oval wooden table that we sit around, like kids at a dinner party. We are supposed to throw out ideas, parse our thoughts while the teacher looks on like some kind of benevolent but detached host. When I walk in, I am almost the last one there. Two seats available. One next to a girl with purple hair, and one next to a cute blond boy. I pick the one by the boy.

Mr. Donaldson is standing by the door, waiting, I suppose, for the last student to arrive. He's looks exactly like you'd expect a boarding-school teacher to look. Gray beard trimmed closely, glasses, tweed jacket, sharp green eyes. The bell rings again; no one else comes. He shuts the door.

"'Morning, everyone. I recognize some of you, but for those who are new, welcome. If you are not here for English 212, now is the time to make a graceful exit."

I'm sure he has said this to classes a dozen times, but people still laugh. No one gets up.

"This semester, we'll be reading from the twentieth-century British and American canon, and you'll be writing three expository papers on whatever books you choose. You'll also pick your own topics. I can provide some if you're stuck, but I really want you to pursue something that interests you.

"The other thing we'll do is creative nonfiction. You'll be expected to compose three stories based on real episodes from your life. This'll probably be challenging, since I want you to write about the real stuff. Events that have changed you, made you see things in a new light. Or, as they say, the precise moment after which everything was different. You'll be reading these out loud in class, so we'll work to establish a deep trust. And the less you hold back, the bigger the payoff."

Some of my classmates are writing this carefully in notebooks, which makes me suspect they won't have anything interesting to say, that they just want to follow directions. I take it all in. Start to worry. My stories are all about Babs. Just transcribing verbatim what she has said to me over the years, with no embellishment, would be taking a risk. And my life has yet to have a moment after which everything was different. So far, it's been just Babs, Babs, and more Babs.

I look at the boy to my left. He's not writing anything down, but his carefully combed hair and Cardiss tie seem to indicate a buttoned-up, sheltered existence. I doubt he's ever seen his mother's pubic hair.

Donaldson continues. "Today, a small exercise to practice."

He grabs a pack of index cards from his desk and drops them in the middle of the table. "I want you to pinpoint a moment this summer when you felt embarrassed and describe it in three sentences or fewer. Write your name and your home-town in the top corner." There is a small murmuring around the table, which dies down as students grab cards and take up their pens.

After five minutes of deliberation, I write:

> Bettina Ballentyne
> Chicago, Illinois
>
> I was sitting on the beach in Cap d'Antibes when my bikini top came unhooked. I couldn't get it back on quickly, and everyone around me was watching.

This of course is a lie, since I and everyone I know always goes topless in France, but I wasn't going to write about the really horrifying things: Babs calling at three in the morning to see if I had gotten my period yet. Leaving Nair on my bikini area too long and getting a rash that lasted a couple of weeks. Borrowing a dress from Cécile and having it rip when I sat down at the dinner table because it was two sizes too small.

When all of us are done writing, Donaldson says, "Okay, now hand your card to your neighbor."

We look up at him, incredulous. We've been tricked. Even if mine is a lie, I don't want the cute boy next to me to read it. He will probably think, *What's the big deal? You don't have boobs anyway.*

Nobody passes on a card and Donaldson says, "I know this might seem difficult, but all of you are taking the same risk."

The cute boy and I swap cards. His reads:

> Lowell Stillman
> New York, NY
>
> I was playing basketball with my friends when I tripped and fell. It hurt so much I cried.

Not so bad. I regret I wrote about my body. Now, at this very moment, I am really uncomfortable.

Donaldson gives us some time to look the cards over and then adds, "Write something positive on the card and hand it back. You'll see it's not as big of a deal as you might have thought."

It doesn't seem that Lowell needs to be shored up, he is so composed. But I write:

> No biggie to cry with your buds there. They probably felt bad you fell.

I hand it back to him. He smiles and gives me mine. He's written:

> Sounds hot! Wish I'd been there.

I wonder if he is making fun of me and I blush. I look at him and see to my surprise that he is smiling in a nice way.

"Nice to meet you, Lowell," I say.

"Likewise, Bettina," he says, holding out his hand.

Maybe Lowell can be my Cape and I can share stories about him with Meredith. All of the details of fooling around. I'm pretty sure he's not major needy, though I have no proof of this.

Seeing Lowell in his blue blazer, white oxford, and rep tie makes me miss Mack in a way I haven't in years. Mack's preppy way of dressing, his tendency to rub his hands through his hair to make sure it's still there, it's all replicated in so many boys here. I thought my desire for Mack would have abated a bit by now. It has not.

I thought Lowell and I could chat some more after class, maybe even flirt a bit, but everyone except me quickly packs up his or her stuff when the bell rings, no lingering. I have a free period after Donaldson, and I can think of nothing else to do but smoke.

I go back to the same bench. This time there's a boy sitting there. He strikes me as the antithesis of Lowell. He wears a coat and tie, as school rules dictate, but pairs them with ripped jeans that have lyrics from the Grateful Dead scrawled on them. According to the C-book, boys are allowed to wear jeans with their ties and blazers. He is also smoking. Marlboro Reds. He has green eyes, and a mop of dark curly hair. He's not handsome, but he is approachable. He has a cool vibe that spills into me. He holds out his hand.

"Hello, beauty," he says, which takes me aback, because of the confidence with which he says it and because I've never been called this in my life. I shake his hand and feel the calluses on his palm. He smokes with his left hand, which makes me believe he is left-handed, like me. A plus.

"And you would be . . . ?"

"Jake Kronenberg," he answers affably. "Have a seat. Plenty of room. Want a smoke?"

At least I have an answer to this.

"Thanks. I have my own." I sit down on the bench, go to work lighting my cigarette with my Cartier lighter. I'll simply join him, as if we were shooting hoops together. Killing time.

"I see you are committed to the endeavor," he says easily. "So, gorgeous, what's your name?"

Now I wonder if he's always this easy with the compliments and roll my eyes. "Bettina."

"Bettina," he says, "don't be so cynical. I'm not bullshitting you. I have high standards, and you more than clear the bar."

"We just met," I say. "How the fuck do you know?"

"I can just tell. See, you said *fuck,* and we haven't known each other two minutes."

"Whatever. I just came to smoke." But I am intrigued by our little game.

He puts his hand on my bare knee and starts rubbing it lightly, using his thumb to make small circles. I'm surprised by how pleasant the feeling is. His fingers begin to trace their way up and down my inner thigh. I am aroused but scared. If he starts to kiss me on the bench, right there, I might even kiss him back. Despite the fact that I'm even less experienced than Holly and have never kissed anyone. And I barely know him. But I can tell he takes what he wants, does not ask for permission.

He reaches my underwear and this jolts me enough to grab his hand, make him stop.

"Jake, I'm sorry, but no. I'm just not . . ." Not what? Not ready? Not it. Not interested? No. Afraid? Maybe.

"No worries. But I can wait. Another time, Bettina."

I don't know what to say.

I look at my watch. Time for biology. I finish my cigarette, throw it, still burning, onto the grass. Maybe this will make me seem daring, show I'm not a prude or a tease.

He grabs my wrist and kisses it. "See you soon," he says.
"Sure," I say.

The day's long with light. When I finally finish my classes,
which promise to be hard but doable, I go back to Bright, still
tired from the jet lag. I want to skip dinner again but know I
can't. I decide to lie down for a bit, refresh myself before walking around the campus and making more of the first impressions that may or may not be important during my Cardiss
career. I climb the steps at the house. The door to Meredith
and Jess's room is open, and I'm surprised to see that Holly has
ventured in there without me.

"Bettina, come in!" Meredith says. I know her enthusias-
tic greeting doesn't necessarily reflect a fondness for me. She
just needs a crowd to be more of who she is. I hesitate but
know not going in would be socially fatal. I pull the door shut
behind me.

Jess sits on her bed, pulling at a bunch of green grapes and
sucking on them like they're decadent candies. Holly and Meredith are on the floor. I think I will just make a pit stop, and
then take a shower.

"So I talked to Cape today and he said he wanted to take a
walk on the lacrosse fields after dinner."

I reach for a cigarette. Now that I have met him, I am curious as to how this is going to play out.

"That's so exciting!" Holly says. Meredith's now her favorite
TV show and she's just happy to sit on the floor and watch the
drama unfold.

"Too bad about the dumb poems," I say, trying to untether
Meredith from Cape, challenge her on the breakup she claims
to want.

She glares at me.

"What are you going to wear, Meredith?" Holly says, trying

to get the conversation back to the excited pitch it had before I walked in.

"Oh, just something that shows off my boobs."

Holly blushes, but I am eager to see them. Meredith must have at least a C cup.

She takes off her top. Meredith's wearing fancy lingerie: a white lace bra with a peach bow at the base of her cleavage. The bra pushes her breasts together, two smooth, sweet cupcakes of flesh. I have the odd desire to lick them, they are so beautiful.

It's brutal for me to think about Cape handling them. He's come to represent the standard Cardiss boy to me. If this is the case, I have no chance of ever fooling around with Lowell. I'll have to settle for an outlier like Jake.

Meredith pulls on a white baby-doll tee and another Laura Ashley skirt. She must have a dozen. The tee can barely hold up to her breasts, and I imagine they might push through any minute.

Jess puts the grapes back in a zip-lock bag and stores them in a minifridge they have snuck into the room and hidden under a large scarf.

I don't see Lowell at the dining hall. Dinner runs from six to seven thirty, so I guess we've missed him. Meredith makes herself a large salad and some Crystal Light from a packet she has brought from the dorm. Holly helps herself to the hot entrée: chicken with Tater Tots. She eats as if she were still in Iowa. We form a little clump in the table by the window, and no one joins us.

I can tell by the deliberate way Meredith holds her fork and scans the room that she is looking for Cape. He isn't there. I do see Jake. He is sitting by himself, reading the *New York Times*. He doesn't seem to be clued in to the fact that you're supposed to eat with other people. Or at least pretend to have friends. His indifference makes me think of Babs. I wish I could be like them. I stare at Jake a bit, and he lifts his head to meet my gaze. Waves at me. I nod back.

This does not go unnoticed by Meredith.

"So you know Jake?" she says, almost laughing.

"Not really—we met over a smoke this morning," I say defensively.

"He's a total slut with major attitude. He's from California and seems to think the East Coast is lame. He's slept with over fifteen people."

"How do you know?" I wonder.

"I know almost everything," Meredith says, pushing a piece of romaine into her pretty mouth. "Seriously, his roommate from last year is a friend of mine and that's what he told me."

"Sounds unlikely."

"Whatever," Meredith says. "Just be careful. Besides, he's not even hot. You could ruin your chances with other boys down the road. Also, he's Jewish."

Did she really just say that? Is everyone in Meredith-land WASPy?

"So am I," I say, just to fuck with her. But maybe I'm not lying after all. For all I know, my father could be.

"No, you're not," she replies confidently. "Bettina isn't a Jewish name."

Huh? Part of me just loves hearing what Meredith considers cast-iron logic.

"Anyway, way more important," she continues, "is that last year, Jake gave this girl, Riley Sayler, a black eye. She dropped out after that."

Jess says, "Mere, Riley said she ran into a door. Also, she was really depressed all year and had to go on meds."

"Whatever. I'd be depressed too if Jake Kronenberg hit me.

But I guess it's your call, Bettina. Don't say I didn't warn you."

Holly seems concerned all of a sudden. "Bettina, you should listen to Meredith. What if he really does hit girls?"

I don't believe Jake is violent, not really, but a dark part of me wants to find out. I also wonder if he really slept with so many girls.

Jake's hand on my thigh earlier did indicate a certain expertise, but where would he find fifteen girls to sleep with? Would I be number sixteen? Kind of a scary thought. I feel like once you lose your virginity, you're in sexual free fall. Open for business. But sleeping with him would give me a leg up on Meredith. And it seems like Jake doesn't give a fuck about pedicures or lingerie.

I decide to go back to the house and take a shower. Meredith looks at me strangely when I stand up. You do not leave the dining hall alone, but seeing Jake has given me just a tiny bit of confidence.

Back at Bright, I go to my room and carefully remove my clothes. Shower. I feel physically dirty, and also somewhat sad, because the adrenaline of defying Meredith is starting to wear off. Why haven't I made more of an effort to be her friend? Why am I so insanely bothered by her relationship with Cape, a boy I don't even know?

I decide to do what I always do when I feel bad. Chase the smash. I've never done it in the shower, but if I tilt my hips toward the stream of water and hold my me with both hands, I know the shower will provide enough pressure. Get me where I want to go. If I have one, two, three smashes, I'll feel better. Will be able to focus on my homework and go to sleep. I close my eyes and think of Lowell, of touching his hair, kissing the sweet spot behind his left ear. Licking his eyelids, grazing his fingers with mine as I do. I am just approaching a smash when I hear the curtain ripped back, feel cold air penetrate the steam. I try to reposition my body, but she sees exactly what I'm doing. Meredith.

No doubt she's come to get ready for her walk with Cape. Apply more makeup. Spritz herself with the L'air du Temps perfume she keeps on her dresser. Why she pulls the shower curtain back when I am clearly in there is a mystery. Maybe it is a bizarre form of hazing? Who knows, but what she finds, me chasing the smash, must be better than whatever she expected.

"Hey, Bettina! That game is much more fun with two players!" she says, laughing so hard I wish I had something to throw at her head.

Babs never once caught me chasing the smash, and it takes Meredith less than forty-eight hours. She's not going to let this go.

There's this girl in my dorm who plays with herself in the shower. Can you believe it? She won't even dirty her lips with the word *masturbate.* Will probably even tell Cape about it tonight. I bet the only times she touches her vagina is when she wipes it after going to the bathroom and sticks a tampon in it during her period.

I want to run out of there and ignore her, but I don't. I calmly step out of the shower and look her right in the eye.

"It's always good to get warmed up before the real thing. You know what I mean, Meredith? I'm surprised you're not doing the same thing."

I don't know where this came from. A total Babs line, but it seems to work. Meredith takes a step back. Like she has new respect for me. But of course she pretends otherwise.

"And who could you possibly be preparing yourself for?"

"Jake Kronenberg, of course," I answer, surprising both of us.

13

Sharp Objects

I GET DRESSED, DRY MY hair, and go outside. I walk across campus to the bench where I saw Jake earlier. As I'd predicted, he's sitting there, smoking. It's still light out. He doesn't seem at all surprised to see me.

"Bettina, my lovely. This is getting to be a habit of yours."

"Hello, Jake," I say. Fooling around with him should not be too hard, and now I have no choice. I should've locked the fucking bathroom door.

"Why so glum?"

I'm surprised he is able to tell what a dim mood I am in. I decide to risk it. See if he's as sexually sophisticated as Meredith says.

"The alpha girl in my dorm caught me masturbating."

"Meredith? Ha! Seems like you did her a favor. Frigid bitch.

"What?" he says in response to my embarrassed reaction.

Talking about sex with Jake is harder than I thought it would be. I am faking it, and this is all going so quickly. I don't doubt that Jake sees this as some kind of invitation.

"Don't be shy. It's not hard," he says, reaching for my inner thigh.

There's that tickle again in my groin. It feels good. So what if he's not Lowell. Maybe this is better. Jake might not write me poems, but he's interested in me in a way that no boy has ever been.

"Meet me at my dorm at midnight," he says.

"Too risky," I say. "I was already caught smoking in the Bright bathroom."

"It's less dangerous than you think. I am in Wentington, room five. Two buildings down from you. I'll leave the light on. Come at midnight. You don't have to decide now, but I'll be ready for you."

When I get back to Bright, Meredith's door is closed. Holly isn't in our room. She must be getting details about the Walk with Cape. Maybe they are talking about me. I decide to go visit Jake after all.

At a quarter to twelve, I quietly pull on my tailored jeans and an agnès b. T-shirt. No bra. Holly's sound asleep. She didn't come back to our room until after ten. I had done all my homework and was pretending to be asleep. I go downstairs and out into the Cardiss night. I am nervous, but not really. Jake wants me to come to his room and I'm going there. It's one of the more straightforward transactions I've ever been involved in, especially when the stakes are so high.

I find Jake's dorm easily enough. He told me his window would have a light, and sure enough, it does. I rap quietly on the window. Jake pushes it open.

"Ahh, I knew you would come," he says, but in a way that is friendly and happy, not smug.

I don't want to seem too easy a conquest, so I say, "I couldn't sleep and thought we could smoke."

"Sure, whatever," he says, grinning. I crawl through the

window into his room. It's filled with Grateful Dead memo-
rabilia. Huge tie-dye tapestries hang on all four walls. His bed
has white sheets and a ripped plaid comforter, and there is a
copy of James Joyce's *Dubliners* on his bedside table. He wears
blue boxers and a white T-shirt. There is a guitar in the corner
of the room.

Once I'm in the room, he hands me a cigarette. "Take off
your clothes," he says so matter-of-factly I'm not sure I heard
him properly.

"What?"

"Take off your clothes. It's warm in here."

He's really going to get down to it. No pleasantries, no
insipid conversation.

"No," I say, more because I hate my body with its lack of
boobs than because of any moral objection.

"Okay, Bettina. I'm not going to make you do anything you
don't want to. But the fact that you came to see me is a tell.
Here's my deal. I love girls, and I love sex. Dating is lame. Anything really worth doing is secretive. What happens here is between you and me, got it? Bright House wouldn't get it anyway."

I say, "Okay," and pause, knowing there's more to come.

"Also, when you are with me, you are with me. I don't share.
And whatever you do, don't fall in love with me. I will probably
always like you, but I will never, ever love you back."

What an arrogant ass, I think. Anyway, I'm just here to save
face. But I'm intrigued by the disclaimer and what is to come.

He reaches over and touches my face, running his fingers
across my eyelids, cheeks, tracing the outlines of my mouth.

Jake pauses and says, "So. Now. At least take off your shoes."

I do. He pulls my feet into his hands and begins massaging
them. His thumbs circle my anklebones. He stops for a second, leans in, and looks carefully at the scar I gave myself after
Babs's deluxe room thrash.

"Tell me about this," he says.

No one has ever noticed it before.

"It's nothing."

"Looks like a cigarette burn."

"When I was eleven, I was mad at myself for pissing off my mother. I ruined what started out as a good evening and wanted to punish myself."

Jake lights up a cigarette.

"Want another one?"

"What?" Who the hell thinks up such things? If it'll stop him from trying to get me naked, it seems worth it. For all the wrong reasons, I say, "Yes."

Jake takes my left foot in his hands and kisses the anklebone. Then he takes his cigarette and pushes it into the space right above it, matching the first one. I wince as he burns my skin, but that's it. Make no other complaints.

After the pain subsides, I think about Meredith. This is more significant than some dumb walk with Cape. Anyone can have that. It takes a special form of intimacy to allow someone to burn you.

"You are such a good girl, Bettina," Jake says and then kisses the burn.

I nod and for a brief moment wonder if he has done this before. But it doesn't really matter; the gesture seems fresh. A first time. I present my face to him. He kisses my mouth. Then he backs away and smacks me hard.

What the fuck?

I am tempted to smack him back. He has unleashed something. I realize that underneath my attraction to this strange boy is a strong hatred. He's not what I want. And it really, really pisses me off.

He pulls his arm back to do it again. I grab his wrist and push him away.

"No!" I say. *I'm not some kind of freak.*

"Each one gets better."

"I don't want any more."

"Fine," he says in a cool voice that is neither angry nor dis-appointed. He's above all that. "Suit yourself. I guess I was wrong about you."

"Yeah, whatever," I toss back. I put my shoes on and leave.

I touch my cheek as I walk to Bright. It's hot. I wonder if his hand has made an imprint.

When I wake up the next morning, I think Jake was right about taking the liberty to burn and smack me. Such violence is already buried in the intensity of my smashes, which I have depended on forever. I will go back to him. Let him push further.

I sneak out almost every night and go see him. He doesn't smack me again. I want to tell him to go full force, but Jake's not someone you tell what to do. We just make out. He is probably punishing me, making me wait. This is boring and tense at the same time. I want him to do something rough, even just bite my lip, draw a bit of blood, but for now he does not.

One night not too long after we begin our game, we meet at the library during study hours in one of the private rooms. I tell him I have a Donaldson story due, and he promises to help me. He reads a book as I work. I decide to write about when I cut my hair, when I was ten. *The day I cut my hair* and completely fuck up the Christmas Card, *I am merely bored, not* a defiant brat *like Babs tells all her friends.* Jake puts our two chairs close together but does not even glance at my work.

After I have written about four pages, Jake throws his books down and I kiss him with as much force as I can muster.

Jake flips off the light in our carrel so the space is completely black. He almost rips the buttons from my shirt as he undoes it, and then he slams his head between my breasts. He takes each one into his mouth and goes right for my nipples. He circles his tongue around them until they are erect. He takes the left nipple fully in his mouth and bites down, hard. I am so grateful he has come back, I want to cry. I put my hand inside his shirt and touch his shoulders, his back. I can feel his muscles, and he is warm, almost to the point of sweating.

He reaches down under my skirt, puts his left hand inside my underpants and then swiftly inside me. He begins a smoothly tempered stroke, in and out, out and in. Despite all my smashes, it hurts. I feel a wetness and know I'm bleeding. Jake brings his bloody hand up to his mouth and sucks on his fingers like they are covered in chocolate. Then with his right hand, he smacks me so hard, I just know he has left the imprint of his fingers. My head's reeling. I'm completely disoriented, but I'm ecstatic. He undoes his belt. I bend over and lick the copper buckle. I want to take the belt from his belt loops and lash him across the back but am not sure this is allowed. He jerks my head up and pulls down his pants.

Jake puts on a condom. He lifts me up and puts me on the carrel's desk. He flips up my skirt and enters me. This hurts more than his fingers, like he is jabbing me with a poker. I just hope it will be over soon. Jake comes after about five minutes. I do not smash, but it doesn't matter. I am completely gone. Jake balls the condom up in some Kleenex and throws it in the trash

As he told me before, there are no *I love yous*, no sweet kisses on my neck, but somehow I still expect *something* tender. Jake has done this many times, I remember, and I'm now just another girl on his list. But maybe this doesn't matter. I am, after all, always one for intensity, and Jake certainly gives me this. If only I could stop crying.

"You won't care so much next time," is all Jake says.

14

Package

OCTOBER 1983

THE CARDISS PO is a small space. A room shaped like an L with nine hundred mailboxes, one for each student. Almost all students go there after morning assembly, and there's much pushing and shoving to get to your mailbox. I really have no hopes about getting mail, just follow everyone else, wanting to keep time with the pulse of the school. Babs is unlikely to put pen to paper, and besides Cécile, no one would really write to me. But today, there's a pink slip in my box. A package. To claim it now, I would have to push my way through the sea of students to get to the post office window. The effort seems enormous. I decide to wait until after third period, when the small room will be empty.

I return in an hour. The post office is deserted. Except for one boy. Not just any boy but, of all people, Cape. After all Meredith's talk about him, he's more a concept to me than a person in his own right, so I don't anticipate conversation. Also don't want to let on how much I know about him. It'll demonstrate an inequality between us and might make me seem like a stalker. After all, I have seen him only once, that breakfast in the dining hall. Still, for some reason I feel like I know him from somewhere else.

I approach the window, where Cape stands empty-handed, waiting. He turns to me.

"They are interminably slow."

"Oh," I say, still holding back. We're going to talk after all. I'm determined to make a good impression. Want to think of something interesting to entice him with.

"First package?" he says.

"Yes," I answer, slowly picking up the thread of a conversation. "You?"

"Second. My mother always thinks I've forgotten something important. Toothpaste. Shaving cream. Socks. She just doesn't believe that I can pick up these things at Woolworth's in town. Any idea who sent yours?" The mention of shaving cream marks his boy-ness and it seems too intimate an item to be discussing with me. I'm happy to go back to *my* package.

"I don't know," I admit.

"Huh." Then:

"I forgot to introduce myself. Cape."

"Bettina."

"I remember you from breakfast the other day. You're in Bright with Meredith, right?"

"Yes."

"She's my girlfriend."

"I know. She talks about you a lot."

"Really?"

"Yes," I say, and leave it at that. So much for drawing him in.

The lady finally returns with his package, which is the size of a jigsaw-puzzle box. The address is written in a blue ballpoint pen, loopy script. I give her my pink slip.

"Just like my mom," Cape says. "She always sends things FedEx even though this stuff can wait."

"What dorm are *you* in?" I ask, not wanting him to leave yet.

"Wentington." Jake's dorm, also Lowell's. I don't want to admit any association with Jake, so I say, "Do you know Lowell?"

"Of course. He's my roommate. Really good guy. How do you know him?"

"English class."

"I've heard all about Donaldson from Lowell. Writing about being embarrassed. Sounds kind of cool."

"Yeah."

This new development in our conversation has stalled his departure.

Cape continues, "I write poetry. Mostly for myself."

I want to say *I know* but don't.

The lady has taken my pink slip but I am still waiting. I check out his package. The return address is Park Ave., NYC.

"So you're from New York?"

"Yes. And you?"

"Chicago."

"Where?"

"Lake Shore Drive."

"Oh," Cape says. "You really *are* from Chicago. I grew up in Grass Woods but left when I was young. My dad died in a car accident."

"I'm sorry." Died in a car accident? I look at him carefully.

"What did you say your last name was?"

"I didn't. It's Morse."

Morse? From Grass Woods? My brain almost hurts as I try to take this in; there is just no place to put it. Cape is Hailer? Cape is fucking Hailer? Is this some kind of sick joke? The boy's real first name is McCormack, after his dad; his middle name is Hailer. How can someone be known by three different names? I knew Cape's last name was Morse, of course, but I thought he was from New York, not Grass Woods. I never would have figured out on my own that he was Hailer. My Hailer. I have waited so long to meet this boy, connect with him, and here he is. At my school, and just a few feet away from me, talking. To me. I guess I shouldn't be so surprised he goes to Cardiss, since Mack went here, but still. Did Babs make this bet when she urged me to apply here? Babs's father went to Cardiss, but Babs is certainly not the sentimental type; she doesn't give a shit about that legacy.

I have to keep myself from either throwing my arms around his neck or throwing up. We can finally talk about our parents. Lament how fucked up our childhoods were. The whole thing will bond us for life, and we will grow as close as a brother and sister, twins even. And together, we will Finally Get Over It. But I know by the easy way he looks at me—like he has seen me only once before in his life and may or may not ever see me again—that he doesn't have a clue about our shared history, is still innocent. Does he need to have his head whacked against something he doesn't even consciously know is there? And if so, is this my responsibility? But he is already on the wrong track. He lets a cruel girl like Meredith put his penis in her mouth and then cries about how much he loves her. He writes her poetry and she laughs about it. If I do nothing, will he spend his whole life in this inane preppy circle, belonging yet chasing after Merediths and other stupid girls? If he knows about his father, maybe he will change. Choose different people to love. Ultimately, choose a different life. *I have to do something about this,* I think. But why, really? No one has yet to do anything about me.

I take a deep breath, rub my hands over my face. I am now Calm. "You know, your father came to some of my mother's parties."

Cape seems interested, but not really. Mack went to a lot of parties. "So our parents knew each other?" he says in the same tone he might ask *So, you have Parker for math too?*

Did our parents know each other? *You have no idea,* I could respond.

Instead, I tell him, "Yes. I would even say they were friends."

"My mother never really talks about the Grass Woods days."

How Mags to leave out the good stuff, I want to say. But no.

"I didn't know him that well, but he was always really nice to me," I say. I heard him fucking my mother in the hallway of the aparthouse. I knew about their nocturnal visits to his country club, about his admiring her centerfold in a golf cart. I even sat and talked to him on my mother's bed about a pearl necklace she'd found just as they were about to have anal sex.

"I'd love to hear what you remember sometime." This is an interesting topic, he probably thinks, but it can certainly wait.

"Sure," I say, nodding. I can follow his lead. Maybe we'll do that sometime, if I don't forget.

"Well, seems my work here is done. Nice chatting," he says, holding his package.

"Yup." I turn my back on him and step closer to the PO window. I have come, after all, to get a package. I hear Hailer walk away and the tinkle of a bell as the door shuts behind him. I know I will have to remind myself to call him Cape.

I wait for at least ten more minutes and start to wonder if anyone is still back there. But then there is a rustle, and my box arrives. It is so huge it obscures the woman who brings it. When she sets it down on the sill, I can tell by the thunk it makes that it is very heavy. I sign my slip as fast as I can so I can check the return address. The aparthouse. Babs.

Once I manage to lug my box across campus and up to my room at Bright, I go to work opening it. Inside, I find a pair of gray suede boots and a maroon cashmere dress. A gold charm bracelet I know Babs got from her parents when she was at Farmington. She never wore it but often brought it out from her jewelry drawers and let me play with the charms. A carton of Duchess Golden Lights. Big bottles of vodka, scotch, and bourbon. A box of Hard Rider condoms. Totally Babs. I dig for a note. Finally find one. Longhand on eggshell-blue stationery, *Babs* in brown script at the top.

Dearest, it reads. *Just a few things. Miss you madly—Babs.*

I'm both excited and disappointed by the package. I can't wear the boots or the dress or the charm bracelet, since they are too rich-looking and out of sync with Cardiss fashion. And the rest is contraband. Could get me kicked out. But I'm not sure Babs really understands there are rules at Cardiss, so I give her big points for sending all this. Trying. And more important, Babs is thinking of me. Misses me. And maybe I could use the booze to rehabilitate myself with Meredith. Like Babs, I can throw a good party.

That morning, I see Meredith walking with a large group of girls, blond and beautiful like she is. They are all laughing and she is walking a bit ahead of them, as if they are a string of beads and she the clasp that holds them together. Meredith waves to me but doesn't stop to say hello. I won't admit it, but I want to be friends with Meredith. And not as part of the clump that follows her, but up front, holding her hand.

15

Party

OCTOBER 1983

T HAT NIGHT, I EXECUTE my plan. After check-in, I knock on Meredith's door. Jess comes to open it. Holly's there too.

"Hey, Bettina," Meredith says from behind Jess, eager for gossip, "tell us something we don't know."

"I've got something better." I hold out the bottle of vodka.

Meredith brightens. Jess and Holly look nervous.

"Where did you get this?" Meredith says.

It feels wrong to say that my mother sent it to me.

"Jake Kronenberg."

"Ah; typical. I heard he has a full bar in his room. Your prep work paid off," Meredith says with a smile. She's no longer inclined to give me a hard time about him.

"I have more in my room."

Holly's now visibly uncomfortable. Knows that she will be expected to drink some. Mount a horse she's never ridden.

"What if we get caught?" Holly says. She is probably thinking about the peer-pressure lecture her mother undoubtedly gave her.

"What if we don't?" Meredith says. "Bettina, come on in and sit down."

I join them on the floor.

"Jess, we need cups." Jess reaches under Meredith's bed. Produces a stack of plastic cups with the Maidstone blue-whale insignia on them. Meredith goes to their fridge. Pulls out a carton of OJ to cut the harsh taste of the vodka. Funny—Meredith has all the paraphernalia for drinking. She's just missing the booze.

Jess makes a cup for each of us, adding two shots of vodka to an inch of orange juice. She hands them out like she's the bartender and Meredith the hostess, even though it's my alcohol. We all drink. Even Holly.

"So," Meredith says, "we were just discussing Cape. I'm going over to his dorm at midnight."

"I saw Cape at the PO today."

Meredith takes a large gulp of vodka and OJ. "I hope you didn't tell him you knew about what happened last summer," she says, with a tad of trepidation that only I can pick up in her voice.

"Of course not, Mere," I say. She adds more vodka to her cup but no orange juice.

"He is really cute," I say, not wanting to ruin what has started as a festive gathering. I take slow sips from my cup. I notice Jess has barely imbibed anything. Too many calories. Holly has had only a few sips.

"Yes, he is," says Meredith. She finishes her drink and goes for another. I like watching her so eager for what I have. She reaches under her bed for her smoking kit.

She drags deeply on her cigarette. Finally smokes like she

means it. She's gone on walks with Cape, but this is the first time she has plans to go to his dorm. I wonder how she'll handle the problem of Lowell, since he and Cape share a room. Maybe Lowell is also having a girl visit.

I look at her beautiful face — it is as perfect and vulnerable as a doll's. If she were a doll you could order from a catalog, she would have a rich name, like Veronica or Cornelia. She would not be the kind you slept with but one that had multiple expensive outfits and was kept on a shelf. If I were a boy, I would have kissed her right then just to get all her attention. I'm even tempted to do it as a girl, to cement our connection. I would push her hair back over her shoulders, maybe even suck on her neck, leaving a mark the color of a wine stain. Meredith went to Chapin, and after nine years at an all-girls school, I'm sure she has been kissed by at least one of them, on a dare perhaps. But maybe not. After the shower incident, I can't afford to be wrong. As the minutes pass, she's less present in the room. Distracted. Focused on leaving. She won't be taking me with her.

I pour Meredith another drink, her fourth. This time I do not add OJ. She drinks in little sips and this seems to silence her. I can tell she's hitting her limit but doesn't want to admit it. She will finish the tumbler no matter what. Since neither Holly nor Jess takes the lead in talking, I say to Meredith, "Do you want to take some vodka with you for Cape? It might loosen him up and stop him from crying after you guys hook up."

"No. Cape . . . doesn't . . . drink. Dad died. Accident, driving." Her words are slurred and she's in that uncomfortable space where she's having trouble maneuvering her body. She's not a seasoned drinker after all. I regularly drank wine with dinner once I turned twelve. Babs didn't want me to make an ass of myself at parties again.

I refill Meredith's cup. Ignore everyone else. This has become an experiment for me. I want to push her as far as she can go.

She can finish only half of it and then places the cup on the floor, as if some waiter from Maidstone will be along to pick it up. She puts out her cigarette in her Doubles ashtray. Stands and tries to steady herself. I watch her take a few wobbly steps to her bed and then fall onto it.

"Not feeling so well," she says in a small voice. She suddenly sits up and says, "Jess, garbage can."

Jess hurries to her with the wastepaper basket. Meredith vomits. It's in her hair. All over her baby-doll tee. She lies back down. It's impossible to take a shower at this hour without Deeds investigating. Even if Meredith changed her clothes and put up her hair, she would still smell and probably could not navigate the distance between our dorm and Cape's. Meredith will have to wait until morning to see him. Her visit to Wentington is now aborted.

Meredith is on the verge of passing out. Holly runs to the bathroom and brings back a cold washcloth. Dabs Meredith's forehead. Meredith lets out a long sigh, then is out cold. I gather up the cups, take them to the bathroom. Pour the remaining contents down the sink. I brush my teeth. Fix my hair. I look in the mirror for about a minute, and I surprise myself. I'm like Babs after all. The boy, not the party, is the whole point for me.

16

Bedtime Stories

OCTOBER 1983

I WALK THROUGH THE DARK night to Wentington. Jake will most likely still be awake, and he can let me in. Surely I can think up a good excuse for being there at that late hour. Cape's room is on the second floor.

Jake lets me in after I rap on his window. He is wearing boxer shorts. Reading *Portrait of the Artist as a Young Man.*

"Bettina," he says, "I wasn't expecting you."

I want to stay with him, but I say, "I need to go upstairs and see Cape Morse."

"That frat boy?" Jake says derisively. "Why?"

"Meredith was supposed to come visit him, but she got sick from drinking too much. I didn't want him to worry."

"Those WASPs just can't handle their liquor." He doesn't seem to include me in this category. I am a WASP, but in my case, it doesn't give me membership in the elite club of blue bloods. I will always be a stand-alone entity, a marginal girl with cigarette burns on her ankles and stories about Babs I can't publish in the Cardiss literary journal.

"What a good friend you are, Bettina," he says, with more than a touch of sarcasm. "Come back if you feel like it. I'm not going anywhere."

I cross the room and open the door.

It's not hard to find Cape and Lowell's room. It's right above Jake's. I knock. No answer. I push the door open. Empty. All the lights are on. Maybe Cape is hanging out in someone else's room?

His loafers are on the side of the bed. I pick them up. Inspect them. Mack's VDB wheat-backs are in the slots. I want to take them out, hold them in my hand, but I'm afraid I won't have the time or skill to slip them back in. I open his closet. Check out his shirts. Some are just plain white or blue oxfords. To the right are the more casual chambray shirts: pink, green, and blue. Worn in and soft. The kind Mack used to wear. I press my head in them, smell. I wish I could steal one and sleep in it. But I have nowhere to hide it.

Cape walks in wearing baggy, faded jeans. White T-shirt. His hair is wet, body showered in anticipation of Meredith's visit. He sees me standing in his room. I watch him narrow his eyes, as if the light has changed. I wonder which one of us will speak first.

He starts trying to act as though he is not surprised. "Hey, Bettina, what are you doing here?"

So many answers to this question. I go with the easy if not quite true one.

"I just came because Meredith got sick and couldn't make it. She didn't want you to worry."

"Oh," he says, clearly disappointed. "Is she going to be all right?"

"I think so. Just had too much vodka and passed out."

"That's not good," he says.

"Where's Lowell?" I ask. I don't really care, am just stalling. I want more time alone with Cape.

"He's studying with some guys down the hall. Has a Latin composition due tomorrow. How did you get in, by the way? The front door's locked. I was about to go down and open it for Mere."

I don't want him to know this, but I can't come up with any other explanation.

"I came in through Jake Kronenberg's window."

"Do you know him?" Cape asks, clearly surprised.

I could say *Sure, we fucked in the library* but instead I go with:

"Vaguely. He helped me with one of the papers I wrote for Donaldson."

"Ah," Cape says, apparently buying it. He continues. "Listen, this sounds awkward, but I need to know. What exactly does Meredith say about me? She seems to be all over the place. Like tonight, for example. We have big plans, and then she gets drunk so she can't come."

I neglect to tell him that it was my vodka. That I did most of the pouring.

"Umm," I say, "a lot of things."

"Like what?"

"She says you are really good at lacrosse."

"And?"

"She calls you Whiplash because your hair is always falling in your face."

"That doesn't sound so bad."

Here comes the point of no return. The reason I'll never have any real girlfriends.

"Umm," I begin again, "she thinks it's stupid you cry during blowjobs, and she hates your poem. She showed it to all of us in Bright and laughed."

Cape looks like I have whacked him in the face with his lacrosse stick. Begins to pace. Moving and thinking, as if I am not there. He stops after a minute. Looks me directly in the face and says:

"I absolutely *do not* cry during blowjobs."

"I am sure you don't," I say, nodding my head. "I'm only repeating what she said."

Silence. Then:

"Do you think I am attractive?" Cape has tears in his eyes but his chin is up, determined. *See, major needy,* Meredith would say.

"Absolutely," I admit. He's one of the best-looking boys in school from what I have seen so far. Even better-looking than Lowell. I can't believe he needs me to affirm it. "Cape," I say, "most of the stupid things Meredith says are just to impress other girls. She's lucky to go out with you."

"Can't tell from what she says."

"For what it's worth, I didn't believe you cried during blow-jobs. But even if you do, that's not so bad."

"I don't," Cape insists. I sit down on his bed and he sits beside me.

"I hope you don't think this is too personal, but have a lot of girls given you blowjobs?"

"No. Just Meredith."

"Just Meredith?"

"Yes."

"Meredith would make anyone cry. She's so aggressive about everything."

"But *I don't* cry."

"Okay, I have an idea." This is no longer about stealing from

Meredith. I feel protective of Cape. I also want him to trust me, in case I decide to tell him about Babs and Mack. I'm tired of trying to make sense of what our parents did by myself.

"What?"

"Think of it as kind of an experiment. I'll give you a blow-job and you can prove to me that you don't cry. That should make you feel better."

"Huh?" he says, confused but trying to seem nonchalant. What fifteen-year-old boy turns down a no-strings-attached blowjob? I've never given one before but am convinced I can figure it out.

"But wouldn't it be cheating on Meredith? I don't want to do that."

"It's not cheating if you don't get caught." This is Babs logic for sure, but here I sort of believe it. "I would never tell her."

"I just don't know, Bettina. Wouldn't it be awkward? We just met."

"You're wrong about that, you'll see."

"Okay," he finally says. I can tell he is still unsure but is too much the gentleman to say no, hurt my feelings, no matter how bold the proposition is. I know he will think about it later, feel bad about Meredith and chew on his fingernails.

We lie down on his bed. He pulls me on top of him and begins kissing me. I hold back, want to keep the clinical air of the experiment I have proposed. Otherwise he might feel like he's indeed cheating on Meredith and then tell her. He rubs up and down on me, but I do not move with him. Finally, he senses my detachment. Does not whisper my name or make little noises to show he enjoys it, which I know he would do were we dating. At last, I feel an erection through his jeans. I now have to tackle his penis. Because I have seen Jake's, it does not seem like a big deal. Just a body part.

I unzip his pants. Pull them off. His erection is now so pro-

nounced it seems to threaten the thin cotton of his boxers. I
take them off and get to work. I start by sliding his penis in
and out of my mouth, careful not to graze it with my teeth.
I'm surprised by how soft the skin is, how my tongue can dart
in the tiny hole at the tip and circle the rim. I try to remember
all the instructions Babs gave me about *raising the mast,* try to
get a nuanced sense of what he might like. But the whole thing
doesn't seem to require tutoring. To me, it seems intuitive,
interesting. *I'm good at blowjobs; they are like my specialty,* I want
to tell Meredith.

Cape tries to reach up my shirt and touch my boobs but
I push his hands away. He tries rubbing my back but I turn
to the side so this is impossible. He finally gives up trying to
please me and just strokes my hair. I focus all my attention on
his penis. I rub his balls, surprised by the loose, relaxed way
they hang in their sack. I can't help thinking about Mack. I
wonder if he ever thought I would be licking his son's penis.
If he were alive, would he send me a cease-and-desist letter? In
the middle of my thoughts, Cape comes, shoots his "hot salad
dressing" down my throat. He doesn't cry. I swallow, marking
the end of our experiment, and sit up on the bed. He lies there
for a moment, looking at me, before he pulls his boxers on.

"Do you do this often, Bettina?"

"No. See, you didn't cry."

"Seriously. Why would you want to do that?"

"To prove you had been falsely accused."

"I still don't get it."

"Don't worry. Feel better?"

"Yes . . . but."

"Don't think too much about it."

"Bettina?"

"Yes?"

"Tell me, is Meredith really such a bitch?"

I say nothing. Don't even nod my head. I do still feel protective of him, but there is only so much I can do. He's going to have to make up his own mind about her.

He sits up and catches his breath. The bed's barely rumpled. Cape has no shirt on, but the scene looks more "before" than "after." Like we have just been sitting there talking. Nothing else.

The door opens. Cape and I both stand up. Lowell. He is wearing jeans, New Balance sneakers, and a faded Nantucket Red polo shirt. He looks at us in surprise. Was expecting Meredith, not me. But for boys like him, there are no awkward moments. I now wonder if he made up the part about falling and crying when shooting hoops in the paragraph he wrote for Donaldson's class.

"Hey, Bettina!" he says. "I know there's no way in hell you are here to visit my idiot of a roommate. I must be late. Sorry to have kept you waiting."

Is he serious? I wonder. Could he really like me a little bit? But I just can't see Meredith and me sitting at Oakley having dinner with these two beautiful boys. Meredith might tolerate me, but she would never let me get away with dating a boy like Lowell. It would be like stealing a fish from her pond.

"Shut up, Lowell," Cape says. "Bettina's friends with Meredith and came with a message from her to me."

"My loss, mate. And if you had any sense, you would upgrade."

Does he really think I am better than Meredith, or is he making fun of me? I don't know him well enough to tell. Cape says nothing.

Lowell continues, now looking at me. "I didn't know Meredith had her own personal courier service. You can deliver a message to me anytime," he says, winking.

Cape's tapping his foot. Looking down. Time to go.

"Good night," I say, like a good sport. I walk out of the room. Take nothing but the salty taste of Cape in my mouth. Lowell gives me a friendly wave.

I get to Jake's room. Jake opens the door, his copy of *Portrait* still in his hand.

"So," he says to me, "mission accomplished?"

"Mission accomplished," I say.

"What were they doing," he asks, "serving hors d'oeuvres up there? It sure took you a long time."

I want to laugh, to tell him everything, but I just can't. He would punish me if he knew the truth. Probably by finding another girl and abandoning me. Right now, I'm not sure I could handle that. For the time being, he is mine.

"Well," I say, "I need to get back."

"Too bad," he says. "Sex in my bed . . ." He leaves the rest to my imagination.

"Next time," I say.

Jake pushes open the window.

17

The Next Day

OCTOBER 1983

MEREDITH IS STILL OUT cold when we all rally to go to breakfast. I go into her room and see Jess shaking her, saying, "You have to go shower, Mere. You reek."

"Hmm," Meredith replies, rolling slowly about in her bed. She finally sits up and strips off her clothes. There's still vomit in her hair. She does indeed smell from our party. She walks over to her closet, grabs her monogrammed robe. Heads for the shower. For the first time since I have known her, Meredith looks like shit. She is pale. There are circles under her eyes.

Somehow, she pulls it together. We all walk to the dining hall. Late, but still within the limits. Meredith grabs a glass of orange juice and a bowl of Lucky Charms. She hates Lucky Charms, is always going on about how stupid it is that Cardiss serves kids' cereals. But after last night, her body craves the sugar. Her hands shake as she carries her tray.

I scan the dining hall for Cape. He's sitting in a corner with Lowell. Meredith's trying to catch his eye, but to no avail. She has no idea about last night. Ha. Welcome to your hangover.

That night, Cape comes to Bright House during visiting hours. I see him from the window and go to open the door. Cape nods at me uncomfortably and asks if I can get Meredith. Did last night have no impact? Or am I now the one who has done something really wrong?

Meredith comes down, fully recovered from the night before. I watch her take his hand as they walk out of Bright together.

I need to distract myself so I go up to my room to write Babs about the package she sent. Thank-you notes are very important to her. I work for almost an hour to get the right tone.

> Dear Babs,
> Thank you for all of the goodies. They are fabulous!
> I miss you too.
> Bettina

Goodies and *fabulous* are Babs words, but they seem appropriate to acknowledge such a gift.

By the time I address the envelope, it is eight o'clock. I hear Meredith walk down the hall to her room, just in time for check-in. I poke my head out and can tell by her red eyes that she has been crying. I think about asking her what's wrong even though I already know. I have inflicted some damage after all.

Jess and Holly are waiting for her in her room, just as they always do after a Cape walk. I decide to join them. I am eager to hear what she has to say.

"I've decided to take a break from Cape," she says, lighting a cigarette and skipping over all the details. "I just can't deal with his neediness."

All he needed was a nonjudgmental blowjob from you and no sub-

sequent bitchy commentary, I want to say, but of course, I restrain myself.

Holly and Jess look disappointed. There will be no good stories for a while. Cape was almost as much their boyfriend as Meredith's.

Holly ventures to say, "Are you sure, Meredith? He's probably doing the best he can."

"Well, it's not good enough," retorts Meredith with an edge in her voice. Only I know the cause of it. She has probably never, in her short, charmed life, been dumped.

"I told him to find a girl who could take it," she says, putting out her cigarette. "I have lots of homework. Let's bag this whole boring discussion."

Holly and I have never seen Meredith study. The situation must be serious. We know to give her time alone.

18

Two Weeks Later

OCTOBER 1983

Two weeks pass, and Cape does not come to Bright to see Meredith. She sticks to her story that this separation was her idea, but I notice she seems to have lost her usual confidence. Her fifteen-year-old body seems to sag a bit. This takes her looks down a notch, and I realize that really beautiful people have engines inside them that generate the outside effects. When the energy wanes, the beautiful don't shine so brightly. It is clearly time for her to find another boy, but she can't seem to admit failure on the Cape front and move on.

In English that day, Lowell passes me a note. I recognize the writing from the poem. Cape! The small paper simply reads:

Bettina—Come to my room at midnight if you can.
Let Lowell know.

I have not been alone with Cape since the blowjob. I've been to Wentington to see Jake fairly often, and our sex has gotten even more intense. He has lashed me with his belt, tied a tie so tight around my neck that I almost passed out, and threatened to cut my hair. Inexplicably, I am not scared but bored. There is still no emotion between us, and the whole thing is starting to feel like a complicated form of calisthenics.

"So?" Lowell asks, waiting for my response.

"Tell Cape yes. But just so you know, Cape's got nothing on you." This is my attempt at flirting, and it has none of the levity of Lowell's. It's like my telling a joke to Babs. She almost never laughs.

It's hard to sit through the day. Time crawls, almost rolls backward, as I contemplate visiting Cape again.

In my room that night, I hesitate over what to wear. I want to dress like Meredith, but lacking Laura Ashley skirts and cute little T-shirts, the closest I come to dressing up is a generous spray of Coco perfume. I wear my black pants and an agnès b. T-shirt, the same thing that I was wearing the first night I went to visit Jake. Hardly a sexy hook-up uniform. But I don't want to look like I'm expecting anything, trying too hard. My recent encounter with Cape at our dorm has tempered my expectations. I dress quietly so I don't wake up Holly. Since Meredith and Cape broke up, there have been no late talks. Holly's usually in bed by ten thirty. Her mommy would be proud.

I walk to Wentington. For a moment, I'm scared about how Jake is going to react to my using his window to get to Cape's room again. Will he allow me to just pass through? I knock on the window, but the room is dark.

Come on, Jake, I think, *don't let me down.* I knock again, this time more loudly. I see movement, and then Jake's face behind the glass. He opens the window slowly.

"Bettina," he says, "you didn't tell me you were coming."

I feel awkward, embarrassed.

"Actually," I lie, "I have to go upstairs with another message from Meredith."

"Well, come down when you are done."

I wonder if he believes me. "Of course."

I walk up the stairs to Cape's room. This time I am officially invited. I knock lightly on the door.

Cape comes to open it. He is again dressed in jeans, loafers, and a white T-shirt. I can't believe how handsome he is, even more so than Mack. Maybe because we are the same age and he is available to me.

"Bettina," he says once I am in the room. "I wanted to thank you for telling me everything Meredith said. We broke up, you know."

"I know," I say, "except she told everyone it was her idea. That you were just too needy."

Cape smarts from this, yet again unprepared for Meredith's cruelty. I know I verge on evil for telling Cape this, but it seems to seal his hatred for Meredith. He pauses, then regains his composure.

"Well, we both know this is a lie." He adjusts his jeans and kicks his loafers a little too forcefully toward his closet. I think of the pennies inside. How valuable they are. I'm too busy thinking about them to say anything back.

"Anyway, it doesn't matter," he continues.

"Why did I have to come to your room in the middle of the night? Why didn't you just tell me during the day?"

"I know how Meredith works; even if she didn't see me talking to you, one of her girls would have reported us to her. And that would have made things hell for you at Bright."

"Well, thanks, but I can take care of myself." I'm disappointed that the whole point of this meeting is once again to talk about Meredith.

"Actually," Cape says, "I wanted to pay you back for the other night."

"How?" He wants to give me a blowjob?

"Um, it was just obvious that you got nothing out of it . . . and I thought I could try . . ."

Try what? I am curious now but don't want to push it. God forbid he comes up with some kind of quid pro quo proposition.

"Don't worry about it." I sit down on his bed and notice a watch with a black croc strap sitting on his bedside table. The straps are curled upward, circling an imaginary wrist.

"Cape? Can I try on your watch?"

"Why?" he asks, confused.

I take it in my hand, flip it over to look at the back. "It belonged to your father, didn't it?"

"How do you know?"

I put it on, even though he has not given me permission.

"When I was eleven, he showed it to me."

"Really? Where?"

In the middle of the night in my mother's room is not an acceptable answer, so I just say, "At a cocktail party of my mother's. I wanted to keep it, but he wouldn't let me."

"Why did you want to keep it?"

Again, I can give only a half answer to this.

"I thought it was cool. He even let me try it on."

"What about your dad? Didn't he have watches you could wear?"

"I don't have a dad."

"Huh?"

"My mother got pregnant and never told anyone who the father was."

"Why?"

"I really don't know."

I can see him looking at me, not getting it. But he's not going to push it. Like Jake said, he is a WASP. He avoids the hard questions.

He leans into me. I think he is going to kiss me, but he's just looking at my face.

"What happened to your forehead?"

"What you do you mean?" I touch it quickly, afraid I have a pimple or a scab there. Nothing.

"Your scar. It looks like it was something serious."

When I hear *scar,* I think about my ankles. But I realize he means the scar from the Hangover-Brunch Cruise Party. When I got all the stitches and left the pink elephant in Mack's pocket. No one has ever mentioned it before, not even Jake. Babs didn't even make me wear cover-up in the Christmas Card to conceal it.

"Umm." I don't want it to sound like all of Mack's life was consumed by Babs's parties. But I go ahead and provide him with the details anyway.

"My mother had a party once and I fell down a marble staircase. Your dad picked me up from the ground and I bled all over his shirt."

"Why didn't he ever tell me about you? Or introduce us? Did he tell you about me?"

"Of course he did," I say. Even though this isn't true, really. For years I thought he was called Hailer, not Cape. I felt such ease telling on Meredith but realize it is not going to be as easy to talk about Babs and Mack.

"Have you met my mom?" he asks.

"Yes," I say. The time I used the bathroom at Tea House. "Have you told her I go here?"

"Yes. She said she knew who you were."

"That was it?"

"Yeah, but she doesn't really like to talk about Grass Woods or Chicago that much. She said once that people stopped inviting her places because she was a widow. I suppose women were afraid she would poach their husbands. Which of course she would never do. She grew up in New York anyway, so it made sense for her to go back."

I take off Mack's watch and give it back to Cape. I know if I were his girlfriend and I asked, he would let me wear it for real.

"So," I say, noticing it is getting late, "Why am I here?"

"I have an idea, but you have to help me."

I know what he is getting at, but I am not going to make it easy for him. Part of me thinks he is drawn to me because of my proximity to Meredith. That whatever we do can be traced back to her. But at least I am included in their union, a point that makes a triangle.

"Okay," I say. I am pretty sure what he has in mind. I dread it and am eager at the same time. I know most of this has to do with his getting back at Meredith, but for now, I don't really care.

"Lie down on my bed." I do. He leans over me and unzips my pants. He pulls them off, along with my underwear.

He moves down and puts his mouth on my me. This is the first time anyone has ever admired my centerfold. The contact feels good, but I'm embarrassed. What do I taste like? Did I wipe thoroughly after my last shit? Are there small bits of lingering toilet paper that will come off on his tongue? It is completely impossible for me to relax, let myself go. Especially since Cape seems to be licking at the lips of my vagina. Will any of my pubic hair get caught in his teeth?

I'm worried, but I think that maybe, with a little practice, Cape will turn out to be a genius in bed, like his dad. If so, I will surely forget myself a few minutes from now and just enjoy an intense ride to a smash. Being aroused is like being drunk: you just surrender and anything goes. But Cape does not have that skill set yet, so I hold back. I don't want to shock him. He lifts his head, starts talking.

"Does that feel good? I have never done this before."

His admitting this just makes things worse.

Unfortunately, it doesn't get any better. Cape can't find my clitoris and is thrusting his tongue inside my vagina, licking his lips afterward. I now know why people (except Babs) call it eating someone out.

I grab his shoulders and pull him up toward my face. Tell him to stop.

"What? Did I do it wrong?"

"No, no, it was just too intense for me. You did a great job."

I see him suppressing a smile. He leans in and kisses me on the mouth. I taste myself on him, and I am grossed out by the idea that the pungent juices all over his lips and inside his mouth belong to me. I have never smelled myself before. Just had clean and precise smashes in the bathroom, or Jake putting his penis in my me. He never asks for blowjobs. I force myself to pretend Cape just drank some exotic, musty cocktail I will probably never taste.

"But you didn't . . ."

Smash? I want to say, almost touched by the innocence of this boy who cannot say *come* or *orgasm*.

"Nor did you," I reply. I see him thinking up some alternative activity. I know he's a virgin, and I don't want him to give this away to me as some kind of payback.

"I have another idea," I say after a few awkward moments. I remember the night Babs told me about the K-Y Jelly and what she and Mack were about to do when she saw the pearls for Mags.

"Okay," I say. "You need to take off your pants and underwear. I am going to flip over on all fours." I know this will hurt, but it will be another thing Cape can add to his sexual repertoire, and I won't have to worry about his technique. Fucking someone in the ass is pretty straightforward, as far as I can tell. Until Babs told me about that time with Mack, I never thought of it as a heterosexual option. But from what I gather, it is an extra on the sexual menu that not a lot of people order, like sambuca after dinner.

Cape takes his time with his pants. I can tell he both knows and doesn't know what is going to happen. When he is finally in position, I can feel his penis on my back. It is surprisingly hard, given the fact that he must be uncertain as to what my next move is. He must still be excited from admiring my centerfold, despite the fact that the whole thing was a disaster for me.

"Okay, Cape, glide your penis into my ass."

Cape would never say *ass,* especially in front of a girl. Meredith would never say *ass* to a boy either. But I know Cape will obey me and we will have our own form of intimacy. Unlike with Jake, this will be a shared moment that will mean something.

"Are you sure?" he asks, but his ragged breath tells me he's up for it.

"Yes, Hailer," I say, and if my anal region could wet itself, this would do the trick. This is what I want more than anything. To get the boy I have known as Hailer since I was ten to hurt me.

"Hailer? How did . . ." he asks, surprised.

"Shh. Just do it."

He repositions his penis and thrusts it in my ass. It is not a good feeling. It is too tight down there and I feel like he is ripping me open. Maybe that explains our parents' need for K-Y. Cape seems to have forgotten his trepidation and is pumping back and forth avidly, gripping my hips so he can go deeper. I am worried I might bleed. I want to yell *Stop!,* but this is what I proposed. I must follow through. My mind drifts to Meredith. If I were here on the bed with her instead of Cape, there wouldn't be this searing pain. She would be all soft skin and puffy lips. I wonder what her lipstick would taste like. Our interaction would be languid and slow, sucking at each other's earlobes and bellybuttons. We would not be a couple, just two girls trying something out new. Just for the hell of it.

But instead, I am here with Hailer/Cape and his painful penis. I wait anxiously for him to come, and for it to be over. His pace quickens, and I know he's close.

He pulls out, puts his penis on my back, keeps thrusting. Like me, he is probably bewildered by what happens to semen when you come in someone's ass. I'm sure he doesn't think he'll get me pregnant, but maybe he worries I'll get an infection or at least smell bad.

He arches his back, and just before it happens, he yells, "Jesus, Meredith!" His come sprays all over the back of my T-shirt, which I have not taken off. I can't really fault him because I have been thinking about her also, and if I were a guy, I would probably have screamed her name too.

I pull away, reach for my pants. Cape leans back into his pillows. I'm about to cry because of both the pain and the fact that I am not, and never will be, Meredith. Cape looks at me and says, "Sorry, Bettina, I didn't mean it. I'm just so used to being with her."

"Don't worry about it," I say.

As he promised, Jake left his light on, and he's sitting on his bed reading. He takes one look at my face and says, "Everything all right?"

"No," I say to him for once, and I climb swiftly out his window.

19

Dance

OCTOBER 1983

THE NEXT WEEK, IT seems all anyone my year can talk about is the Lower dance. The dance is not really the point; who you go with is. I'm more than curious to see what Cape will do. Will he ask Meredith? Even though they broke up, I know that he is still into her, since he called out her name during our ass-sex (as I am now referring to it). A small part of me hopes he'll do something different and ask me. But once again, I indulge myself in a good mind-fuck.

Jake wants to take me to the crater, a no man's land behind the railroad tracks where students get drunk and do drugs. It's far enough away from campus to be off the radar of Cardiss teachers. I'm slightly disappointed because I want to go to the dance and show the school, and especially Cape, that I have a boyfriend. But Jake told me up front that dating wasn't part of the deal.

We convene in Meredith's room to discuss details. Holly is going with Ned, an insipid boy from her math class. He's from Milwaukee and I wonder if he'll bring her a corsage. Jess is going with Nathan, a bohemian type from her art class who has a ponytail. I wonder if she has any dresses to wear to the dance. She is always just this side of dressing like a boy. I tell them I'm going out with Jake but don't go into details. Maybe he will just smash my head into a tree.

Meredith is strangely quiet. Despite her popularity, I don't think anyone has asked her. Any boy other than Cape is probably afraid of being rejected.

"I happen to think the whole thing is stupid," Meredith says. "I'm going home to NYC for the weekend to see my friends. They're going to have a keg party and we're going to play strip poker with some boys from Collegiate." I think of Meredith's adverse reaction to my vodka and wonder if she will risk drinking again. Probably, but she will stop in time to fool around with someone. I wish could go with her. See her sitting on some guy's lap in her bra and underpants.

"You can come with us," Holly says, thinking she is being helpful. "I'm sure Ned wouldn't mind."

Meredith would, however, and says, "Thanks, Holly, but I'm just not up to it. No offense, but I sit behind Ned in math, and the back of his neck is always sweating."

Holly has never noticed this or thought to add it to her list of boy faults. She pretends her nails are suddenly fascinating.

Jess says, "Come on, Mere, if you aren't at the dance, it won't be as good. Maybe you could ask someone. No boy would say no to you."

"I'm really not interested, sorry. I went to the dance last year and it was lame. All of those paper streamers in school colors, and the fucking balloons. It looked like a birthday party for a six-year-old."

They give up on trying to convince her. Maybe she really does want to go to NYC after all. Recharge herself after the Cape debacle.

That evening, we have visiting hours. I am forced to suffer through Ned and Holly making small talk as I struggle with my calculus.

"Where do you want to go to dinner?" Ned asks.

"It doesn't matter. If it's too expensive, we can just eat at the dining hall," Holly replies.

Ned laughs. "Holly, that would be so lame. What do you like to eat?"

"Anything!" she says, still not catching on that cool girls aren't interested in food. She has probably gained ten pounds since the beginning of the year.

"Okay, I will just pick somewhere. I better get a kiss for this."

Holly blushes. "We'll see." I know she is both embarrassed and happy that she might be able to impress Meredith with a kiss from Ned, despite the sweaty-neck situation.

On and on they go, navigating the particulars of the evening. I put my red Sony Walkman on and flop down on my bed, work on my math.

Since our door is open, I can see everyone coming and going. Since there are only four of us in the house, there's usually not too much traffic. All of a sudden, I see a tall boy and a flash of dark hair. Cape. I have the absurd idea that he is going to come into our room and ask me to the dance. But no, of course not.

Cape keeps walking and knocks on Meredith's door. His strides have a new confidence, which I attribute to our nocturnal activities. He now feels himself on a par with Meredith, as confident as she is. Will win her back. I consider telling Meredith that we hooked up, but I don't want to ruin my chances with either of them, become a girl who sits in the corner and plays by herself.

I imagine that when Meredith opens the door and sees

Cape, there will be a tinge of surprise in her hello. She won't be expecting to see him.

Or maybe in Meredith-land, she knew, in the end, he would come. She is never let down, never embarrassed or humiliated. She just changes her plans.

Cape is there for about an hour. She's making him work for it.

After visitation, we all meet up in Meredith and Jess's room. Meredith and I smoke. Her mood is now ebullient.

"I've bagged my trip to NYC. Cape asked me to the dance. I said no initially, but then he looked so dejected—like a lost dog—that I took pity on him and said yes."

"That's great, Meredith. Now we can all get ready together. It wouldn't be right if you missed out," Holly says.

"Yes, and you can even borrow my Clinique foundation. I noticed that your skin has more than a touch of acne."

If Holly is offended by this, she doesn't let on. In her mind, Meredith is being constructive, not critical. Holly touches her face and says, "Thanks, Mere. I appreciate it."

"Bettina, could you bring some of your booze? I am going to give Cape a blowjob, and I can take it to another level with a good buzz. Also, he might try to go down on me, and some rum will make the whole thing less awkward."

"Nathan told me in such a situation, you should give your pubic hair a trim and flush the hair down the toilet. It makes it easier for a guy to navigate down there. You can use my nail scissors," Jess says.

"Did you do it?" asks Meredith.

"Yes," says Jess. "It looks much neater down there. Nate will have a clean workspace." I am shocked that Jess has such bold sexual plans. That she will let a boy touch her anorexic body, with its sharp bones and flat-as-cardboard chest.

Holly looks intrigued. "I never even thought of that."

I know if Cape admires Mere's groomed centerfold, he will never want to go near mine again. I suddenly hope Meredith will ask Jess for the scissors and do it right there. I want to see if her vagina looks different from mine. Maybe if I got close enough, I could smell her and see if she is cleaner and fresher than I am.

"Thanks, Jess. Brilliant idea. I was going to wear a thong and expose my ass, but this is much better."

"No problem."

"You can wear my diamond studs if you want," Meredith says. This is a big deal. All of Meredith's friends have them; they are like sorority pins. They're not for special occasions; the girls wear them all the time, even during sports.

For once, all the girls in Bright look richer than I am.

20

Haircut II

I DON'T HAVE A DRESS that is suitable for the evening of the dance, even though I'm not actually going, but I still have plenty of traveler's checks left from the wad that Babs gave me in the beginning of the school year. I decide to walk into town and buy a dress. Jake might not care what I wear, but I do. For once, I want to participate in the ritual of getting ready with all the other girls.

I walk through campus until I come to the one street that represents the "town" of Cardiss. There is an ice cream shop, a bookstore, a tanning salon (bizarrely), a few homey restaurants that serve soup with hearty hunks of bread, a hamburger place. There are only two stores that sell clothing: Mrs. M., which caters to middle-aged women who have not frequented the gym in a while. The store has monochrome pantsuits in bright colors, the pants at three-quarter length and the over-size shirts with droopy bows.

This store does not attract the core of the female faculty

at Cardiss. Most teachers are more like Deeds. Fit from work-
outs, the women look like they are still in college. To find
something in her size, Deeds must buy her clothes on trips to
Boston or order them from the L. L. Bean catalog. A small part
of me wishes she would go with me, like a big sister, but I
think of the five cookies she put out on my first day. Know
she will never give more than just enough. I wish I had had
the foresight to go to Boston, but the dance is tomorrow. I will
have to make due with Cardiss's meager offerings.

Next door to Mrs. M. is a store called Wow! I normally
eschew places that have exclamation points in their names, but
now I have no choice. Wow! has two sections: teen and adult. I
examine the teen dresses, which go to the floor. Pouffy sleeves
and muted colors, just this side of wedding dresses.

I walk over to the adult section. Peruse the rack and find a
plain black shift that hits just above the knee. There is a shoe
section, and the saleslady helps me pick out a pair of black
pumps. Simple and elegant. My outfit is almost an exact replica
of what Babs wore to Mack's funeral.

Near the counter is a cluster of jewelry. No gray pearls with
diamonds, but I see a silver necklace that would be perfect to
put my father's medallion on. I'm still afraid to take the next
step and find him. After the Cape incident, I don't think I ready
to risk rejection so soon. What if my father has a real family, a
wife and a son or daughter my age who would keep him from
wanting me? But maybe, just maybe, I am a secret that he has
begrudgingly kept all these years because Babs told him to, but
he really wants me to know. I still can't figure out why Babs
kept his identity a secret. Maybe because she wanted me all to
herself? Not because she loves me, but because she didn't want
me to love anyone else? Maybe the coin doesn't even belong
to him. Was it just something Babs gave me to stop my questions? I know I will be devastated if this is the case. I know how

many times Babs has twisted my hopes into humiliation, and I am just not ready to climb this staircase yet.

Though she said almost nothing while helping me pick out shoes, the saleslady now acts like we know each other well enough for her to offer an opinion. She tries to dissuade me from buying the black dress.

"Is this for the dance?" she asks.

"Yes," I say.

"We have more festive togs. I can help you pick something."

Togs? Is she fucking kidding? I thought that was one of those words that no one actually uses in conversation. I'm also pissed that she thinks to give me fashion tips. Does not understand that I don't want to be like other girls. Their dresses seem too hopeful, mine just right.

"I like this one, thank you."

She shakes her head and rings me up. I don't care what she thinks. Babs would never take fashion advice from someone who works in a clothing store. Maybe from one of the designers who make dresses just for her: Halston, Ungaro, Blass. But not from someone who earns seven dollars an hour and folds things in tissue paper. All the stuff Babs buys gets sent to the aparthouse in heavy hanging bangs, the items covered in plastic sheaths.

My dress, shoes, and silver chain total one hundred and sixty dollars. I'm sure the saleslady expects me to pay with my parents' credit card. Instead, I give her two hundred dollars in traveler's checks. She doesn't understand these at first, spends a bit of time looking over them. I bet she's never left the country. I'm about to explain to her that they are just like cash and she can call American Express with questions, but she doesn't say anything. Just opens the cash register and hands me my change.

"Enjoy the dance!" she calls after me, like she's happy to have helped me pick something out. Maybe she has no daughters.

"Thanks!" I say, as if I am as excited as she is. All the parties I have ever been to have ended badly, but she cannot tell this from just looking at me.

My next stop is Hair We Come, the town's beauty salon. I decide on a thorough bikini wax and an extreme haircut. I want to top Meredith's well-groomed vagina, even though I know Jake could care less. I have never had a bikini wax. Have only accompanied Babs to hers and chatted with her as a Czech lady ripped the hair from her crotch. One of Babs's rules is never, ever shave your privates. The hair will just come back as stubble, a kind of female beard. She would be proud I am following her advice.

I check in at the desk.

"I would like a bikini wax and a haircut, please."

The woman looks at me. Shakes her head.

"We don't do waxing. Not really much need for bikinis this time of year. But we do offer hair removal with tweezers."

Tweezers? It would take at least a week to clean me up. I could work on it at night after I finished all my homework, I suppose. But the idea of plucking hair follicle by follicle seems overwhelming and painful.

"Um, no, thanks. Just a haircut."

"Sweetie, we could fix those brows of yours. They are a little thick."

A part of myself I had never thought to be self-conscious about. I imagine angry red lines on my forehead.

"I do them myself. It's just been a while."

She shakes her head, not ready to let it go. "Well, hon, it's time."

There is no reason to be nice to this woman who has criticized my looks. I have clearly come to her beauty salon to address the problem. I smile, a promise that I will Get to It.

"Just a haircut, then?" she continues, satisfied she has made her point. "We have a special rate for Cardiss students. Fifteen dollars."

I worry about the price. This is what Stacey gave Geoff as a tip at Zodiac. Can a haircut be any good if it's this cheap? Twenty percent would be three dollars. Could a person buy anything with that meager a tip? I'm tempted to tell the lady I'll pay more, as if I were buying some kind of good-cut insurance, but I know it doesn't work that way.

"Great," I say. "Thank you."

"Go see Barb in the corner."

She points me toward a brown Naugahyde swivel chair near the window. Barb is short and wears bangles on both of her wrists that jingle as she takes my hand. As I'm getting settled, she says, "What do we have in mind today?"

The *we* is reassuring to me, like we are working on a project together. I look at the mirror in front of her station and see a cosmetology license taped on it. The paper is stamped with the seal of New Hampshire. Geoff did not have his credentials on display. Maybe he didn't have any. I wonder if she has to make small talk with all her clients before and during the haircut, if this is part of a hairdresser's code. A kind of Hippocratic oath, but just for hair. Geoff clearly didn't have such principles when it came to me.

"I am going to a dance and want a new look," I say. My hair is long, to the middle of my back, but it has none of the body of Meredith's. I want something that will make me stand out, not something that looks like a failed imitation of her.

"How about a color rinse and a perm?"

Babs always makes fun of perms. People want curly but get kinky. *If you want body, pick up some hot rollers.*

"I was just thinking of a cut. Maybe a bob."

"Are you sure? That's pretty drastic. How about I just trim the ends?"

Is Barb worried she can't pull this off? But seeing her license gives me confidence in her.

"No, I'm sure."

She walks me over to the washing station and shampoos my hair with two applications of green-apple-smelling shampoo and follows it with a thick conditioner that smells like lemons.

We return to her chair and she cuts. The hair falls in my eyes, but I keep them open, watching.

Holly's horrified when I return to our room.

"Bettina! Your hair. What happened?"

She clearly has never read an issue of *Vogue*. Her reaction makes me feel like I made the right decision.

"I was just sick of it."

"It's the day before the dance. What if Jake doesn't like it? You can't fix it."

"It doesn't matter what Jake thinks. It's only hair."

"Well, if you're sure. Are you going to tell your mom?"

"I really don't think she would care."

When we walk to dinner, I check myself out as we pass the enormous windows of the library. See a girl who might have grown up in Paris or even New York instead of Chicago. I almost as glamorous as Babs. Maybe I *should* call her and tell her about it.

We arrive and spot Jess and Meredith at a corner table. They are sitting with three other girls that I recognize from Meredith's field hockey team: Serena, Lake, and Elizabeth. They're all pretty, like Meredith, with slight variations in their noses and mouths. If I didn't know Meredith, I'd be hard-pressed to tell the four of them apart. The way they're leaning in to her, giving her their full attention as she talks, it is obvious that she is the leader of the pack. Holly and I go through the line. Join Meredith and her *cercle des amies*. Meredith raises an eyebrow when she sees my new look. The other girls don't seem to notice or care since I'm not one of them. I don't count.

"Daring," Meredith says.

"Not really." I wonder what Meredith will think of my new dress, if she will deride it but secretly think it is cool. Maybe she'll want to borrow it someday.

I scan the dining room. Cape is sitting with Lowell, not three tables from us. Meredith peacocks for Cape, sitting up straight and shaking her blond hair over her shoulders. Surprisingly, he seems to be looking at me, as is Lowell. Who knew boys gave a damn about hair, especially the short kind? Maybe they think it's ugly. I don't care. Cape's looking at me does not go unnoticed by Meredith. She pouts.

We finish our dinner, but I linger, going back for another cup of black coffee. Finally I'm confident enough to sit alone. Only Holly says goodbye. Her voice betrays the tiniest amount of pity. In Iowa, I bet only babies and menopausal women have short hair. I fit into neither category.

Cape and Lowell are still at their table. Meredith doesn't acknowledge Cape as she flounces out since he made no eye contact with her during dinner. If he notices her dramatic exit, he doesn't show it.

I finish my coffee, dump the Styrofoam cup into the trash. I'm not ready to go back to Bright. Don't want to hang out with Meredith's posse of non-Bright friends. They always look slightly offended when I am there, as if they are waiting for Meredith to tell me to go away. But thankfully, she never does.

I decide to go to the boathouse for a smoke. I want to feel the cool air on my neck where my hair used to be.

Outside, I feel a tap on my arm from behind. I turn, expecting Jake. Surprise. Cape.

"Where are you headed?"

"To the boathouse for a smoke." I know from Meredith that

Cape finds smoking disgusting. Has never even held a cigarette between his lips. So this is my way of telling him to go and leave me alone. I'm still furious he's asked Meredith to the dance.

He says, "Can I go with you?"

I say, "Sure." Shrugging my shoulders, but curious why he wants to come with me.

We walk in silence until we get to the boathouse bench. I fish in my bag for a cigarette, but he stops me by reaching over and ruffling my new short hair. I sit up and look at him.

"What's the fuck, Cape?" I say.

"I just wanted to apologize for, you know . . ."

I am not going to let him get away with this. "'You know'? What does that mean?"

"For saying Meredith's name when we . . ." I so want him to say what we did, but at least the boy has some insight.

"Oh, how nice," I say in my most sincere voice. "But I rather enjoyed it."

"Really?" he says, rethinking his strategy.

"No, not really, Cape," I say bitterly. "Everything about the whole night sucked."

"I'm sorry. I never thought things would end like that."

"Whatever." I reach for my lighter.

But before I can light up, he leans in and gives me a soft kiss on the lips. Why? Is it my new hair? Does he just want me to come to his room late at night so he can hone his sexual skills?

As nice as the kiss is, I hold firm.

"What the fuck are you doing? Last time I checked, Meredith was back at Bright."

"You have to understand. Meredith and I go way back. I met her when I was really young. St. Bernard's had dances with Chapin. Her parents and my mother are good friends. I feel comfortable around her."

"Why did you tell her you loved her?"

"Because I thought I did. Meredith was my first girlfriend. The first girl I really fooled around with."

"Why did you ask her to the dance after all the mean things she said about you?"

"I didn't know who else to ask."

I want to reply *Why not me?* but this seems to verge on desperate. Instead, I say, "You're telling me that out of the nine hundred students at this school, the only one you could come up with was Meredith?"

"If you want the truth, I would have asked you. But I thought Mere would be really mean to you about it. And all the other girls I think are cool are already going with someone else. They would also say no to me out of respect for Meredith."

"Sounds like you have really thought this out," I say. "But I would have turned you down. I already have someone."

"You do?" he says. Like this is impossible. "Who?"

"Jake Kronenberg."

Cape does not comment on this. It barely seems to register.

"Well, do you want to come by tonight?"

"I'm not sure," I say. "I don't want to piss off Jake. I do after all have to climb through his window to get to your room."

"Why do you care what he thinks?"

"I'm not sure I do. But it's just rude."

"Well, I could come down and open the front door to Wentington if you give me a specific time."

"What are we going to do, play Scrabble? I have a big paper due tomorrow for Donaldson."

"We can do whatever you want, Bettina," Cape says.

21

Cape, Midnight

OCTOBER 1983

AFTER MY WALK WITH Cape, I go to the Cardiss PO. I'm not really sure why, but it is something to do. I think I miss Babs after all my interactions with Cape. Maybe she has sent me another package. There's something in my mailbox, but it is not a pink slip. Instead, it's a postcard.

I pull it out and carefully hold it with both hands. I hate postcards. Showoffs send them when they are on great trips. But this is different. On the front side, instead of a picture of blue water lapping a pristine island, there is a charcoal drawing of a young girl. Brown hair, brown eyes. She is pretty in the way only young girls can be. No makeup. A smile that is not directed at the person drawing her but at the world in general.

I flip it over, and the words are written in a confident hand, in black ink. No mistakes. The card's back is divided in two: one-half for my address, one-half for the message. I read it.

Dear Bettina:
    I drew this right after I first saw you in Chicago, but

Babs said to send it when you were older. I'll never
forget that night. Your dance was so creative. You were
brave to get up in front of everyone. I'm sorry how it
all ended. I always regret, as your cousin, not taking
you to the hospital, and not being in contact earlier.
Babs isn't easy, but she does love you. Write if you
want.

Love, Lucas

I finish reading. Feel like tearing it up and throwing it away.
He's a grown man who listens to Babs about when to send me
mail. And there's what he said at the party: *Let's go dance to the
Duch and pour pink champagne over people,* leaving me bleeding
in the kitchen. I look at the flip side of the card again. Study
the portrait. I stare at her for a few minutes before I realize:
It's me.

I return to Bright House. I don't want to join the other girls
in Meredith's room to talk about the dance to come. Of course
I can't tell them I'm going to see Cape tonight, and they would
never understand the real story about Jake.

I use the time before sneaking out to work on another
assignment for Donaldson. I sit at my desk and write about
the Daddies' Breakfast at Chicago Country Day. It isn't the best
story I have in my inventory, slightly vapid in my opinion, but
I know the other students might laugh at Wendolyn Henderson. Also, it wouldn't earn me concerned looks from Donaldson. Or a trip to the school psychiatrist, like the girl who wrote
about how much she loved to binge on Twinkies and then
make herself puke. My classmates might be taken aback by the
Bettina-has-no-daddy angle, but so what. It's a wound I seem
to have gotten used to.

I get into bed but am too excited to sleep. At eleven thirty,
Holly's asleep and our room is pitch-black. I turn on my desk

lamp and cover it with an Hermès scarf to dim the brightness. Instead of my customary black pants and agnès b. T-shirt, I decide to wear my new black shift and pumps, along with my father's medallion, as if Cape and I really are going to the dance.

I dust my face with a little blush and apply lipstick. As I look in the mirror, I see there really is an attractive girl looking back. As if Lucas has upgraded my features. Has erased the plain Jane Babs always saw.

I stuff two pillows in my bed to make it look like I am under the covers sleeping in case Deeds changes her habits and comes in to check. Lots of students sneak out the night before the dance, all filled with anticipation and needing to blow off steam.

The pathways of the campus are dotted with streetlamps, so it's always easy to see where you are going. It's five until midnight. I pick up my pace and make it to Cape's dorm on the dot of midnight. I rap gently on the door, and sure enough, he opens it.

I am somewhat dismayed to see that Cape is wearing his pajamas: L. L. Bean red plaid flannel pants and a white T-shirt. As if he just rolled out of bed. My dress and pumps look ridiculous. As always, I'm trying too hard. Thank God Babs taught me that pantyhose are decidedly middle class and I should never wear them except on the most formal occasions. When I take off my pumps and hook them by the heels on the fingers of my left hand, I am barefoot like Cape. I don't want to clack up the stairs to his room.

Once in the room, Cape says, "Bettina, you look beautiful."

He reaches in to kiss me, soft and sweet like at the boathouse, but I hold back.

"This isn't about Meredith?"

"Of course not." He says it like I'm crazy to ask such a thing. But all of a sudden I am not so sure. Maybe he is still a virgin and wants to have sex before the dance so he won't look foolish in front of Meredith.

This whole thing is really starting to really piss me off. But what was I expecting? A blazer and a picnic basket for a late-night snack?

"Do you really want me to be here?" There is definitely an edge to my voice.

"Of course," he says. This isn't going as he had planned.

"Prove it," I say.

"How?" he asks. "What would convince you?"

I am not sure. Then I see his penny loafers sitting haphazardly by his closet. I come up with the ultimate test.

"Give me your pennies," I challenge him.

"What?" he asks, surprised, thinking I'm expecting him to forage in his desk for change.

"The ones in your shoes."

"I can't," he says.

"Why not?"

"They were my father's. I never take them out of my shoes."

"Let me see them, at least?" I ask as if I'm no longer really interested. I know, however, that I'm not leaving his room without them.

Cape goes over to his shoes and struggles to get the pennies out. He walks back to his bed, where I am sitting in my black shift. Hands them to me. They are indeed Mack's 1909-S VDB wheat-back pennies. I clutch them in my hand, the way I so wanted to do every time I saw Mack wearing them in his shoes.

"I will bring these back the next time we see each other," I say resolutely.

"Well, then, don't you think you should give me something of yours that is of equal value?" I think he expects me to have nothing comparable. That he's won this game and I'll be forced to give the pennies back. I finger my father's medallion on the chain that hangs out of view, between my breasts. I pull it out, undo the silver chain, and hand the silver coin to Cape.

"What is this?"

"This was my father's. My mother gave it to me when I was younger. As you know, I don't know who he is. My mother would never tell me."

"Why don't you find out?"

"How?"

"It's right here on this coin. The Latin translates to 'by faith and courage,' and the griffin is the mascot of the Ryder School. We play them in squash."

I had no idea Cape was such a Latin scholar. Ryder is a small academic school on par with Groton. My father's not only smart but must have some money. Not a doorman in the building of the aparthouse, which I'd thought was one possibility.

"You could call the school and have them look up who won the Latin prize that year. Then you would know."

I had many expectations for this evening, but I never imagined that Cape would give me the clue to finding my father. And how easy it would be to do it.

"Fair trade?" I ask Cape.

He says yes, with the caveat that under no circumstances can I lose the pennies. They must be returned at all costs.

"Of course, the medallion too," I say. But the medallion is almost worthless to me now that Cape has decoded it. It's just an interesting piece of jewelry.

After this exchange, I finally believe that Cape's for real. He wants me there. He's willing to give up the pennies, at least temporarily, for an evening with me. He takes the pennies from me and sets the coins and the medallion down on his trunk, which doubles as a nightstand. He comes over to the bed and sits next to me. He goes in for a kiss, more forceful this time. More caressing of my short hair. He then moves away and takes my face in his hands. After a moment of inspection, he says in a low voice, "Bettina, I'm so damn attracted to you."

I'm now wearing only my bra and underwear, but for the first time I'm not embarrassed. My body's not perfectly thin or even toned like Meredith's must be from field hockey, but Cape doesn't seem to care. It takes him a while to unhook my bra, but I think his concentration on doing it is cute. He takes each of my breasts into his mouth, and my wetness intensifies. I am almost worried that I will smash before we get where I'm sure we are going.

I pull off his T-shirt and his pajama bottoms. I feel his hard-on against my leg, and he's so erect with anticipation it almost hurts as he pushes against my thigh. I want nothing more than to take his penis into my mouth and suck him so hard that he passes out. He lifts the covers off the bed.

Instead I reach down and pull him inside me. I notice the tip of his penis is already slippery from excitement. I start to rock my hips, but he pauses.

"Wait," he says. "Let me get a condom."

I don't want to lose the momentum, so I say, "Just pull out and come on my stomach."

A condom makes me think of Jake, whose facility with the application seems only to accentuate all his experiences with girls other than me, his facility with sex itself.

Cape's breathing so heavily now, he's really in no position to argue about skipping the condom. "Okay," he says between ragged breaths. Only two minutes into it and already he is about to smash. Then there's a knock at the door.

"Shit, Lowell," Cape says, though he's almost past talking.

"Wait!" I call out.

I feel Cape wither inside me, the moment broken. He rolls over and pulls the bedspread up to our chins. I want to cry because Cape didn't finish, smash inside me, and also laugh because I know Lowell will give us both a hard time about this. There's no hiding what we have been up to.

There's the sound of a key in the door, and I hear a deep voice say, "I am keying in now." Faculty members are required to say this when opening a locked door, but they never give you time to cease whatever illegal activity you're engaged in.

The door opens and it's Mr. Carlson. Cape's dorm head.

"Shit," Cape says, barely recovered from our romp. We both understand at once that we are in big, big trouble.

22

Busted

~~~~~~~~~~~~~~~~~~~~~

OCTOBER 1983

M R. CARLSON WAITS OUTSIDE in the hallway while I
get dressed, which I am grateful for. I've heard stories
of teachers who stand and watch while you put your clothes
on. I pull on my shift and pumps. While Cape hunts for his PJ
bottoms, I surreptitiously grab the pennies from the top of the
trunk.

Mr. Carlson says nothing as I follow him down the steps of
Wentington and back to Bright.

He rings the bell when we arrive. I had hoped he had the
keys and that I could walk unnoticed to my room. But no. Part
of my punishment consists of facing Deeds at this ungodly
hour of two A.M. She arrives quickly and lets us in. Her room
is on the first floor. She is wearing boxers with DARTMOUTH
printed on them and an oversize green T-shirt.

She sees me with Carlson, but given how late it is, it takes
her a couple of minutes to wake up and understand what has
happened. Carlson waits a bit, then says, "I found Bettina in

one of my boys' rooms having sex." He then gives me a little shove.

"Thanks, Mike," Deeds says, and she takes me by the upper arm. Uses more force than is necessary. I wonder if she regrets not reporting me for smoking in the bathroom the day I arrived. We head into the house.

"Bettina," she says, in a cold voice, "this is a big deal. Until the faculty disciplinary committee meets in a few days, you are on probation." She walks me upstairs to my room. I know I'm no longer a Cardiss student in good standing. I am in a liminal space—somewhere between being kicked out and being reinstated. I am worried but still in the positive fog of having slept with Cape.

Once inside my room, I take off my dress and pumps and leave them in a pile by my bed. There will be no visit to the crater with Jake. I wonder if he'll be mad and stop speaking to me or won't really care. Either way, I know things between us are over. I have unequivocally broken our contract.

I change into the Cardiss T-shirt I sleep in. Lying in bed, I review the evening and all its implications. Cape and I might get kicked out, but Meredith will be punished in a way too. I imagine her sleeping soundly now, no idea that I have not only ruined her evening at the Cardiss dance but also fucked her virgin boyfriend. Will she forgive him? I doubt it, especially since he was found with me, someone who's not even in her league. I start to dread breakfast. I should be the one to tell her, but I'm not sure I am up for it.

I wait until it's light enough to go out for a smoke. I know this is probably a bad idea but what the hell.

23

Admission

I COME BACK TO THE dorm around seven, having smoked almost half a pack. I thought the girls would've gone to breakfast, but I can still hear their voices in Meredith's room. They hear my Converse sneakers in the hallway and yell for me to come in.

"Bettina," Meredith calls. "Come here. I have something to show you. While you were out, we had a little party to practice getting ready. Sometimes you just have to bend the rules in search of a higher good. I think we can skip breakfast today, no?"

I wonder what she will think of my "higher good."

"Check it out," she continues.

Meredith is dressed but her feet are bare. She spreads her toes, and I see they are painted perfectly white with a maroon C on each big toe.

"What do you think? It's a surprise for Cape. We might just hit the shower." They are beautiful, and under any other circumstances, I would have said so. Before coming in here,

I decided that Cape would have to deliver the bad news, but now I know I have to. I can't stand here and let her go on like this.

"Meredith, I have some bad news. Can you close the door?"

She looks nonplussed, but does as I ask.

"You might want to smoke," I say, bizarrely trying to be helpful when I am the one who's wronged her. I sit down on the bed.

"No, thanks. You know how much Cape hates smoking."

"Um, there is not going to be a dance."

"What do you mean? Did they call it off?"

"No, but . . ." This is going to be harder than I thought. Holly and Jess are staring at me, waiting to hear more and undoubtedly wondering what would happen to the pretty dresses in the closet.

"Well, um . . ." I am stuck.

"Just spit it out, Bettina. You're starting to annoy me." This is pure Meredith and gives me the confidence to tell her. Take her down with me. Maybe even draw blood.

"Last night, I got caught in Cape's room and we're both are on probation. We can't go to the—"

"I fucking know what probation is. What the hell were you doing in his room anyway? A bit of stalking?"

"No."

"Well, then, what? I know you've always had a crush on him by the way you stare at him in the dining hall. He must be horrified by the whole situation."

Bring it on, I think.

"Well, if you must know, Cape invited me."

Despite my bravado, I know I'm wandering into dangerous territory. I should be sucking up to Meredith since she is on the student judiciary committee. Now she won't be lenient. Will crucify me.

"He invited you?" Meredith asks, then pauses. "I don't fucking believe you."

"I have the pennies to prove it."

"What pennies?"

"From his shoes." I had slept with them curled up in my hand and had even taken them to the boathouse that morning. I continue:

"They were his father's and he gave them to me so I would trust him."

"Ha!" Meredith says, desperately searching for another scenario to explain them. "You probably went in and stole them, he walked in, and that's when you got caught." But this seems improbable, even to Meredith. I can see her looking at her toes, wishing perhaps that she could put the big ones in her mouth and gnaw off the Cs.

"Why would he have wanted you to trust him?"

Here was the point of no return.

"Because," I say slowly, "he wanted to have sex with me."

"And did he?" Meredith can't stop herself from asking about the details.

"Yes," I say.

"Why would he sleep with you? You aren't even pretty. You must have ambushed him. You pathetic little slut."

"Well, I just wanted to give you the heads-up so you'll be prepared when you hear people talking about it on campus."

"Get out of here, you freak." If Meredith were given to easy crying, this would be the breaking point.

I get up to go. Meredith hurls her math book in my direction. It narrowly misses my head.

I have one more confession to make in the next week. I hope it will go better than this one.

24

That Day

I FEEL SOME RELIEF AT having told Meredith about that night myself. She probably pictures it as being an awkward encounter. Clothes on, my dress wrinkled. A few kisses and a quick in-and-out. Which it pretty much was. Maybe she will forgive me in time.

I go to breakfast without the other girls, who stick to their guns about skipping it. It will take them a long time to parse and digest what I told them. But I don't have the luxury of breaking any more rules, given my status. I have no appetite after what has just happened and dread walking into dining hall alone.

I grab some coffee and check out my seating options. Cape is there, sitting with Lowell and some other boys from Wentington. He seems a bit subdued but still looks at ease as he eats his waffles and drinks his OJ. I don't dare sit with him. All the students are watching us. Then I see Jake, sitting by himself with the *New York Times,* as usual. Maybe he doesn't know yet. Or if he does, maybe we should officially break off our arrangement. Not sure how this works.

"Hey, Jake," I say tentatively.

"Sit," he says. I am relieved to hear no trace of bitterness in his voice.

"I missed you at the boathouse today," I venture. So far, so good. "It was a beautiful morning."

"Listen, Bettina, I prefer honesty to all your cheerful banter." Now his voice has a bite to it.

"So," I say softly. "I guess you have heard."

"I want to hear you say it."

"I was caught in Cape's room last night and am going up for action."

The irony is not lost on me; I will be going up for action for having gone up for action.

"And . . . you were . . ." Jake continues.

"Having sex."

"I can't believe you would have sex with a pussy like Cape."

"It's not that simple," I say, taking a sip from my coffee. "We have . . . a history."

"Whatever," he replies, now sounding bored.

I'm almost bummed there is no big confrontation. "Can I sit here and finish my coffee?"

"Sure. Knock yourself out." He takes his paper, grabs his tray, and leaves.

I am now sitting alone at a table, as he always is, but I don't have the confidence to pull it off.

Around six clock, I sit on my bed. Can feel the shift in the air as girls all over campus get ready for the dance.

I watch as Holly blow-dries her hair, applies eye shadow — a snow-cone blue like Stacey used to wear — and dons her pouffy dress. Of course she is on Team Meredith, so she does not so much as acknowledge me. I leave our room to go to the bathroom. As I walk down the hall I pass Meredith and Jess's room, and I am surprised to see that Meredith is getting ready. I am tempted to go in and remind Meredith that Cape is not coming, but surely she must know this.

When I return, Holly's gone, presumably to the living room downstairs so Ned will not have to call up for her.

Just then, I hear a familiar voice yell, "Hey, Meredith, you ready?" Lowell. She shouts back, "Coming, darling!"

Lowell? How did Meredith pull this off? Surely he must have had another date, must have asked another girl. But now he is showing up at Bright to collect Meredith like he is the next song on a mix tape. Maybe Cape begged him to do it, or maybe Lowell was attracted to her all along. Maybe he was just nice to me because I was in her dorm. But he's a hot boy like Cape, and Meredith will not suffer much for my having slept with Cape; I have not ruined her evening.

When they're all gone, I pull the pennies out from my underwear drawer and rub my index finger over the faces. I wonder where Cape is now.

I think back on our night together. My me is starting to get wet. I get up and lock the door. Technically when you are on probation, you are supposed to keep your door open, but I am not going to risk the shower again and I need to chase the smash. Meredith's gone, like everyone else, but maybe Deeds will come to check on me. Is having sex with yourself against the rules? I go ahead anyway. Just like when I was a child. It will alleviate my anxiety. I lie on my bed and pull down my pants and underwear. I am still wearing the underwear from last night. It is now a souvenir, like the pennies.

Wanting to feel that Cape is there with me, I put the pennies in my me, just far enough to feel them inside me but not so deep that I can't retrieve them when I am done.

I won't wash them before giving them back. It's like we have had sex all over again. I unlock my door and fall into a deep sleep.

25

Phone Call

Eight o'clock that night. I'm sleeping but wake to Deeds calling, "Bettina, phone."

I thought phone calls weren't allowed during probation. Apparently they are. I have the hope that it's Cape calling from Wentington to lament our mutual imprisonment. Our missing the dance.

The phone's downstairs in Bright's living room, a yellow rotary that rests on a table next to the couch. It looks antiquated, like something bought at an estate sale. Something a granny would use to call her family or to receive requests for brownies or crocheted blankets.

I put the receiver up to my ear and muster a cheery "Hello?"

"You sound pretty upbeat for someone who has managed to fuck up her Cardiss career." Babs.

"I'm, I'm not, Babs," I manage to reply. I have not spoken to her in over five months.

"Well, let me tell you, I'm quite pissed. One, that you got caught, and two, that you didn't have the balls to tell me yourself. I'm paying a shitload of money to send you to that school, and you don't even have the courtesy to pick up the phone to give me the heads-up."

"I'm sorry, Babs," I say quietly.

"It's not about being sorry," she says. "I want you to take responsibility. Some dean calls to tell me and is fucking flabbergasted when he realizes I'm the last to know. And Hailer Morse! This reeks of some kind of sad cry for help. You want my attention? Well, you got it. But I'm not going to give you a teary hug, go into therapy with you."

"It wasn't like that, Babs. I like Hailer. Or Cape, as he is really called."

"Okay, Cape it is. I don't have a problem with you screwing him. I have long waited for the day when you got some really good sex under your belt. But I never thought you'd be stupid enough to get caught."

"Babs," I try again. "I'm really sorry."

"That's not going to cut it, babe. The worst part of this whole thing is that I'm expected to attend the fucking meeting of the disciplinary committee. I have better things to do. And I'll probably have to sit next to Mags and make nice while she pretends not to know who I am. Does Cape know about Mack?"

"No," I say.

"Well, if his mother was too chicken to tell him, then I will."

"Please don't," I say.

"Full disclosure," Babs says. "No reason to spare your fucking prince the gory details. Maybe he'll even learn something."

Though I had been considering telling him all about our parents' affair, now I have no choice.

"So, I'll see you Wednesday," I say, now sounding dejected rather than upbeat. "Will you be staying at the Cardiss Inn?"

"I don't do inns. They always try to get you to make friends with the other people staying there. No room service, just that offensive breakfast in the smarmy dining room — fresh-baked muffins with tubs of butter next to them, and pots of jam with spoons stuck in the them. Vile coffee and no smoking. I'll stay at the Ritzy-Titsy in Boston and have a car take me up to campus."

"Okay," I say. "Thank you."

"Don't thank me," she says. "It's your mess and I'm not coming to clean it up."

She slams down the phone. I stand there, going over the conversation in my mind while listening to the dial tone. As bad as the call went, it gave me the bizarre impression that Babs loves me. Since the time she smacked me at the Hangover-Brunch Cruise Party, she has not let herself go and get really mad at me like this. She is actually going to alter her schedule and come to Cardiss. Sure, she will not play the dutiful mother, stay at the Cardiss Inn so she can be close to my dorm, be able to walk five minutes to see and comfort me. But she's still coming. That counts for something.

26

A Chat with Cape

OCTOBER 1983

THE DAY AFTER THE dance is Sunday. We have a half day of classes on Saturdays, so Sundays are the only days when we have nothing scheduled. We can sleep in, hang in the quad throwing Frisbees, and don't even have to go to meals. Sunday is also the day to catch up on homework and, for most students, to make the weekly phone call home. After my exchange with Babs, I am not inclined to talk to her again until she comes for the trial, as I am now calling it.

Even though nothing has happened yet, I can't help but feel uncomfortable.

I haven't been kicked out, but every time I walk outside, I have the feeling that I am trespassing. I also cannot believe Cape and I have not rehashed the events of the evening. Some small part of me believed that he would seek me out, but, as usual, I'm the one who has to chase after what I want. Not that I'm in a hurry to see him. When I do, I'll have to tell him about Mack so Babs won't blindside him with this information.

I go to the dining hall for brunch and spot Cape and Lowell. I sit at a table nearby, alone. Drink my coffee and eat two slices of buttered white toast.

Then I dump the contents of my tray. Walk to Cape's table.

"Hey, Bettina," Cape says, friendly but cautious. As if he is afraid I am about to propose we have sex in the dining hall, or at least make out.

"Umm," I respond, as both boys stare at me, "I was wondering if we could go for a walk."

He pauses. "I would love to, but I just don't want faculty to see us and think we do what we did on a regular basis. That we show no remorse."

"We could meet at the boathouse."

"Deal," he says. "You leave first and I'll see you there in twenty minutes."

It's early in the school year, and Cape and I are the first students to go up for action. Not that no one else engages in this behavior. They have just been more careful. When I walk, the students give me a wide berth, as if they are afraid they could catch what happened to Cape and me. I feel sad. Each one who now avoids me is a friend I might've had. I was just so focused on winning over Meredith.

I get to the bench and wait.

Cape arrives after about twenty minutes. Takes his place next to me on the bench.

"So, I suppose you want to discuss strategy."

Surprised by his confidence that this is my agenda, I say, "Yes."

"Just so you know, kicking students out is more an art than a science. They take all sorts of things into consideration, things that have nothing to do with the offense. One student may be allowed to stay and another one asked to leave even when they have both done the same thing."

"How does this work?" I ask, surprised by this information.

"Well, first they consider if you are a legacy or not. My father went to Cardiss. You?"

"My grandfather. Does that count?"

"Not as good as a father, but it helps. Next is the money factor. They are reluctant to kick out a kid who comes from a lot of it. My family is well off, but not rich. My mom has been pretty much living off my father's life insurance, and she has some family money of her own. What's your situation?"

"My mother is a chocolate heiress." I wince at having said this, but the conversation seemed to require it.

"As in Ballentyne Chocolate?"

"Yes."

"Is your mother philanthropic?"

"She just gave a million dollars to Miss Porter's and they used it to build a new dining hall." I don't tell Cape how ironic this is, given how much Babs hates food.

"Good, good. The head of development is on top of what goes on at other schools and will surely alert the faculty. Now, is there anything you're particularly good at, something the faculty would be loath to lose?"

"I'm good at French and English, but that's about it."

"That won't really help. It has to be something like sports or music. For instance, I don't mean to brag, but the lacrosse coach will fight to keep me."

"Oh, I see." Wishing I had extracurricular activities besides smoking and chasing the smash.

"So we both have certain things that will make it hard for them to kick us out. Your money, and my being a legacy and the lacrosse."

"Won't they want to make an example of us?"

"Of all the infractions, sex is not so bad. Cheating and haz-ing are the worst, followed by drugs and drinking. The thing about sex is that the girl might get pregnant, and the school would be held responsible."

I thought about the fact that we had not used a condom. But what would Cape have done with it after we got caught? Would he have had to turn it in as evidence?

"Does that make sense? I think we are in fairly good shape."

"Yes," I say distractedly. Knowing somehow that we aren't.

"Cape," I begin, "there is something I have to tell you." I put out one cigarette and light another.

"What?" he says, a bit surprised that there is more to discuss after he has explained what he perceives to be a fairly good game plan.

I pause, knowing the rest of what I have to say might be bad strategy on my part, but I just can't let Babs tell Cape about Mack.

"I wasn't completely honest with you. My mother knew your father outside of her parties. He visited my mother quite often."

After a significant pause, he asks, "What does *visited* mean?"

Shit. Here goes.

"They had an affair. It lasted about six months. I'm sorry."

"How do you know this?" he asks, searching for sources, definitive documentation, as if I have written a paper with a flimsy thesis and questionable footnotes.

I decide to spare Cape the details of my camping out on the stairs and listening while Babs and Mack had sex. How Babs told me later about whatever I couldn't see or hear.

"I saw his shoes in the front hallway late at night."

Cape says nothing for a good minute and then cracks his knuckles. He does not have a cigarette to dilute his feelings about the situation.

"Oh, that explains the fucking pennies. Which I need back, by the way. Why the hell didn't you tell me before? I *never* would have slept with you. Does my mom know about these visits?"

"Yes. It was pretty common knowledge."

"Jesus Christ, Bettina. Think how my mother must feel that out of all the girls at Cardiss, I got caught with you. She was crying when I talked to her the other day, and she never cries. In fact, I have seen her cry only once: when we drove back from my father's funeral. Why are you bringing this up now? Do you want me to hate you?"

"It wasn't my fault, Cape." I'm not sure how to explain to him that unlike his mother, Babs does whatever the fuck she wants.

"Maybe not, but you were still there all those nights my mother must have waited up for him. And it seems you sought me out, perversely, as if the whole thing titillated you."

"Cape, I was around eleven years old when this happened. And I loved your dad. He was nice to me."

"Oh, how cozy. Well, I'm glad he showed some affection somewhere. Because he basically ignored me. He was always gone or distracted."

I hear the hatred in his voice and start to cry.

"Bettina, I'm not going to pity you, if that's what you want."

I can't help it. My tears get more intense, slide out like tributaries over my face.

"Cape, do you really have to hate me? I didn't want to have to bring all this up. I just thought you would want to know, given the circumstances."

"What do you expect me to do?"

"I don't know. Tell me you know it wasn't my fault? Forgive me for not having brought it up earlier?" I venture.

"Well, that's not going to happen," he says. He's trying to sound mean, but I know he wants to cry too. He starts to walk away, then turns back, having regained his composure. "Look on the bright side: you can always write a story about it."

27

Monday

THE TRIAL'S THREE DAYS away. I've achieved the status of a quasi-celebrity on campus. Everyone's excited to know the consequences of our infraction. Will we be kicked out or allowed to stay? The crime's particularly interesting because it involves sex. Most of the students in the school are too focused on academics to have lost their virginity.

Meredith's still furious, and the other girls at Bright follow her lead. They no longer make cruel remarks; they just ignore me. This is hard for Holly, since she's a genuinely nice person. Cannot bear to tell her parents the fate of her roommate, who had seemed to share their values. I imagine her on the phone saying, *Yes, everything is great. Bettina and I are getting along very well.*

This semi-goodwill is completely shattered when word gets back to her that I'm not some poor scholarship student but the daughter of Babs Ballentyne, chocolate heiress. I am related to food, as they originally thought.

Holly hears this from some of the older students from Chicago who called home with news of me going up for action. Their parents know all about Babs and her money. Now Holly has reasons of her own not to talk to me. I have lied to her and her family. The fact that I didn't mean to doesn't really matter.

I am unclear when Babs is coming to campus. Am afraid to call her and ask. She could come Tuesday night and take me to dinner in town. She could wait until Wednesday, right before the trial. Or maybe, just maybe, she won't come at all. I'll have to wait and see.

After dinner Monday night, there's no one in my room, but on the wall by my bed someone has scrawled the word *liar* in big brown letters. I walk closer and discover that the epithet has been written in chocolate. On the wall behind my pillow is the word *slut,* also written in chocolate. I'm ashamed, but also furious. This gives me the courage to face Meredith, Jess, and Holly.

I storm into their room. Am stunned to see Holly smoking. She doesn't really have the hang of it yet and coughs after every puff, but I am sure she will master it by the end of the semester, in December.

"What is it?" Meredith asks in an impatient voice.

"I want to know what's up with your fucking art project on my walls. I must say the use of chocolate was original."

Meredith doesn't address my question but instead turns to Holly, who looks me dead in the eye and speaks.

"I found out the truth about your family. How dare you let my parents believe you had no money? You even took ten dollars from my dad! What were you doing, laughing at us?"

Under any other circumstances, I would have tried to explain, even apologize. But I'm so mad about Holly's defection, her defacing my walls, I can only glare at her.

"You know this counts as hazing," I say. "That's more serious than what I'm going up for now."

Holly turns pale, looks to Meredith.

Meredith just says, "Holly should have added *snitch* and *bitch* to her list of your glowing descriptors."

I would never report them, but I take satisfaction in their reaction to my bluff.

"Fuck you, Meredith," I say and go to the bathroom to get a washcloth. I wet it and start cleaning my walls. At least Holly did not use indelible ink.

Once the walls are clean, I sit down and tackle my homework. Why? Can think of nothing else to do. Then I notice: all of Holly's things are gone. She must have moved down the hall to the empty double next to Meredith and Jess's. So what, I tell myself. I see she left the foot warmer her mom made me. The fucking Combs family and their stupid, hopeful gift. It was their fault after all that I lied about the money. I don't know if I should mail the foot warmer back with a fifty and a note saying *Donna, maybe you can go to WeightWatchers or buy yourself some attractive shoes* or just throw it away. It would look stupid in the aparthouse anyway.

28

Phone Call II

I CAN'T FACE JAKE OR CAPE so I'm in my room skipping breakfast when the phone rings. Deeds is nowhere to be found so I run down and pick it up.

"Hello?"

"Bettina, darling, it's Babs." *Darling?* Under the circumstances, it rings false, but who cares.

"Hi, Babs," I reply, not certain where this conversation is going.

"Listen, I shouldn't have gotten mad the other day. I think it's fabulous you had sex. Fuck the school that considers it a crime."

I hesitate before contradicting her. "But I really like Cardiss."

"You like Cardiss or Cape?"

"Both," I reply.

"Well, if you are kicked out," she continues, "think of all the fun we'll have. We can travel. Stay up all night watching movies. Shop. You can apply to another school for next term.

Miss Porter's has to accept you after all the goddamn dough I've given them."

Babs wants to have fun with me? Maybe she has no one to fuck and is bored with single women her own age, just finds them depressing. Maybe I would be just a placeholder until she can set up a suitable new cast for the Babs show, but who cares. I would choose Babs over Cape any day.

"I'm coming to Boston this afternoon. Want you to come to the Ritz and spend the night. We'll go out to a *fab* new restaurant, Touché, and close the bar down at the hotel. I've got a suite."

As great as this sounds, I know I can't go. How to explain this to Babs?

"I don't think I can, Babs. I'm on probation until I go up for action and have to be checked in by seven. I don't think they will let me leave Cardiss, even with a parent."

"That's bullshit," she says. "I'm your mother and I pay the bills at that crummy school. Let me talk to Ms. McSoSo."

I put the receiver down and run upstairs to get Deeds. She is hunched over her desk marking up papers on *Le petit prince* with a red pen. She looks up at me. Annoyed.

"Yes?" she says curtly.

"Um, sorry to bother you. My mother wants to talk to you."

"Okay," Deeds says, straightening up to assume the posture of a dorm head. She follows me down the stairs. She is barefoot, toenails trimmed but not polished. She picks up the phone.

"Yes," Deeds says, trying to project some level of authority. Even though I can't hear Babs's monologue on the other end of the line, I can tell Deeds is not buying it.

"I'm sorry, Mrs. Ballentyne, Bettina needs to be back at Bright by seven o'clock. She also isn't allowed to leave campus except to go into the town of Cardiss. Maybe you could drive up and visit her?"

Pause.

"I understand, *Ms.* Ballentyne, but Cardiss doesn't make exceptions for heiresses."

Pause.

"I *know* it's the night before she goes up for action. That's why it's mandatory that Bettina follow all the rules. There are no exceptions."

Pause.

"Yes, you *are* her mother, but by sending her to Cardiss, you made the school in loco parentis. Unless you want to take her out of this school for good, you can't override our rules.

"Please, I'm sorry you are upset. And no, I don't want to discuss my personal life with you."

Pause.

"No, from what I gather, Cape won't be leaving the area with his mother."

Deeds is now gesticulating wildly as if Babs can see her. Forgets I'm standing there.

"Okay, I'll put Bettina back on the phone. I hope I've made myself clear."

Deeds passes the phone back to me, shakes her head. Goes back to her room and *Le petit prince,* I presume. A fantastical book, but whose plot, syntax she can understand. Unlike Babs's and mine.

We resume our conversation.

"What a fucking lawn ornament," she says. "No sense of priorities. Zilch sense of humor."

"So, I guess we will have to wait until Wednesday. I really would've liked to come, Babs. Sorry it didn't work out," I say, thinking that Babs has taken Deeds seriously. But of course Babs doesn't take anyone seriously.

"Are you kidding me? I'm still sending the limo to get you."

I take more than a second to answer. If going to see Cape was risky, leaving midday in a stretch limo is downright destructive. If I do it, I'll get kicked out for sure.

"Bettina?" Babs, incredulous that I might follow the rules now that she's concerned. "This whole in loco parentis crap is bullshit. I'm your mother. I get to decide what is or is not okay."

I think of her care package. Was she trying to be cool by sending it? Or did she want me to get kicked out all along? Probably both.

I say, "I'm sorry, Babs, but I can't. I hope you have fun."

"Have it your way, you fucking chicken," she says, all the chummy excitement gone.

Conversation over. Dead air. I hold the receiver as if it is some kind of amputated appendage. Hope I've made the right choice.

29

Tuesday

OCTOBER 1983

ONE DAY LEFT BEFORE the trial, and I can't think of anything productive to do. I consider what Babs would do in this situation and decide to shop. I need something appropriate to wear to the trial. Not only is my black shift too sexy, too evening, I can't show up in the same outfit I got busted in.

Back to Wow! The same saleslady is there, waiting to help me. I'm sure she remembers my odd choice of *togs* for the dance.

"I need a dress for tea with my grandmother," I say. A lie, but good shorthand for "virginal, frumpy."

"I think I have just the thing." She walks to the back of the store. Digs through all the racks.

"You are a size eight, yes?"

The dress she hands me is the exact opposite of the one she sold me before. A floral jumper with a Peter Pan collar, and it hits below the knees. Perfect. Now for the shoes. I pick out a pair of black patent-leather flats and hope they don't give me blisters. No time to break them in, and I don't want to limp to the trial.

The saleslady (I find out her name is Bev) rings me up and once again is bothered by my use of traveler's checks. She folds the dress into a Wow! shopping bag, covering it with tissue paper. She tucks the shoes into the side.

"I hope you enjoy your tea," Bev says.

"Huh?" Forgetting the story that conjured this dress. Once again, I can't seem to get out of a situation without lying. "Oh, yes. Thank you," I say. A tinkly bell on the door marks my departure.

I continue my walk through the town of Cardiss. Arrive at the hamburger place, The Dog and the Fiddle. I stop and read at the menu hanging outside. Look in the window. Sitting in the front booth are Cape and Mags. They have their heads bowed and are holding hands, as if they are praying.

I feel a sudden longing for Babs. Why couldn't she have stayed at the Cardiss Inn, taken me out to lunch, reassured me? Suddenly, I have the idea to go into the restaurant and join them. Mags might have given me a chilly reception at Tea House years ago, but maybe this time will be different. Even though she cried on the phone to Cape when he told her the news, she is a mother after all.

I open the door and walk to their table, my Wow! bag swinging in my hand. Cape spots me coming, although he averts his eyes and pretends not to. I reach their table and stand by the edge, the same spot a waitress would. Wait for them to ask me to sit down. At first, neither one says anything. They just stare.

At last, despite the awkward situation, Cape remembers his manners.

"Mom," he says coolly, "this is Bettina."

"We met once, as I remember."

Then, silence. As if they think that if they don't say anything, I will get the idea and leave.

But stupidly, I still believe they might ask me to sit down. We're all in this together, after all. Then again, maybe not.

"Out shopping?" Cape says, as if I were insane to be hitting the stores with such a momentous day ahead of us.

"Not really. I just needed to pick something up."

"Oh," he says. "Bettina, could you please let my mother and me finish our meal?"

But I'm not ready to leave just yet.

"Mrs. Morse," I say, "I just want to apologize that Cape and I got into this situation. I wish we hadn't." I think this might melt her resolve, show her that I'm not Babs, that I do have the capacity for remorse. However, Mags remains unmoved.

"It's really too late for apologies, Bettina," she says. "I don't know if your mother put you up to this, but it wouldn't surprise me."

I want to say that Cape wasn't the victim here and that Babs had nothing to do with this. But I'm not sure that this is entirely true.

30

Judgment Day

FINALLY, WEDNESDAY. STUDENT JUDICIAL committee meeting at four, followed by the faculty trial at five. Stud Jud, as it's known, gets one vote on our fate, almost a formality with no real consequences. Just ensures that we have the embarrassment of being judged by our peers. I haven't forgotten that Meredith is on the committee. Wonder if she's the tiniest bit mad at Cape or if she will pin the whole thing on me.

I sleep poorly the night before, and despite my resolve, I leave Bright at five A.M. for a smoke or, rather, for many. I tell myself I will brush my teeth vigorously and spray enough Coco to mask the smell. I sit on the bench of the boathouse and watch the river rush by. I know Virginia Woolf killed herself by walking into a river with stones in her pockets. I am not quite at the jumping-off place, but close. I'm now really worried that because I refused to go to Boston, Babs will bag the whole event and fly back to Chicago.

I put my first cigarette out and catch sight of my ankles, a burn on each one. They no longer make me feel powerful; they make me feel damaged. How did I manage to fuck things up so badly? I am tempted to go for the whole I-have-major-problems package and put a cigarette out on each of my wrists, but I know such a thing can't be undone. And maybe, someday, when Babs dies, I will have a shot at a normal life.

Today, Cape and I aren't required to go to classes. The school expects that we'll spend the early part of the day with our parents. They're allowed to visit our rooms before we go up for action. I know that Mags will probably be in Wenting-ton after breakfast, but as for Babs, who knows what her plans are.

I return to my bed and sleep for a while, since my previous night's sleep was so broken. When I wake up, I go to the grill and order a vanilla frappe. It's all that I feel like eating; screw the calories. I go back to my room and try to read *Anna Karenina*, but I am too distracted to make any progress. I keep thinking about Babs. I decide to call her at the Ritz, though I don't know what my reception will be.

I go downstairs and pick up the rotary phone. It's too complicated to use my calling card, so I call collect. The operator at the Ritz miraculously accepts the charges and puts me through. The phone rings and rings until Babs finally picks up.

"Hello?" she says in a groggy voice. For most people, being groggy makes them more vulnerable, but for my mother, it is just Babs on low.

"Babs, it's Bettina."

"I figured as much."

"I was just calling to see what time you are coming to Card-iss. The first meeting is at four."

"Hmm. Let me get this straight. You flatly refuse to come to Boston yesterday after I had gone to all the trouble to plan girlie time, and now you expect me lug myself up to Cardiss. Tell me why the fuck I should do this."

"Well, Babs," I begin tentatively, knowing whatever I say will decide whether she shows up or not, "parents usually come."

It's unbearable to think of going through this alone.

"Since when have I been lumped into the category of parents? What, I want to know, is in it for me?"

I pause. Don't really have a good answer to this. If I have to work to get her here, chances are she has already made up her mind about coming. Maybe her attachment to my being at Cardiss will convince her. Or maybe watching me get kicked out will be fun.

"Students who have their parents there usually have a better chance of not getting kicked out."

"And why would I give a shit about that?"

Now I am barely above begging. I opt for a new strategy.

"You could see Cape. He looks a lot like Mack."

"Ah, yes. I *was* looking forward to that."

"I already told him about the whole thing so you don't have to."

"Good for you, my girl! Points on the fearless score."

I try one more time. "Please come, Babs. I need you."

I know Babs detests neediness in all forms, but I can't think of anything else.

"I'll see how I feel after some coffee and a few ciggies. *Ciao,* babe."

She hangs up, her visit still up in the air. I go back to my room, no real progress made. It is ten thirty, and I have the whole day to kill. I make my bed, straighten up my desk, and organize my clothes in different drawers. Cape's pennies sit on top of my dresser. I decide I'll take them to the trial.

31

That Day, Continued

THREE O'CLOCK. TIME TO get dressed. I put on the granny-tea dress and black flats. I decide not to wear any makeup. Just opt for a good scrubbing of my face with Noxzema and cold water. I don't put on lipstick, just a swipe of lip balm. I look in the full-length mirror and almost don't recognize myself. I look innocent in a way I didn't even look when I was ten, when Babs picked out all my clothes.

I sit on my bed and smoke. Don't want to go to the boathouse and chance running into Jake. Cigarettes are a great way to kill time without actually doing anything. Am ashing into an empty Diet Coke can when there is a knock at the door.

Will Deeds ever get tired of catching me at things I shouldn't be doing?

I tentatively open the door. It isn't Deeds but Babs.

32

Maternal Instincts

BABS WALKS INTO MY room without so much as a hello. She's wearing a maroon suit with gray fur around the collar and cuffs. Cardiss colors. I'm almost surprised she knows what they are, but then again, she is always attentive to a theme. Has on a ruby necklace, a ruby bracelet studded with diamonds, and a ruby cocktail ring. She sits down on the bed, then says:

"What a dump! This place looks more like a prison than a dorm room. What the fuck is this?" She points to the rug with the *B* on it.

"Holly's mom gave it to me on my first day here."

"Ah, the joys of kitsch. And your sheets—standard-issue Cardiss. I would've thought with all the money I gave you, you would buy some new ones. And what the hell are you wearing? You look Amish."

"I thought it would make me look contrite for the trial."

"You don't look contrite, you look like someone who has zip taste in clothes."

"I'm not going to change, Babs. I don't have any other dresses."

She goes to my closet and takes inventory.

"What about the one I sent you? Or this black one? It's almost chic."

"I thought it was too risqué. I was wearing it when I got caught."

"Well, have some balls. You are from Chicago, not Kansas."

I back down. I will do anything to placate Babs. I am that grateful she showed up. I pull on the dress. Still wear my new black flats.

"Bag the flats," she says. "You are too short to swing them. Go with the heels."

"I'm not sure, Babs."

"And put some makeup on. This crunchy shit is not going to fly. I don't want you to embarrass me."

The spiral staircase all over again. I put on a minimal coat of makeup, and it's time to go.

33

Trial

OCTOBER 1983

THE ENTIRE PROCESS TAKES place on the top floor of the Madson library. There's a special room the school uses for big-deal occasions. Trustee meetings, search committees for new department heads, discussions about changing the curriculum. Babs wants to drive to the building in the limo, but since the library is a two-minute walk from Bright House, I persuade her not to.

"Have it your way, babe," she says.

We set out across the lawn, me struggling with my pumps in the grass. Babs lights up a cigarette.

"Um, Babs, there's no smoking on campus."

"Maybe for you, Bettina, but I don't go here so I don't give a fuck."

I pray she puts it out before we reach the library. Thank God, she does. We arrive early. Look like we take the whole thing seriously. We take the elevator to the seventh floor. Down the hall is a wooden door that is cracked open.

Babs strides confidently toward it. As if this is something

she does every day. That's the thing about Babs. The chocolate money makes her feel at ease anywhere.

I follow behind. I have never been in this room, and I am surprised to see that, despite all its mystery, it looks like any other classroom at Cardiss. A big oval table with wooden chairs around it. There are six folding chairs on the side where we are to sit. Implies Cape and I each have two parents to get us through this mess. Which of course we don't.

Cape and Mags are already there. Cape wears a blue blazer, khakis, and a Cardiss tie; Mags wears a Liberty print shirt, blue poplin skirt with pantyhose. Grass Woods all the way. I still can't believe that clothes don't matter in this process. If I still had my pink-and-white-checked sundress, I probably would have tried to wear it.

They hold hands. If Mags is troubled by Babs's arrival, she doesn't show it. Just pulls a mint from her purse and offers it to Cape.

I take in the twelve students who compose Stud Jud. They wear blue blazers, each with the Cardiss insignia on the right lapel. Meredith sits on the far end of the table, her blond hair up in a bun, as if she were a teacher. I wonder where all the blazers are kept. I have never seen one in Meredith's closet. It's not the kind of thing you wear around campus.

Even though none of them are smiling, I can feel the palpable excitement in the air. There is a copy of the C-book in the middle of the table, should any of the students need to refer to it. The only other person I recognize is Jade from my bio class. We dissected a pig together. My incisions were jagged and cost us an A. She never spoke to me again, and I know she's probably not sympathetic to my case.

The only adult in the room besides Mags and Babs is Mr. Carlson, Cape's dorm head, the one who busted us. I suppose he's going to present the official charges against us.

He knocks the table with a gavel and asks all of us to stand.

"Repeat after me," he says.

I start to follow along before I realize he's addressing only the students at the table. I feel like an idiot.

"We, members of the student judiciary, swear to consider each of the students before us without personal prejudice and only in light of the infractions committed."

They all repeat this and retake their seats.

I look at Meredith and discern no smugness in her bearing but rather a somber attitude I've never seen her sport in real life.

The next order of business is for Mr. Carlson to present our crimes. He remains standing. I feel Babs twitch beside me and know she's craving a smoke. I wonder if she'll light up right there or excuse herself.

"First," Mr. Carlson says, "I want to remind you that each of these students, Bettina Ballentyne and McCormack Hailer Morse, should be considered as separate cases, even though they were caught together."

He continues.

"On the night of October twenty-third, I entered Cape's room and discovered Cape and Bettina in Cape's bed, engaged in sexual activity. Both parties were naked, and it was past midnight. Both are charged with illegal visitation and sexual congress. Bettina is also charged with leaving Bright House after hours, a dangerous activity in and of itself, as it undermines campus security."

It's not lost on me that my leaving my dorm is the only infraction that gets a qualifier.

Having finished recounting the crime, Mr. Carlson sits down.

We're not to have our say in front of Stud Jud. They're judging us solely on our infractions, not factoring in our achievements at Cardiss. We're dismissed to the hallway while Stud Jud votes on our fate.

The bench we're to sit on is fairly small. Awkward. Babs sits next to Cape and I'm next to her. Mags is on the other side of Cape. Cape seems to want to protect Mags from any contact with either Babs or me.

Babs strikes up a conversation with him. I pray for a benign *Hello*, but of course this isn't Babs's style.

"Too bad your father isn't here to see this. The whole thing presents a nice symmetry, don't you think?"

Cape just sits there rigidly. Chooses to ignore Babs. I feel like grinding the heel of one of my pumps into her toes. Why, I ask myself, did I want her to come? As usual, she is making things worse. But there's nothing I can do to stop her. To make her be anything but herself.

Ten minutes pass. The door opens and Mr. Carlson reports the vote. The Stud Jud has voted for both of us to be allowed to stay at Cardiss. I'm stunned. Maybe Meredith has less influence than I feared.

They all file out, no longer wearing the blue jackets. They are now just students like us. No one says anything except Meredith, who is eighth to walk out. She bends down and whispers to me: "I voted for you to stay. Leaving Cardiss would allow you to escape all of the fun we have in store for you."

Then Meredith walks over to Cape. He stands to greet her.

"I voted for you Cape," Meredith says. "I know Bettina, and I know it was not your fault."

He doesn't deny this, just says, "Thank you, Mere." Kisses her just where her hairline meets her forehead.

Mags stands up and gives her a hug. "Thank you, dear Meredith."

"Of course," Meredith replies, then walks down the hall to

the elevator. I can't help but wonder: *Is this some kind of fucking cocktail party?*

Now all we have to do is wait for the faculty. We sit in silence as they trickle in. They are not wearing special jackets like Stud Jud, just their regular blazers and ties. I suppose their being on this committee at Cardiss cloaks them in enough authority that they don't need a special uniform. The identity of the faculty members on the committee has always been shrouded in mystery. Unless you go up for action, you will never know which teachers preside over Cardiss students' fates.

I look around to see who is there.

The dean of students, Mr. Watson, sits next to Donaldson. I hope he's read enough of my Babs stories to feel sorry for me. Deeds is there, which is worrisome, since she caught me smoking and Babs tried to bully her. She's the only woman. The rest are male teachers I have seen walking on the paths but don't know personally.

Watson, as dean, is in charge of the whole procedure. I note that he has two folders in front of him on the table. A thick one that reads MORSE on the side tab, and a slimmer one next to it with a tab that reads BALLENTYNE. I could worry about this, but I don't.

Carlson stands up and describes our crimes. The report is almost verbatim what he said to Stud Jud, except he doesn't need to remind the faculty that our cases are to be decided separately, and that they are not to let any personal interactions they might have had with us affect their judgment. Mr. Watson then reaches for the folders. He picks up Cape's.

"These are in no way expected to excuse the crimes but are meant to provide insight into what each candidate has contributed to our school."

I want to raise my arm and call foul since this last sentence seems to negate the impartial decision that they promised just minutes earlier.

He opens Cape's file.

"Mr. Morse is a legacy; his father attended Cardiss. His mother endowed all the gardens at the entrance to the library. Mr. Morse maintains a three-point-seven GPA and belongs to the Young Republicans' club, Students Against Hunger, and the debating society. He is a superlative lacrosse player and is known for not only his athletic skills but also his sportsmanship. He is expected to make captain this spring, the first Lower to do so in twenty years." Watson closes Cape's file and opens mine.

"Miss Ballentyne is a legacy of sorts: her grandfather attended Cardiss. He gave generously to the school while alive and included Cardiss in his will. Miss Ballentyne matriculated at Cardiss as a Lower, so she has no grades reported yet. She is on no sports teams and has joined no clubs."

My record, as he presents it, seems to suggest that in the two months I have been at Cardiss, I have left my room only once, and that was to sleep with Cape.

"Now we have the chance to hear from the students," he continues. I was unaware that we were expected to make a speech or a plea. I'm not good at public speaking. Cape goes first and I am grateful.

"I know the severity of my crimes, and I am deeply ashamed of the dishonor I have brought upon the school and my family. It's my hope that the committee will see how dedicated I am to the school and give me a chance to continue my activities, and perhaps even take up some new ones. I promise also to serve as a role model, tutoring other students and telling them how important it is that they follow Cardiss rules. Thank you for your consideration." He finishes and takes his seat next to Mags.

I stand, even though I really can't think of anything good to say.

Babs looks intrigued, curious to know what I will come up with.

"Um, I too realize what a grave crime we've committed and know no amount of apologies can make up for what we have done. I also know that I haven't had as accomplished a career as Cape has, but it has taken me a while to acclimate myself to boarding school. I've applied myself to my studies and hope for three-point-eight this term. In the spring, I plan on joining some clubs and maybe a sports team."

I sit down, knowing my speech is riddled with the hypothetical but hope the faculty will see in me the potential of a productive future at Cardiss. Of course, I have never played any sports, so making a team is pretty unlikely, and I'm not sure I have the pep or conviction to join a club. Students Against Domestic Violence? Pennies for Puppies? Maybe, just maybe, I can push myself to be like the other students. Focus on getting into college. Making friends along the way.

Babs does not pat me reassuringly when I return to my seat but instead puts up her hand.

"Yes?" Watson asks, surprised.

"Would it be okay if I spoke?"

"Well," he replies, "it's not customary for parents to comment, but I suppose we can make an exception. Go ahead."

Babs stands. My hands shake. I wish I had gone to Boston that night. Now it's payback time.

"As Bettina's mother," Babs begins, "I have of course known her all her life. When I heard the news that she had been caught in a boy's room, I was disappointed but not surprised. Bettina has always been defiant, but before, it was always little things. Still, I do not consider sex at her age a crime. She has good grades, and as far as I'm concerned, what she does with her body is her business.

"I believe this so strongly that I am willing to take her out of a school that punishes teenagers for being teenagers. Do you actually expect them to get to college without a little experimenting? But I know Bettina loves Cardiss, so I am willing to pledge a million dollars to the school if you change the policy on sexual practices and allow Bettina to stay. Add a sex education course if you have to, but don't punish students such as her for this."

She sits back down, satisfied. She has made a good case. No swearwords, and what institution could possibly turn down all that money?

I look at the faculty. They say nothing, stunned.

We are asked to leave the room while the faculty deliberates. This time Babs leaves the library. Goes outside, I'm sure to have a smoke. Cape and Mags still don't talk to me, but I can sense they are uncomfortable. If Babs can buy my way out of this, it undermines the whole system.

Twenty-five minutes go by. A faculty member motions for us to come back in. Babs has not returned. Maybe the elevator is stuck. She doesn't do stairs. The faculty begins at once, not bothering to wait for her.

I keep my head down as they read their decision. Stare at my pumps. They have bits of grass on the heels. I start to count all the blades. The suspense is so intense it almost hurts. The verdict will not only decide my fate but also prove or invalidate what I have always believed about Babs: that she gets whatever she wants. This time, she appears to want something good for me. Will she get it?

The dean delivers the faculty's verdicts. But somehow I hear none of it. Or I do, but it does not register. Maybe it is just too hard for someone my age, sitting there by herself, to take in. I leave the room and see several students standing in the hall. Lowell is there, and he pats Cape on the back. Another boy approaches them. Asks, "Hey, what's the deal?"

Another boy from Wentington I have seen Cape pal around with answers loudly, as if I'm not standing right there:

"Cape in; Bettina out."

I see a glimmer of relief on Mags's face. Finally, things are as they should be.

I push my way though the throng of students, out of the library. There's no one there on my side. No one says sorry, or wishes me luck. I go to look for the only one who cares about my fate. Babs. I search for her outside but can't find her anywhere. I walk back to Bright. Surely she's there, sitting in her limo smoking, or in my room starting to pack. This is another thing she's good at from all her trips. She loves to fold and organize. But no. My room is empty. I'm not sure why she left before hearing the outcome. Did she just assume the chocolate money would prevail? For now, it doesn't really matter. I have to finish the rest of this alone.

After being kicked out, a student has twenty-four hours to vacate the campus.

Even if I were ready to leave, it is unlikely that a cab could get me to Logan Airport in time to catch a flight to Chicago. I pull out my LV duffel and start packing. It takes me about ten minutes. The only thing left hanging in my closet is the Peter Pan collar dress. I take it out and throw it into the garbage. Would it have made a difference in the outcome? Probably not.

Just then I remember something: Babs's care package. The genesis of this whole mess. It's under my bed, but I can't leave it there. What to do with it? I can't take the bottles with me. Too heavy, and Babs has some at home anyway. Nor can I empty them into the dorm toilet. There would be nowhere to throw the bottles away. I decide to take them to Meredith's room. A thank-you present for voting for me. Despite her threat to torture me if I stayed.

I pick up the box, walk down the hall, and rap on Meredith's door.

"Come in," she sings cheerily. I half expect her to add, *Ding-dong, the witch is dead.*

I open the door, though it is hard to balance the heavy box in one hand. I drop it on the floor. Sit down in front of Meredith. Holly is there too, and she faces me squarely and says, "Sorry about the news, Bettina." She is the first person to say this to me and I think about how nice she still is. I could have used a best friend like her, but I blew it.

"I brought this for you guys, thinking you could use it."

Meredith peeks into the box. "I hope you're not using this as a ploy to get us put up for action."

"Of course not."

"Well, this time, *I* will get a good buzz before visiting Cape."

"Cape?" I say, stunned to hear her mention his name after all he has done to her. Maybe I am not significant enough for what he and I did to count as unforgivable. "What about Lowell?"

"Lowell? Oh, we had a good time at the dance and then he walked me home like a gentleman. But that's it. He's no Cape."

"So, Cape . . ." I continue despite myself.

"He's going to take me out to dinner with his mother tonight."

"Oh" is all I can say. I had thought he might come by to see me. Feel he owes me one last goodbye.

"Thanks for the gift, Bettina, but I have to go shower before dinner," Meredith says dismissively.

I go back to my room. Glad that I have saved the bottle of bourbon for myself. Maybe I'm not *fearless,* as Babs deems drinkers, but I sure feel better after a few slugs. As for my getting caught, it doesn't matter. Cardiss holds no more punishments for me. Soon, the walls start to sway. I decide to lie down on the bed. I want to go and see Cape, kiss him, have his hands run over my body. Pretend things are the way they were before we got caught. Before I told him about Mack. I stand up, but I find I can barely walk. This does not stop my thoughts of Cape. Drinking, besides blurring your senses, brings you back to your losses. Mine now stretch out and encompass me. Maybe this is why Babs doesn't drink. It keeps her unstuck from the past. No morose thoughts about the loss of her parents. Not devastated by Mack's death. Content with the chocolate money.

Drunk, I am sad to the point of tears that I may never see Cape again. There will be other boys, I know, but none like Cape. I lie back on my pillow and pass out.

I wake up around nine, still drunk but with a massive headache. There is drool on the side of my face, and I am desperately thirsty. I stand up and stumble to the bathroom.

On the way out of my room, I trip over a white envelope with my name written on it. I recognize Cape's handwriting. He did come after all. Maybe he knocked on the door and in my stupor, I did not hear him. So he left me a note. I am sure it will be sweet, apologizing for getting so mad about our parents' affair and taking it out on me. I pick up the envelope and hold it to my chest. It is surprisingly heavy. I carry it to the bathroom, determined to clean my face and drink some water to cure my dry mouth before I read it.

Back in my room, I think, *Meredith, take this!* I sit on the floor, have another swig of the bourbon. My hands are shaking from the anticipation. I slowly open the envelope and tumbles my father's medallion. I take it in my hand and rub the crest of the Ryder School. That's all that's in it. I suppose he expects me to return his pennies this same way.

I'm suddenly angry in a way I have not been all day. Not angry, even. Furious.

Emboldened by the alcohol, I leave my room and walk across campus to the boathouse. I don't even bring my cigarettes. I want what I do to be clean and decisive. I reach the boathouse.

There's a fence blocking the river from the bench, and I take the bourbon bottle and smash it across the wood. The bottle shatters, and the rest of the bourbon sprays all over me like a slick, foreign perfume. I see the glass in the grass and feel a satisfaction that I have broken something else that cannot be fixed.

I reach into my pocket. Pull out the pennies. It's dark and I cannot read the faces, but I can make out the marks with my fingers. I clutch them in my hand. I take off my shirt and my bra and stand before the river topless. I rub the pennies over my skin. I think of when I used them to smash. This time, I'm not aroused. I just want to feel the intimacy of the copper making small inroads, invisible tattoos on my body.

I take the pennies and toss them into the river. They arch out of my hand and make a satisfying plink as they hit the water, sink.

I put my bra and top back on. I stare at the river to see if they will float back up, like dead bodies, but nothing.

34

Goodbye

OCTOBER 1983

THE NEXT MORNING, I wake up around nine thirty, hung over. I make my bed and check that all my things are packed. The next task is to make travel plans to leave Cardiss. This is the only item on my agenda. There's nothing of mine in anyone else's dorm room. I have no more goodbyes to say. I'm just a girl hanging about.

I go to the dean's office to set up my itinerary, since it is almost impossible to make long-distance calls on the Bright rotary phone. The dean's secretary is named Sallie. She has a pronounced Boston accent and is on the larger side. The type to accessorize with scarves and brooches to distract from her fat.

Babs thinks brooches are stupid. Real jewelry should hit the bare skin. Necklaces, bracelets, rings. Babs would even prefer a navel-piercing to a brooch.

I shake Babs out of my head, remembering that even though Sallie might not be at the apex of fashion, she is still making an effort, and, more important, she's always been nice to me the few times I have been in the dean's office. She never forgets anyone's name.

She looks up from her newspaper. Sees me waiting to get her attention.

"Bettina, I'm so sorry. You'll be missed." No one else has said this to me. I am grateful. Even if she might not really mean it.

"Sallie, thank you," I say. Then I explain the reason for my visit. "I need to use the phone to make travel plans home."

"Sure," she says. "It's right over there. I'm about to go on break, so please remember to keep your calls as brief as possible."

The phone is silver and has real buttons to push. I reach in my wallet and pull out my American Airlines frequent-flier card and a platinum AmEx. Babs gave me the card for emergencies, she said, but mostly so I could buy her expensive clothes in the south of France.

I dial American Airlines. I am placed on hold, and I see Sallie get up from her chair. She discreetly waves at me. Heads out for her coffee break.

I wait for about ten minutes before a female voice answers. She helps me book a three P.M. flight, Boston to Chicago. It is terrifically expensive, but so is an aborted year at Cardiss. I then call the cab company and tell them to get me at twelve thirty. I am leaving the same way I came: with a small bag and no parents.

Sallie is still not back. I have made my calls, but I'm disinclined to leave. Something keeps me there. After about two minutes, I grab the receiver and dial 411. I am not really ready for this but I do it anyway. I don't know why I have waited so long; maybe because still, after all these years, I have no real plan.

I get the operator and say, "The number for the Ryder

School, please. Concord, New Hampshire." As Cape told me, my father's alma mater.

She spends a minute looking, then spits out seven numbers. Ryder is in the same area code as Cardiss.

I hang up. Stare at the phone number. Need to act, one way or another. Sallie will be back from her break in about five minutes. To dial the number has the impulsive feel of calling a boy you're not sure likes you. Not to seems like throwing away a good book you haven't read. Maybe Ryder doesn't have records of Latin prizes. It's just a call, after all. I'm not committing to anything.

I dial. Ask for the Latin Department. A chummy-sounding male voice with an English accent answers the phone.

"Hello?"

"Um, my name is Meredith and I'm a student at Cardiss. I found a silver medallion at a tag sale the other day. The front has Ryder's emblem, and the back has 'Latin Composition One, 1958.' It seemed like it might be important to the winner and so I hoped you could tell me who it belongs to so I could return it. If it's not too much trouble."

"Trouble? Not at all. I have all of the winners for the past seventy-five years painted on two wooden tablets hanging on my wall. What year did you say it was? Okay, just a second."

Just a second? This is going way too fast. Should I hang up?

"Here it is," says Latin Scholar.

"Wait." I stall. "Is it a hard prize to win? I mean, there can't be that many students taking Latin. Not that many contestants."

"Oh, yes, you're right. But some years we don't give it out because the work isn't outstanding enough."

"Does it always go to a senior?"

"Usually, yes."

"Do most students study Latin before they get to Ryder, or do they pick it up while they are there?"

"We have both." Latin Scholar is beginning to tire of this conversation. Finds my questions strange. Why all the interest if I just want to send back a medallion to an alum?

"Do you want the name or not? I don't have his address but you can check with the alumni office for that."

"Yes," I say. "Please." I'm not quite ready yet. But I won't ever be.

He tells me.

"Thank you," I say slowly, and then quickly hang up the phone. I am sure he says, "You're welcome," but I don't want to hear it.

Part III

35

The Matchbook Book

BABS AND I SIT in the dining room of the aparthouse. We're having dinner or, more accurately, smoking and not eating. Despite my trepidation about returning home, Babs has been surprisingly nice. She doesn't apologize or explain her departure from campus, but she's called Miss Porter's and they will gladly take me in January.

I don't tell her that I know who my father is. I'm afraid of her reaction. She did give me the medallion after all, an easy way to find out, but maybe she thought I would never follow up. In any case, I don't want to do anything that might upset our relationship. She seems to have new respect for me. Because I have finally had sex? Because at my age, I'm so little work? But neither of these things promises any continuous stability between us. So I keep my discovery a secret.

I wonder what I'm going to do in the meantime. Get a job? I won't be sixteen until March. Hang about the aparthouse and chitchat with Lily and Franklin? Something will come along, I tell myself, and until it does, I will just enjoy the company of what appears to be a new, subdued Babs.

That night, Babs provides me with a project. After Lily serves our coffee, straight black in demitasse cups, Babs takes a sip, lights up another cigarette, and begins to talk in an upbeat voice.

"Bettina, now that you're home, I have an idea of something we can work on together. I am fucking sick of Tally's success with all of these inane books she cranks out. I know I could do better with a book of my own."

Tally is still writing her Diary of an Heiress series but has also branched out in her subject matter. She has ventured into self-help. Her latest book, *The Libido Effect*, argues that if readers channel their sexual energy into pursuits outside the bedroom—office work, exercise, or even tennis—they'll have enormous success. Tally gets invited on talk shows and even leads retreats. Even though Babs is famous in Chicago, she's never been on TV. I know this pisses her off.

"What did you have in mind, Babs?" I ask. I imagine the worst. A sexual handbook with a chapter devoted to each of her top ten fucks. She would write about how every man had different needs. List the activities she performed for each, perhaps in menu format. There would most likely be an exhaustive section on masturbating.

She continues. "I know people are curious about my life as a chocolate heiress. Rather than write a memoir, which is passé, I thought I would show the reader all of the places I have been. With matchbooks instead of pictures. I will annotate them, and they will give my readers a detailed account of not only how I live, but also how rich people in general live."

Babs doesn't really think that memoirs are passé. She just doesn't have the sustained attention required to write one. I encourage her nonetheless. It sounds like she might even sell a few copies. No real plot or conflict, but interesting just the same.

"Great idea, Babs. You could have it published in a scrapbook format, which is rarely done, and call it *The Matchbook Book*. Instead of a paperback with regular pages, each book would be laid out in a leather scrapbook with facsimiles of each matchbook. The readers would feel like friends of yours, reminiscing with you about the restaurants and clubs they have also been to. And there are would-be fans who are eager for a thrilling peek inside the daily life of a chocolate heiress."

"Brilliant. I love it!"

I am fairly sure that some publisher like Rizzoli would take it on, or maybe Babs will decide to publish herself. But I know deep down she couldn't give a fuck if anyone buys it. She could throw a huge party and give the books away as favors, if it came to that. She's just badly in need of a project.

"What I want you to do, Bettina," she continues, "is to put all the matches in chronological order. I've written the dates in the inside cover of each matchbook so you know what follows what."

I can do this, I think. Maybe I'll even get credit as a coauthor. Babs and I haven't worked on something together since the Hangover-Brunch Cruise Party. And this time I will have real responsibility. There's the possibility that Babs really is different now that I am older. Unlike when I planned my dance number, I know I can do a good job. Finally please her after all this time.

Babs pushes her chair away from the table and walks up the spiral staircase to her room. I follow as if these stairs are just like any other. We go into her shoe closet. It isn't a closet, per se, more of a room with at least three hundred shoes. Organized by color in specialized racks. It looks like the shoe department at Saks, only with more offerings and all in Babs's size.

She reaches in the back of the closet and pulls out three shopping bags full of matchbooks. There must be at least two thousand matchbooks total. She hands them to me.

"This should keep you busy. I know it's a lot of work, but you have nothing else to do. Nothing cures boredom like a good challenge. And I so appreciate it, my darling girl."

I float on her praise as I lug the bags back to my room. Then reality hits.

This project could take me until January. Despite what Babs has said about us working on this together, it won't be true. Just me alone in my room trying to make sense of this mess. Another room thrash, just not as messy and more prolonged. I will have to stay up late, make order from chaos. No mother-daughter bonding after all.

I put the matchbooks on the floor by my desk. I pull one out, Maxim's, and open the cover. *September 1976* in Babs's handwriting, just as she said. None of the matches inside are missing, since she uses lighters for her cigarettes. She always says that only tacky people use matches to light cigarettes; they make cigarettes taste bitter and remind her of gas stations. Matches are only good as souvenirs.

The bars and restaurants on the matches might be different, but the story is always the same. Babs absent from the apart-house, wearing fancy clothes, drinking fancy water, talking in her invented vocabulary. Absent from me.

I have no clue how to start this project. Should I dump them all out on the floor? Pull them individually from the bags and sort them as I go? I finally decide I will sort them by years and then continue from there. This plan seems clever to me, and I work until I can no longer keep my eyes open. Fall asleep, four A.M.

I wake up at noon the next day. I have made a lot of progress and can't wait to tell Babs. I go down to the kitchen. She is up, wearing a waffle robe from Raffles in Singapore and talking on the phone. Tally? Some friend I don't know? I pause in the doorway before she can see me, and listen.

"Yes, the kid is home and will be until after Christmas. Porter's is taking her, no surprise there. It will probably cost me another building."

Pause.

"Of course she's bright, but getting caught having sex at her age is just fucking stupid. Whole thing probably took three minutes. Cost three years at Cardiss."

Pause.

"Yep. You heard right. Mack's son."

Pause.

"Best part for me: Mags was beside herself. Can you believe that bitch still won't let it go? But I did the ladylike thing and said nothing. Or almost nothing. I even played the good mother and offered them some dough to let her stay. I knew Cardiss was too fucking earnest to take that bait, and it probably forced them to kick her out. They couldn't be seen taking a bribe. But I know it horrified Mags."

Pause.

"No, the last thing Bettina needs is therapy. You have to be interesting to go a shrink, otherwise you'll bore the shit out of him."

Pause.

"Just organizing stuff for me. But I'm sure she is going to fuck that up too. I already hired an assistant to start after Christmas. I just needed to get her out of my hair."

Pause.

"Sorry to bore you with all this. No, I'm not going to talk to her about it. I feel how I feel and that's it. I will just do my

best nicey-nicey and soon she'll be off to Porter's. Slim chance
of her getting busted for sex, unless she tries the whole lesbo
thing. Even then, not sure this is against the rules."

Pause.

"Bye. I'll be in touch, darling." She hangs up.

I back out of the doorway before Babs can see me. Walk
upstairs to my room, reeling. Two scenarios about the project. One: Babs has played me. She's punishing me for getting
kicked out. For proving that, for once, the chocolate money
can't buy her whatever she wants. She doesn't really expect
me to do anything useful with the matches, just waste my
time. She's already planning on hiring an assistant to do it all
over, erase all traces of me. Babs will be nice because she likes
watching me trust her and enjoy what I think she's giving me.

Two: She really is happy to have me home. Wants to work
on the project together. What she says on the phone is just
how she talks to people. She can't admit to anyone, even herself, that I have finally won her over.

I want scenario two, of course. But her conversation went
on so long. Needs to get me out of her hair. Do the whole
lesbo thing. Offering Cardiss money not to save my ass, but to
piss off Mags.

The real question is, why I am giving myself options? Why
am I still bothering with this fucking book?

I gather up all the matches that are strewn about my bedroom floor. Put them back in the shopping bags. I change out
of my pajamas and leave the aparthouse. Go see a movie at
Water Tower Place. Sit in the dark and eat a bucket of popcorn
and drink a large Diet Coke. I don't really watch the movie,
just think until I have a plan. One that will test which is more
important to Babs, the matches or me. I think I know the
answer. I imagine my father's reaction to all this. If Babs tells

me to leave once and for all, at least I will have somewhere else to go.

I succeed in avoiding Babs the rest of the day. That night she goes out to dinner. I eat meat loaf with Lily in the kitchen. Excuse myself early, saying I am still tired from the night before.

I go to sleep. Set my alarm for three; Babs will be home and asleep by then. She's not fucking anyone at the moment. When the buzzer goes off, I gather up the bags of matches and go downstairs. I stop in the living room. I like the darkness: it enables me to see the cars speeding down Lake Shore Drive, with their bright headlights and their definite places to go. I also like the dark waves of Lake Michigan that crash on Oak Street Beach. A machine working overtime, since there are no people sitting in the sand watching me.

I walk around to the terrace of the aparthouse. Babs once told me she fucked lots of men there, but unlike Mack, they were not bed worthy, and she never invited them to stay over, sully her sheets. Across the way, the John Hancock Building is dark. People have left their offices, and in the apartments on the upper floors, everyone has gone to sleep.

I walk to the railing and stand there. I think about the medallion she gave me, the tutorials about sex, the package she sent to Cardiss. Gestures that seem to me like Trying. Maybe she just doesn't know any better. But at this moment, this is no longer enough. I know I have to act quickly or I will lose my resolve, get swept up in the fantasy of a Babs who is doing the best she can. I love her, after all. But, finally, I realize I want to be loved back.

I slowly reach for the first bag and dump it out into the nighttime air. My pouring is tentative and slow. With the next two bags, I gain momentum, throwing the matches over the railing like they are heavy buckets of water. I watch as the wind catches them, and they slowly float down, making patterns in the sky before landing in the street. Like the Splushes I discarded when I was a child, the matches are gone forever. Unlike the solid pebbles of chocolate, they will have a more graceful landing, float to the sidewalk like butterflies.

But no matter. I have taken what Babs probably sees as her life's work and scattered it about the street. Thrown it away forever. There will always be more Splushes, but the matchbooks are irreplaceable.

I leave the empty shopping bags on the terrace and go upstairs to bed. I don't bother to tiptoe up the steps; I let them creak under my weight. At that moment, I feel no remorse. I don't need to get in my bathtub and chase the smash to alleviate my anxiety. I get into my PJs, crawl under my covers, and sleep soundly.

36

Goodbye, Babs

I WAKE UP AROUND NINE and go downstairs for breakfast still wearing my PJs. I see the three shopping bags that
once contained the matches sitting in the back hall. Lily must
have found them outside and decided to keep them since Babs
likes to save such sturdy bags to pack odds and ends for the
country.

I greet Lily in the kitchen and eat the omelet, fresh-squeezed
orange juice, and black coffee she has made for me. Normally,
I just push the eggs around on my plate since they have so
many calories, but now I don't care. I know Babs won't be up
for a couple of hours, so I get dressed and go for a walk on Oak
Street Beach. Given how cold it is, there's no one else there.

I take off my shoes, stand in the lake. It feels like liquid ice,
but I make myself stay there. I begin to think about how Babs
will react to the matchbooks that I have jettisoned from the
perch of the aparthouse. It's a very different equation during
the day. Part of me doesn't care. Part of me is incredulous that

I have betrayed her in such a way. I know our relationship will forever be altered. But I feel liberated, standing in the cold water, knowing how much I've changed.

Babs is in the kitchen when I get back.

"Hey, Bettina," she says cheerily. "How's the project coming?"

"It's not," I say flatly, not really wanting to give up the friendly greeting she has given me with a curt reply, but there's no turning back.

"What do you mean, 'It's not'? Is it too fucking difficult for you to sort matches? I guess I can hire someone who's more competent than you." Once again, there will be no sustained kindness. Babs is always right. Doesn't do conflict.

"Haven't you already got someone else lined up to work on this project?" I challenge.

"Actually, yes. I had a feeling this would happen so I have an assistant starting in January. But I wanted to give you a chance."

So she was telling the truth during the phone call after all.

"Well, Babs, you needn't have bothered." For the first time, I'm not afraid of what she's going to say. I've had enough.

"What do you mean?" she asks. I'm surprised to have caught her off-guard for once.

"I decided the whole project was stupid. I threw out the matches." I try to emulate a Babs voice, dismissive and authoritative, but I can't quite pull it off.

"Well, you can just get them back," she says, probably thinking they are in a garbage can somewhere. She is getting impatient and annoyed.

"No, I can't."

"Fuck, Bettina, where are they?" She acts like she is simply trying to get an answer from me and is indifferent to the ultimate outcome, since she knows she has the power to fix anything. But the tremor in her right hand gives her away. Things are not going as she expected, and she is pissed.

"I threw them over the balcony. They're scattered about the Gold Coast."

"That was stupid, Bettina. Stupid." As if this is some kind of preamble. Her hand is still shaking. I am waiting for her to smack me, resume combat. But she does nothing.

"Just go away," she says, quietly but evenly. "I don't want to look at you."

She turns on her heel and leaves it at that. This is much worse than her yelling or hitting me. That would mean I count in her life. But somehow I know she has abandoned the mother role once and for all and will never come back.

"I'm going up for a bit of a nap," she says over her shoulder to Lily and leaves the kitchen without another word.

This is not typical for Babs. She may sleep late, but she eschews naps. She thinks they are for people who are Letting Themselves Go.

I now understand that what I did is devastating to her, because she seems to be so emptied out by it. But I would do it again, just the same.

One week after I throw the matchbooks away, Babs is crossing Michigan Avenue. She has her head down, lighting a cigarette, and isn't paying attention when the light changes. She is mowed down by a brown Toyota with dents in the sides. I know this would have horrified her—she would have preferred to be hit by a car that rich people drive: perhaps a British racing green Jaguar with biscuit interiors. In any case, the Toyota is just as powerful and sends her flying. When she lands, her beautiful legs are broken, and her head smashes on the pavement like a carton of eggs. It was Franklin's day off, and she was walking to Zodiac for a blow dry.

There's no need for an ambulance, since she is so obviously dead, but the police come to make the final report. The driver of the Toyota is a young girl with bad acne. She is crying, trying to explain.

The police search the body that a few hours ago was Babs and find her wallet in her pocket. This is unusual because she rarely carried one, but perhaps without the matches, she felt insecure, as if she needed ID to prove who she was. The police show up at the aparthouse about an hour after the accident. Babs is moved to a morgue and they want me to go identify the body.

I am absolutely undone that I am asked to go see my mother's dismembered body, but I don't cry. Yet. I just sit with the horrifying thought that maybe she ignored the light change on purpose.

Lily's still there when I get home. She hugs me, crying. "Sugar," she says, "you know your mama loved you." I hug her back but am still too numb to cry. I can't figure out if Babs's dying is the best or worst thing that has ever happened to me.

I sit with Lily a bit and then tell her to go home. I want to spend the night in the aparthouse by myself. I am fifteen, but it will be the first time I have ever done so.

I go to my room, and the air feels light, like all the times Babs left the aparthouse on trips. But the whole space now seems different. The bunny-fur rug and canopy bed seem decadent, yet wonderful. Babs did have real imagination, I think, unlike me, who relies on books for alternative realities. I lie down on my rug, rub my cheeks against its softness.

I get up, walk down the hall to Babs's room. There will be no more staircase sex, no yells from behind her closed door, no more blowjob tutorials. I suddenly feel grateful to Babs for giving me all this information, sorry for all the kids, like Cape, who had to figure things out on their own.

I go into her shoe closet. Up above the shoes, on a high shelf, are boxes that contain artifacts from Babs's parties. I spot the one labeled HANGOVER-BRUNCH CRUISE PARTY and open the stepladder that is folded in the back of the closet. I sit on the floor and open the box, pulling out all the highlights of the evening. There is the DRINK UP, THROW UP, SHOW UP shot glass, the Lucite wave cube with the drowning swimmers, the tiny bottles of rum and vodka, and the luggage tags. I line them up carefully on the rug. Then there is my costume. My bikini with the blue sequined *Bs* looks so small I can't believe I ever wore it. Next, I find my *A Chorus Line* cassette. No matter that it caused such a disaster; Babs kept everything that had to do with her parties, the way other mothers might hoard report cards and letters from camp.

At the bottom of the box is her white bathing suit, captain's hat, and blue stilettos. I think about the makeup she wore that night, the sparkly blue eye shadow, the gashes of rouge. I am strangely sad not to find the makeup in the box. This was the best part of the evening for me: watching Jasper put it on Babs while Frances and I sat on the floor. Babs looked so beautiful when they were done, more so than anyone else at the whole party. And then it was all ruined because she was so worried Mack wouldn't come. She might have smacked me, but maybe it was because she was angry at Mack. And the bleeding had nothing to do with Babs, it really didn't. I was the one who was stupid enough to fall down the stairs.

The day's ending and no one has called to offer condolences, see if there is anything to do. I know it is early, and people probably still don't know. But I take inventory and wonder who would call: Who would want to assume the role of the weepy best friend? Or even be in the inner circle, someone who brings lasagna and helps me write the obit. All this makes me sad for Babs. Despite all the chocolate money, she had no real friends. But even though I don't have any either, I still have one person to call. Lucas.

He is probably the only one who will care that Babs is dead. He answers on the fifth ring. This is the first time I have ever called him, and I don't quite know what he will say, hearing from me out of the blue. But he has always been nice to me, even if it's in a haphazard and distracted way. Despite everything, he's her cousin, after all. I will tell him this news, and then let him take the lead, see where it goes.

"Lucas," I say without preamble, "Babs is dead."

There is a pause on the line, then:

"Bettina? Jesus, what happened?"

"She was hit by a car crossing Michigan Avenue. This morning."

"Oh, fuck. Are you okay?"

"Yes," I say succinctly, the way I think a grownup would. Then I start to cry. I want to tell him everything. Getting kicked out of Cardiss. The matches. How it was really all my fault.

"I think it was my fault, Lucas. I messed up . . ."

"No, Bettina. No more than anyone else."

"But I slept with a boy, got kicked out of Cardiss . . ."

"I know. She told me on the phone."

So that was him on the other end of the conversation that day. I am disappointed that it seems he did nothing to stick up for me. But now that Babs is gone, maybe things can be different.

He lets me cry a bit, then says, "Do you want me to come out and help you with her affairs?"

I pretend to consider it, even though of course I want him to.

"Yes." Then I remember my manners, and though the situation might not quite merit it, I say, "Thank you."

I do need him to be here. Even though I'm her only daughter, I can't help but think he knows her better than I do.

"I'll be there in the morning," he says. "Will you be all right until then?"

I nod, but then remember he can't hear that.

"Yes," I say. "I'll see you then. Thank you again, Lucas."

We hang up. If he will be here in the morning, I realize, he'll be taking a plane, and I remember how much he hates to fly. This is a good sign. If he stretches himself for Babs, he might just stretch himself for me.

That night, I decide to sleep in Babs's room. I wear the Raffles robe she had on the morning I told her I had thrown away her matchbooks. I can hardly let myself think it, but these things are no longer Babs's. Everything in the apartment belongs to me now.

I put my father's medallion in the pocket of the robe. I know it is finally time to tell him. Soon, I think. There will be no repercussions from Babs, and the worst that can happen is he will reject me. That's a big worst, but better to know once and for all. If he does not accept me as his daughter, I can bury the idea of him with Babs, lose both my parents at the same time, just like Babs did. If she survived this fate, so can I.

I pull up the peach satin bedspread and settle into the crisp ironed sheets that have *Babs* sewn on them. I feel both cocooned and lonely. I know Babs's response to this would be *You're on your own, kid,* and there would be no challenging her. After all, for the first time, I really, really am.

Lucas arrives the next day. I'm already awake and dressed, wearing the black shift I bought in Cardiss from Wow! and a gold cuff from Babs's jewelry drawer. I don't really want to wear this dress, since it's the one I got kicked out in, but I have nothing else that is black. It seems obscene to go shopping the day after your mother dies. I know Babs would have no qualms about hitting Saks were the situation reversed, *Life fucking goes on,* but I still have my own set of fairly conventional rules. Maybe someday I will adopt Babs's, but not yet.

Lucas is also dressed in black: black suit with a black tie. I know these are only worn at funerals, and realize he has been through this before. He has most likely been to a lot of these, has known many people who have died. Unlike me, this isn't his first round with death. Thank God.

The only thing that is off about his outfit is that he is wearing paint-splattered Converse sneakers. I know they must be different ones than he wore at the Hangover-Brunch Cruise Party, and so must be his signature footwear. I imagine that they are important because they represent the paradox that is his life: the paint marks him as an artist, marginalized from his class, but at the same time, thanks to the chocolate money, they show that he is able to wear whatever he wants, even when dealing with his cousin's death.

He gives me a big hug and kisses me on my hairline. Then he stands back, assessing.

"Bettina, my girl, you've grown up so much since the party."

Yes, I think. *Too bad you weren't here to see it.*

We are due to meet with Babs's lawyers at two, an hour from now. I'm not sure what we are supposed to do until then. I am not up for a deep talk about endings and new beginnings. I suggest we go out on the back terrace, maybe talk about his work, his family in New York.

"Do you mind if I have a drink?" Lucas asks me.

"What would you like?" I say, disappointed that he needs one to interact with me.

"Whiskey, no ice."

I pour one for him, wonder what Babs would say. Is he not *fearless,* or does this day mark an exception to the rule?

I grab a Diet Coke, and we go to the terrace, the place where I threw out the matchbooks. I still want someone to absolve me, tell me it was not my fault. But Lucas doesn't know about these things, and I might not ever tell him. He might think I have been a *defiant brat* all along.

He asks me, "Did you ever see the paintings I sent Babs?"

"Yes, she hung them in the playroom. I used to look at them a lot."

"What did you think?"

"I didn't really understand why they were so gray, what you wanted to get across."

"I usually do more realistic paintings, but Babs said she wanted abstract. I rarely got to see her or you, and I wanted to have a place in the aparthouse, to remind you both I was out there. Even if it was only in New York."

I want to tell him he succeeded, but still I am disappointed he didn't do more. He must have intuited what Babs was like as a mother. Why didn't we see more of him? Did he really hate to fly or was that just an excuse?

Lucas nurses his whiskey. I can't quite handle his apologies. As difficult as she was, Babs was always in my landscape, somewhere. I excuse myself and go to the kitchen to fix a Babs drink. I pour Perrier in a wine goblet and cut it with fresh orange juice. I smoke two of Babs's Duchess Golden Lights, which are sitting in a silver cup by the phone. There is an Imari plate next to it that she used as an ashtray. I have not tried one of her cigarettes since the ankle burn, but smoking them makes me feel closer to her. I can't believe she will never smoke again.

I walk to the pantry where she has hung all of our Christmas Cards. I know the backstory to each one, of course, but in the final proofs, we look happy, united. There seems to be no diluting our duo, the way my father might if he were on the scene. Maybe Babs knew this and really wanted me all to herself. She didn't do groups. She had only one best friend, one lover at a time, and when they were gone, she always had me.

It is now almost one thirty and I go get Lucas. I remind him we have to go to the lawyers.

"Okay. More time for talking later. Let's just pull things together and get through with it. This'll be tougher than you think. When my father died and left me all his chocolate money, that's when it really hit me he was gone. Money should make you happy, of course, especially when you get as much dough as I did, but you never forget how you got it."

Babs did not seem to have this problem, I want to say, but I don't. Lucas stands, leaving his glass, ready to go.

Franklin is downstairs in the garage waiting, and we get into the stretcher. I'm amazed to sense that there are still some Babs particles in our car and I don't want to disturb them. I smell her perfume and see a pack of Duchess Golden Lights tucked in the door. I decide to light up, wave the cigarette during the pauses that come between my inhales, creating a kind of Babs incense.

Lucas and I sit there. He grabs my hand and holds it, marking a place where we should have so much to say. I want to enjoy it, but I still don't really trust him. He seems to be trying for a connection with me, but I can't forget the smack, the bleeding, and his ultimate resolution to the crisis: *Let's go dance to the Duch and pour pink champagne over people* . . . Maybe he's just a watered-down version of Babs: a Ballentyne after all.

We arrive at Harris and Grasser, take the elevator to the thirty-third floor. There's a female attorney waiting for us in the conference room. She reminds me of Wendolyn Henderson, my homeroom teacher at Chicago Day. She is fat and wearing a black suit and a red silk shirt that does little to cover up the rolls of her belly. She has on black shiny pumps and pantyhose that are just a shade too tan. The pumps don't show off muscles in her calves, just accentuate her puffy knees. I know Babs would be horrified that such a woman will be executing her last will and testament.

The lawyer's name is Constance, and she takes out a folder crammed with papers. Lucas is nervously tapping his foot, and, like Babs would, I wish I could smoke. Constance stands, begins to read from one of the papers.

"'I, Tabitha Ballentyne, declare this to be my last will and testament. In the case of my death, I do not wish to be buried, but wish to have my ashes scattered in Lake Michigan.'"

This seems completely out of character for Babs. There will be no party, no pomp and circumstance to mark her farewell. Even though no one has yet called to offer condolences, I know they all would come to the aparthouse to celebrate her life. Then I remember her standards: a theme, elaborate invitations, good music, and lots of booze. She probably thought I could not pull such a party off; that for all my efforts, I would embarrass her.

Constance continues. "'As for all my possessions, I leave them to my daughter, Bettina Ballentyne, to be held in trust until she is twenty-one. I name my cousin Lucas Ballentyne as trustee, and he will be paid a fee to execute his duties. Bettina will have the right to draw on her trust to pay for her living expenses as Mr. Ballentyne deems appropriate. I estimate she will receive three hundred million after taxes, in addition to my apartment and all my possessions. If she decides to sell these, the proceeds will also be held in trust to be managed by Mr. Ballentyne until she is twenty-one.'"

"Signed, Tabitha Ballentyne."

Lucas and I sit there silently, taking it all in.

I know I should be thrilled, but somehow I'm not. What

the hell am I going to do with all this money? It seems very scary. I'm no longer just a girl who lives in an aparthouse with a chocolate-heiress mother who is often mean but, in the end, never boring. Away from her, I could nearly pass as normal. But Babs had no choice. Almost everyone in Chicago knew about the chocolate money. She had to play the part: buy jewels, have parties, go speed shopping. It was just expected, whether she wanted to do these things or not. No wonder she came unhinged.

Now that I was the *fucking chocolate heiress,* would I have to do the same?

Three days later, Lucas and I walk to the edge of Oak Street Beach. The lake's small waves lap at the shore, instead of crashing into it. It's dark. We didn't want to have to explain to anyone what we were doing, so we chose this time. Lucas carries the red polka-dot tin box that holds Babs's remains. I find it bizarre that Babs would want her ashes scattered here, since she never came to this beach, considered it middle class. Why not the Côte d'Azur? Portofino? But since she's dead, I guess it doesn't really matter. Maybe she was afraid she would end up sitting on the mantel of the aparthouse until I could execute such a trip.

Lucas takes off the top of the canister. Among the ashes, there are tiny chips of bones, pieces of her arms, legs, skull. Lucas slips his hand into the ash and sifts it through his fingers, fishing for the bones as if they are seashells.

"Bettina," he says, "do you want to throw Babs in the water?

I can't quite believe the woman who ripped up my Brooke Shields cocktail napkin and made me clean up the mess naked is now just a pile of ashes that we call Babs. I take the box from Lucas's hand and say, "Yes.

"Should we say something?" I ask.

Lucas thinks a moment, and then says, "Here's to Babs, who had the best of times always . . ."

I'm disappointed by this. Seems to indicate that Lucas doesn't really understand what life in the aparthouse was really like.

I want to add something but can't think of anything to say with Lucas there.

It seems too intimate to hurl insults at Babs in front of a man I barely know.

Instead, I just toss the ashes, watching as they arc into the lake. It takes a few throws before the tin is empty and she's finally gone.

Lucas puts his arms around my neck for a hug. A real one that lasts longer than five seconds.

"Let's go back, sweetheart. It's getting cold." We are bundled in sweaters and jeans, but they are no longer adequate against the chill. I start to cry again when he calls me sweetheart. It seems deliberate, directed specifically at me, not a generic moniker that's less intimate than my name.

"You can tell me everything back at the aparthouse. I'm not going anywhere. Actually, I'm taking you with me."

I will. Tell him everything. It's about time somebody, some other person besides Babs and me, knew.

We go back to the aparthouse and Lucas says he'll cook dinner.

"I'm not much in the kitchen, but I can always manage pasta."

I'm not really hungry, still really spent from the day, but go along with him anyway, showing him where the pots are and setting the table. When all is ready, we sit across from each other. Given the circumstances, the air in the aparthouse is not light enough to carry small talk, and we eat for a while in silence, as if we're on an awkward date.

I use the time to look at him closely. With his blond curly

hair and brown eyes, he looks nothing like Babs, or even Mack. His hands are large and he doesn't have delicate fingers. I can easily imagine him holding big paintbrushes, pulling swaths of color across his canvases. When he reaches for his glass, I notice he is left-handed, like me. He's handsome, but not in an obvious way. You would have to get to know him to see this. But because I, too, am understated, easily overlooked, I understand his looks at once.

We continue to eat, and as nice as it is in many ways to not be alone, to have a grownup on my side for once, I start to feel angry. Why do I get his help only at the end? He might think this is when I most need it, but of course it really isn't. Why didn't he come more than that one time and stand up more forcefully to Babs over the years? If she told him not to, couldn't he at least have come up to Cardiss with Poppy and taken me out to lunch? Is that too much to ask? It would have promised nothing but given me so much.

Finally, emboldened by these thoughts, I decide to talk to him about the One Big Thing. I don't know if Babs told him or not, but I have to know the specifics. All of them. I pick up my wineglass and take a sip before proceeding. Lucas seems lost in his pasta, but fuck it, I think. Why should I give him time to check his fly, smooth down his hair, and get ready?

"Lucas." I look at him intently and say in a low voice, "I know."

He stops chewing and meets my eye. Stares. At least he doesn't insult my intelligence and respond, *Know what?*

Instead, he says, "Did Babs tell you?"

"No, not really. She gave me your Latin medallion from Ryder and I didn't follow through on the information on it until I was leaving Cardiss. I was afraid to know. I also didn't want to piss Babs off. I always thought she gave it to me as a dare."

Lucas's face is slack, taking it all in. At last he says, "We always promised we would keep it a secret. Of course, the whole thing was an accident. I had had too much to drink, and you know Babs liked to push the envelope. When she told me, I never thought she would have you. The whole thing was just so indecent. In addition to our being cousins, I was married to Poppy with JoJo on the way.

"I thought she would take care of it, figured she did not want children yet. But she was furious at me and not only had you but had her tubes tied, so you would be the only one. We would always be linked by this, and her lack of fertility would be all my fault. Not that I thought she especially wanted more kids."

"So you wanted Babs to get rid of me?" I want to hear him say it again, not sure he realizes the implications for me sitting across the table for him.

"Well . . . at first, of course. But once you were born . . ."

"You loved me as your own and were upset Babs wouldn't let you see me."

"Well . . . no, not exactly, but I did think about you a lot and wonder how you were doing with Babs."

"Gee, thanks. Did you tell Poppy? Does she know? Especially since I will be coming to live with you?"

"No. Look, Bettina, it's complicated."

"Oh, right. For me or you? Look, I don't expect some kind of weepy reunion between us. I don't really even want an apology. Babs certainly never told me to expect those. I'm not sure what the fuck I want. Don't worry, I'm not going to call you Daddy. I'm not going to tell anyone. Just don't feel sorry for me. Maybe someday you will get to know me and regret it, but if not, I don't really care."

Lucas tries to reach out and take my hand. I pull away and stand up. I throw my napkin down on the table and tell Lucas,

"Maybe you could do the dishes. That would be just great."

I go back up to Babs's room, where I decide to spend my last night at the aparthouse before leaving for New York the next morning. My whole body is shaking. I didn't really mean most of what I said to Lucas, but his opening gave me no choice. I am through with begging, trying to prove to someone that I am worthy of love. I will just go to live with him in New York, put that idea away, and pretend I am an orphan with a dead mother and a lot of money.

I change into one of Babs's nightgowns, put on her Raffles robe, crawl into bed, and fall asleep quickly. All the emotions of the evening have drained me, left me spent.

Later that night, I feel a soft touch on my shoulder. I slowly open my eyes: Lucas. He leans down and kisses my cheek. I can't help it; I start to cry. Hard. He tries to catch my tears with his hands. We say nothing, and after about ten minutes, he leaves.

Poppy fusses over me when I get to New York. She's constantly hugging me and always gets up to make breakfast for JoJo and me. She takes me to Saks to round out my wardrobe and never once comments on my body.

I find her gestures somewhat earnest and naive, as if she thinks I cannot do such things on my own. But I know she is trying to accommodate my arrival in her life. Thankfully, she says nothing about my smoking. She must think it is my way of grieving, my way of staying connected to Babs. I don't disabuse her of this idea, even though my smoking is not symbolic; it no longer has anything to do with anyone but me.

I go to Brearley, then Williams. I make friends, but they are always the quiet, bookish type that Meredith would have made fun of. Despite her ebullience when I got kicked out, I still miss her. Even though I have a clean slate to reinvent myself at these prestigious schools, I never manage to transform myself into the bitchy blond girl who people fight to be friends with, who makes her own rules, no matter how mutable they are. I ask myself *What would Meredith do?* when confronted with difficult situations, but I can never bring myself to execute the solutions I come up with. Meredith's is a petty form of power, I know, but I still aspire to have it. I even have the absurd notion that someday she will seek me out. Maybe she even included a tiny picture of me on her senior yearbook page. I know this is an idea I have made up, so I never allow myself to check.

My biggest regret, however, is Cape. I look for him among the boys at Williams. Many of them resemble him, and I often catch my breath as they pass. I always tell myself that I stumbled on him once, so why not twice? But of course, he's not there.

37

Adults, Past and Present

SEPTEMBER 1991

I'M NOW TWENTY-SIX AND still live in New York. The chocolate money is at last mine outright. I buy myself a two-bedroom prewar on East Seventy-second Street, with two fireplaces, built-in bookcases, and a walk-in closet. I have it professionally decorated. The colors I pick are muted, and despite the cost, the result is subdued, not ostentatious. I anonymously give $200,000 to Cardiss to endow a prize for a student who produces the most fearless writing. Despite the fact that I was kicked out, any anger I had has transformed itself into sentimentality and a reverence for the kind of things they teach there.

The truth is that spending the chocolate money scares me. I want to have a normal life, if such a thing exists. I don't want to join the tribe of the smug few who do nothing but shop and party. Of course, in New York, unlike Chicago, fortunes don't seem to be such a big deal. I see the last names of kids from Cardiss plastered on important monuments: Rockefeller Center, the Frick Collection, the Sackler Wing at the Met; even on such everyday products as Heinz ketchup. Somehow, I never noticed that there were other people at Cardiss besides me who had the same kind of money. I have the idea of starting a support group with them in order to figure out how these kids handle their money. But deep down, I know that being rich does not count as a real problem, just a neurosis some people have, and I abandon the project.

I work at a literary journal, *Blue Sea Press,* and make sixteen thousand dollars a year. I get this job based solely on my college GPA and major in English lit. I've never worked before and have no references. I want to "pass," so I accept my meager paychecks, act like they are the only thing getting me through the month. The truth is that sometimes I leave them in pockets or at the bottom of my backpack and don't even bother to look for them. I always wear ripped jeans or clothes from thrift stores. I also have Converse sneakers, like Lucas. These are perfect, as they seem to belie the possibility that I have ever had any exposure to real fashion.

One day on my lunch break, I'm walking down Madison Avenue, peering in the store windows. I never go in, but the dresses on the mannequins remind me of Babs. I take note of the dresses she would buy and the ones she would hate. This is my way to feel that she's not gone for good, merely on an extended trip somewhere. I know she would tell me to *Go the fuck inside* and buy some real clothes. That my downtrodden outfits are *a goddamn embarrassment.* But I know no one would wait on me, the way I am dressed, and this protects me from any temptation I have to emulate her, and allows me to hold on to the idea that I am now my own person. Can dress however I want.

I'm absorbed in my activity when someone calls my name. I hesitate before turning around. Is it a writer who has been rejected from *Blue Sea Press*? A boy from Williams who would force me to make awkward conversation? I still have not really mastered small talk with people my age.

I do a slow about-face. Now that Babs is gone, things are almost never as bad as I fear. When I see who it is, I freeze. Color heats up my cheeks like a fever.

It's Cape.

He catches up to me quickly, still tall, taking long strides.

"Hey, Bettina," he says, leaning in for a hug.

I pull away. After all these years, I'm still mad at him. The cold way he returned the medallion. The fact that he got to stay. That we were never really in it together after all.

"How are you?" He's not at all deterred by my backing away.

"Good, good," I say, but I am still so shocked I can barely manage more than a whisper.

"I heard your mom died." Cape says this so affably I start to wonder if he remembers what happened after all.

I nod.

"I'm really sorry, Bettina." This time he modulates his tone, genuinely sorry or just feigning it, I can't tell.

"Listen," he continues, "do you have time for lunch?"

I do want to hear what he is doing, but I should be getting back to work. Although I know that I can call in with some lame excuse; that's just the kind of place Blue Sea is.

"Sure," I say. Just this side of friendly.

"We can go to Café Montalembert. It's right around the corner."

Montalembert is Mad Ave. fancy: starched white tablecloths, tiny glass vases with white roses, real silverware. I'm not especially bothered by my grubby clothes. In New York, only tourists and people who consider the menu expensive worry about dressing up. I order a Pellegrino and orange juice, and Cape gets a scotch. I think it's too early in the day to be drinking, but unlike Babs, I never comment on what other people order. And after all, what do I care? This boy does not belong to me, and never has.

Sitting across the table, I finally am able to take all of him in. He looks mostly the same: tousled brown hair, blue eyes, perfectly straight nose, the kind Jewish girls break their own for. He is wearing chinos, a pink-checked shirt, blue blazer. I look to see if he still bites his nails and I notice he's wearing Mack's watch, and, more surprising, a wedding ring. Now I don't want to talk about where we have gone to college, where we work. I just want to get to the story of the present.

"So, you're married," I begin.

"Yes," he answers, reaching to twist the ring, seemingly needing to touch it to remind himself this is true.

"Who?" I say, not adding *is the lucky girl.*

"No one you know."

Why is he withholding this? Isn't this the lunch where he reiterates that I'm not worthy of him?

"Oh," I say lamely.

"Listen, Bettina, I owe you an apology."

At last. "For what?" There are so many things he could say he was sorry for, I wonder which one he will pick.

"For blaming my father's affair on you."

So that's what he wanted to tell me. Absolve me for something I didn't even do.

"Thanks, Cape," I say drily. "But I don't really see how a ten-year-old could have orchestrated an affair between two consenting adults. I might have been wrong to tell you about it, but some kid from Grass Woods might have shown up at Cardiss and filled you in anyway. And that kid wouldn't have loved you like I did."

Cape says nothing, but looks uncomfortable. I know the

word *love* has thrown him. He is probably still drawn to women who belittle him, like Meredith.

"Anyway, Cape, why did you decide to apologize now? I don't get it."

He leans forward, eager to speak.

"Six months ago, I went to a party at the Yale Club."

The Ivy League. So Cape must have made good on the promises of the Cardiss trial: tutored kids, upped his grades, played superlative lacrosse.

"It was two months before my wedding to Lolly." *As in lollipop?* I want to say, the way Holly might have. But I know it is probably short for Lucille, Isolde, or something equally pretentious. But in the end, I don't really care.

"Anyway," Cape continues, "that night at the YC, I ran into Anna. A girl I dated for two years who ultimately dumped me because she said I wasn't intellectual enough. I tried reading Virginia Woolf and Faulkner, but she still wouldn't take me back. When she graduated, she took off for Tibet and did whatever Yale graduates do there.

"That night at the party when I saw her, she looked fresh as ever: no makeup, simple blue dress. I figured she was there to approach potential donors for whatever cause she was currently interested in. I walked up to her and asked her to dinner that night. I wasn't hungry, just wanted a chance to spend more time with her.

"We were two of the last ones to leave the party. I had had too much to drink and had to grab her elbow to steady myself. I hailed a cab for us, and our legs touched as we crawled in."

I'm getting bored with this story and can't figure out why he wants to tell it to me, of all people. Was this run-in today an accident or did he call my job and some stupid intern told him where I might be? I want to say *Speed the fuck up,* but he seems determined to include all the details.

"When we were in the cab, I tried to put my arms around her, give her a hug, just like I did when we were twenty. I was still buzzed, so I missed and kissed her on the lips. She kissed me back and we started making out in the cab."

"And . . . ?" I ask as he reaches into the bread basket for a roll and starts to butter it.

"That's it. I took her to her place and got out of the cab so I could walk a bit and clear my head on the way home. When I got there, Lolly was sitting on the couch in my Brooks Brothers pajamas and finalizing the guest list for the wedding. I almost took her wrists and told her what had just happened, but instead I went to take a shower."

"So what do you want me to do? It was only a kiss and technically, you were still single." I want to laugh at his earnestness, at what he perceived as the gravity of the situation.

"I want your advice, Bettina. You have always been one of the smartest girls I know. You also know about my father's affair. I want your opinion: Am I like him?"

Slowly I say, "If you were like Mack, you never would have told me. You don't bring third parties into affairs—which you did not have—by the way, unless you want to get caught. Don't tell Lolly. One mistake is not worth ruining a marriage for."

"But what if I have more slips?"

"If you're so worried about it, do the right thing and divorce her before you have kids. But I know you won't do it again. I just do."

Cape looks relieved. Like he really believes I have all the right answers.

"What about you, Bettina? Aren't you worried you will turn into Babs?"

Even though this is my biggest fear, I say confidently, "You can't *turn into* people, Cape. Even if I make all the same mistakes she did, I will still be me."

He takes this in, says nothing at first. Then:

"What about the pennies? Do you still have them?"

So after all these years, he hasn't forgotten about the two fucking cents he gave me.

I don't want to tell him how angry I was that day, what I did with them.

"I'll look into it. They must be around somewhere."

"You promised me you wouldn't lose them, remember? And I gave you your medallion back. By the way, did you ever track your dad down?"

"Um, yes. He was dead after all." It's not worth going into with Cape, I decide. If he has married someone called Lolly, I somehow know we will never be close friends. That this lunch is probably it: the last time I will see him.

"I'm sorry, Bettina."

We eat spaghetti with clams and talk about his honeymoon. They went to Bali. The bill comes and Cape pays for both of us. I say thank you and lean in for a kiss. Some part of me hopes he will kiss me back, just like he did with Anna. I too am a girl he once slept with. But then I remember we never dated.

We get up from our table and walk outside.

"Goodbye, Bettina," he says. And once again, he's walking away. "Call me if you ever find my pennies."

"Sure," I say, not adding *Drag the Cardiss river.*

I hesitate before turning and watch as Cape disappears up Madison Avenue. As I stand there, I imagine the sidewalk turning from concrete into grass, extending itself into a huge lawn. Cape is no longer a man in a blazer but an eleven-year-old boy wearing white shorts, a white polo shirt, and the plaid hat I saw in the foyer of Tea House so many years ago. He turns toward me, standing there in my pink-and-white sundress, and then breaks into a run. He knocks me over when he reaches me, and we roll about the lawn, wrestling like puppies. We don't look but can feel the presence of our mothers sitting on the porch talking and laughing, drinking iced tea, perhaps. Finally, we're done with our roughhousing, and he takes my hand and pulls me up, wiping the dirt off his knees, then draping his arm casually about my shoulders.

But quickly, I snap back to the present. I can still see Cape walking up the sidewalk, getting smaller and smaller as he goes. He does not take notice of the stores, just dodges people as if he were navigating traffic in a car. Not once does he look back at me. See a girl just standing there, alone.

But Cape is just another one of those things that Babs took away from me, something I might have had.

Acknowledgments

My husband, Alex, and our three chickens, Alexander, Vanessa, and Camilla. Our nanny, Katie Nicolas, who holds it all together in our nest.

My immediate family: Abra, Jeremy, Peter, and Madison; Anthony, Eve, and Lucille Mia; Jonny, who will always be missed. Christina. Jim Wilkin and Pamela Sherrod Anderson. The Norton clan (I apologize for all the profanity).

The best friends I am so lucky to have: Lola Vautrin, Betty Wang, Jean McMahon, Rebecca Stedman, Brooks Brown, Kristen Smyth, Elizabeth Cutler, Meredith Rollins, Kathleen Seward, Carrie Karasyov, Kate Hope, Christine Frissora, Scott McCormack, and Rick Fiscina.

Phillips Exeter Academy, for providing much of the inspiration for this book as well as the first writing coach I ever had, David R. Weber. Andrew McKinnon, for loaning me his middle name and his superlative looks (perhaps unwittingly).

Dr. Barbara Gerson, Dr. Michael Teitelman, and Dr. Lee Cohen, who pulled me from the abyss, and all those who carried me and my family during that dark time. Lisa Brown, who understands and is perhaps the coolest person I know.

Adrienne Brodeur, my amazing editor, who believed in *The*

Chocolate Money enough to buy it and never lost enthusiasm for the project. Her gentle touch on the page and attentiveness carried me gracefully over the finish line. Stephen Simons, Tracy Roe, who worked miracles with my face and my prose, respectively.

Bill Clegg, Bill Clegg, Bill Clegg. Without him, there would be no book. Thanks as well to his assistant Shaun Dolan, who answered all of my rookie questions with thoroughness and care.

The Blécon family, who taught me much of what I needed to know.

Finally, to the rooms.